# «All Under
Control »

# « All Under Control »

based on the television stories

ALL UNDER CONTROL

and

DOWN AMONG THE DEAD MEN

Sandy Mitchell

First published in Great Britain in 1996 by
Virgin Books
an imprint of Virgin Publishing Ltd
332 Ladbroke Grove
London W10 5AH

BUGS the television series is produced by
Carnival Films Ltd and broadcast in the UK by BBC1

Text copyright © Sandy Mitchell 1996
adapted from screenplays by Duncan Gould and
Stephen Gallagher

Cover photographs © Carnival (Film & Theatre) Ltd, 1995

The moral right of Sandy Mitchell to be identified as
the Author of this Work has been asserted by him in
accordance with the Copyright, Designs and Patents Act
1988.

ISBN 0 753 50020 5

Typeset by Galleon Typesetting, Ipswich
Printed and bound in Great Britain by
BPC Paperbacks Ltd, Aylesbury

# « Prologue »

The light in the room was muted, shadowless, carefully controlled to prevent reflection from the semicircle of computer screens at its centre. Icarus found the effect relaxing, but then he'd designed it to be. Here, surrounded by his monitors, he could become one with his equipment, soothed by its almost subliminal hum, unhindered by the petty distractions of the outside world.

Usually. But occasionally the petty distractions forced themselves on him, even here. Tearing his attention away from the block of machine code on the screen in front of him he turned to face his associate, who was hovering nervously by the door.

'What kind of complication?' he asked.

His associate shuffled his feet. 'Ms Langford. The manager at the airport.'

'I know who she is,' Icarus said, unable to keep an edge of asperity from creeping into his voice. His associate had an irritating tendency to state the obvious when he felt under pressure. It was a way of marshalling his thoughts, Icarus supposed. But it was vexing, nevertheless. Icarus liked precision in everything. He waved a hand at the empty seat next to his own, and adopted a more friendly tone. 'And do sit down. You're making the place look untidy.'

'Thanks.' The man sat, the expression of unease fading from his face.

Icarus waited for a moment, then prompted him. 'Jerry Langford. What about her?'

'She's called in a security expert. I think she's on to us.' The man's expression grew troubled again. 'Suppose they get a lead before we're ready to strike?'

Icarus considered the implications. It didn't sound all that likely. But still. 'What kind of an expert? Computer security?'

'No.' The associate shook his head. 'He's trained as a pilot. Australian. Young, and rather abrasive.' A trace of a smile appeared on his face. 'He's ruffled a few feathers in the Security Division already. I made sure of that.'

'A pilot. Probably.' Icarus nodded thoughtfully. 'Then I don't think we've got too much to worry about.'

'Why not?' His associate was unconvinced. But then the man was a worrier. Sometimes that could be a strength, a positive contribution to the partnership; it made him aware of the details that sometimes even Icarus had overlooked. But, on other occasions, it made him incapable of grasping the obvious as well.

'Because if she had any idea of what we're planning she'd have called in an electronic security team. If she's gone for an aviation specialist, it shows she's thinking about direct physical sabotage.' He permitted himself a thin smile. 'Which is precisely what we want her to think.'

'I see.' His associate nodded. 'It's all going according to plan, then.'

'Exactly,' Icarus reassured him. He returned his attention to the computer equipment. 'This time next

2

month we'll be rich. And what's more important . . .'
He began amending a complex block of computer code
from one of the keyboards. 'The whole world will
know what we did. And how we did it.'

Chief Petty Officer Stokes loved mornings like this.
Bright and clear. An edge to the wind, spiced with the
scent of the sea. Most of his adult life had been spent
with a faint flavour of salt in his mouth. But he was less
than a year from retirement now. He wouldn't feel a
deck under his feet again this side of civvy street.

Sometimes he felt like one of the hulks in the
graveyard dock, stretching out around him now in a
panorama of decay and dereliction. This was where
Marine Command sent its old ships to be cannibalised
for usable spares. To be scrapped. Its old salts too, he
often joked with his colleagues in the mess. But, like
the obsolete vessels stored here, he still had something
of value to contribute to the service.

These days he was an instructor with a shore training establishment, playing nursemaid to a gaggle of
officer cadets, hoping to turn them into sailors. He
liked the assignment. Liked the sense of continuity.
Individuals came and went, but Marine Command
was always there.

His charges would take what he taught them, and
use it, and add to it, and pass it on in turn to the next
generation. Some of them would make Captain, a few
might even rise to flag rank. In a way, he supposed, he
was shaping the future of the service. Leaving his mark
for years to come.

But here and now there was a job to be done. He
slammed the rear door of the dark blue minibus with
his shoulder, carefully balancing the armful of equipment he'd collected, and turned back to his working
party. Half a dozen midshipmen, at parade rest, in

what he supposed they fondly imagined was a straight line. Five carefully composed expressions of alert interest, and one vacant stare.

'Are we going a bit too fast for you, Midshipman Windette?'

'Yes sir! I mean, um, no, Chief Petty Officer.' The young man straightened his back a little, resuming his habitual expression of eager expectation, while the others almost managed not to grin. Stokes kept a straight face easily, but then he'd had years of practice.

'Try to keep your mind on the job,' he said. 'She'll still be there this evening.'

Windette flushed, and a half-suppressed snigger snorted into silence somewhere in the middle of the line.

'You wish to add something, Midshipman Groves?'

'No, Chief Petty Officer.' The young woman stared impassively ahead.

'Good.' Stokes walked down the line, handing out the equipment. One waterproof notepad computer and a beltful of tools for each member of the party.

The breeze picked up a little, whining through the derelict frigate behind them, rattling loose cables against the metalwork. It was the *Arrogant*. Stokes could put a name and a service history to every one of them, illustrious and obscure alike. Technically, of course, the hulk was nameless now. A new *Arrogant* had been launched the previous year. Tradition. The lifeblood of the service.

'Each one of you has been assigned a vessel. Identify it by the number of the bay in which it stands. If you have difficulty locating it, access the map of the dock-yard which has been pre-loaded into your notepad. When you find the vessel, open the blueprint file. This will show you the simplest route to the component you are to salvage. It will be required for repairs to

4

an operational vessel, so remove it with care. Any questions?'

An expectant silence, broken only by the squealing of the circling seagulls.

'Good.' Stokes hesitated. It was only a rumour, but from a reliable source. His friend in the provost's office wasn't a man to exaggerate, even after a pint or two. Maybe it was better not to worry them. On the other hand . . .

'Apparently someone's been breaking in and nicking stuff. God knows how they're getting past security. Or why, for that matter. So if you see anything suspicious, call in.' Everyone nodded. 'Right then. Radio check.'

Each of the midshipmen sounded off in turn, their voices echoing tinnily from the speaker on the dashboard of the van, before replacing the miniature transceivers in their toolbelts. Stokes nodded, satisfied.

'Salvage party . . . Dismissed.'

He returned their salutes and watched them scatter, sighing quietly as Windette started out in the wrong direction and had to retrace his steps. Then he settled himself in the driving seat of the minibus, and retrieved his thermos and a newspaper from the glove box. With a bit of luck he'd have time to finish the crossword before they got back.

Thirty-seven, thirty-eight . . . Windette counted off the bays along the wharf, comparing them to the map on the screen of his notepad. If he was here, then that meant bay forty-one should be right over there.

'Oh great.' He stared at the derelict. It shouldn't be that low in the water, surely. He called up the blueprints. No doubt about it. She should be riding higher than that.

Oh well. Maybe the bilges were flooded. He checked the location of the valve he was supposed to collect. No problem. Piece of cake. Of course, he'd make it sound a lot more exciting and dangerous when he told Sally about it this evening. She really went for the action man stuff. Maybe he'd get to hold her hand in the cinema tonight. Maybe even . . .

'Ouch!' Preoccupied with delightful daydreams he slipped on the narrow gangplank, landing heavily on his left knee. He climbed cautiously to his feet again. The Chief was right, he thought. I need to keep my mind on the job.

He checked the blueprint on the screen again, and headed for the companionway marked with a flashing red icon. Just follow the lights to the treasure. Easy. He opened the hatch.

Not so easy. The ladder led down into darkness, and the unmistakable acrid tang of enclosed seawater. Windette unclipped the torch from his belt and shone the beam downwards. The light rippled, reflected back from a silent pool.

He should call in and wait for help. The rules were clear. Entering a flooded vessel alone was strictly forbidden. But it didn't look all that deep. No more than knee-high. And he was damned if he was going to end up the only one not to complete his assignment. Groves would be straight in there. 'What's the matter, Windy? Scared of getting your feet wet?'

On the other hand, the Chief would give him the bollocking of his life if he flouted the safety regs. His hand dropped to the walkie-talkie. Fell away again.

What the Chief didn't know couldn't hurt him.

The water was freezing. Windette eased himself carefully down the ladder, probing carefully with the toe of his boot. It was deeper than he'd thought, but not by much. No more than halfway up his thighs. He moved forward awkwardly, trying to minimise the bow wave, flashing the torch in front of him as he moved. The beam reflected eerily off the walls and the rippling shadow of the liquid floor.

The corridor was clearly marked. He moved carefully, his breath misting in the chill air. Gradually, the water level rose, the floor tilting almost imperceptibly downwards as he moved aft. Maybe she was holed below the waterline. As the chill passed his crotch Windette paused, restowing the radio in his breast pocket, next to the notepad.

'This is really, really stupid.'

He went on anyway, while the toolbelt gradually submerged. Another few yards, he thought. Then I go back.

Something splashed in the darkness. Windette turned, flashing the torch back the way he'd come, but the sound folded in on itself in the tightly enclosed space. He took a deep breath. There were bound to be noises in a wreck like this, he told himself. Metal shifting. Water dripping. Fish tap-dancing, for all he knew.

Where was that blasted valve? It should be somewhere up ahead. He fished out the notepad again, and rechecked the blueprint.

The next compartment. Great. He pushed on, the water lapping against his chest. Through the open hatch.

There, on the bulkhead in front of him. At last.

Windette pulled the spanner from the toolbelt, and began to work on the nuts. They came free surprisingly easily. He'd expected them to be corroded solid.

Another splash sounded loud in the compartment. Windette turned, adrenalin surging through his body. That was close. Not imagination. Something brushed against his leg. He pulled back, swinging the spanner like a weapon, flashing the torch into every corner. Nothing.

Something exploded from the water in front of him,

7

a grotesque parody of a human shape. A diving suit. Windette swung the spanner at its head, the rational part of his mind still trying to make sense of the situation, while his primitive instincts screamed *Fight! Kill! Fight or die!*

Stokes checked his watch again. Five of the midshipmen were back, grimy and tired, flushed with success and the weight of their booty. One was overdue. Windette. Of course, it had to be Windette. He leaned in through the open door of the minibus, and picked up the radio handset.

'Midshipman Windette. Respond, please.' He released the thumb switch. Static. 'Salvage party to Midshipman Windette. Please respond, over.'

Nothing. 'Maybe he's still below decks.'

This from Groves, hovering at his elbow, the inevitable strand of hair hanging loose from inside her cap. She brushed it away, spreading a tick of grime across her forehead. 'These are low-powered sets. With all this metal around, it could block the signal.'

'I didn't know you were an R/T specialist, Groves.'

Anyone else would have folded, but Groves was constitutionally immune to sarcasm. Stokes was never sure if she really did take everything he said at face value, or was just playing some sort of game for her own amusement.

'I'm taking the course, Chief Petty Officer.'

'Ah. Right.' And she was correct. If Windette was still inside the hull, he might not be receiving. The question was, what to do next.

'Did you take First Aid as well?'

'Yes, Chief Petty Officer.'

'Good. Come with me.' He raised his voice. 'Everyone else back in the bus. Midshipman Chandler, drive back to the main gate. Carefully. Report to the Duty Officer and wait for me there. Any questions?'

'Well, he was here.' Groves pointed to the fresh scuff mark on the gangplank. Stokes nodded, and raised the personal radio he'd taken from Midshipman Chandler.

'Midshipman Windette. Are you receiving? Over.'

Nothing. Just more static. He led the way up the gangplank.

Bay forty-one. The *Lawford*. He'd served on the *Napier*, her sister ship. Must have been twenty years ago now. Setting foot on the deck of the old destroyer felt strangely familiar. If he remembered correctly, Windette would have come this way.

'Windy!' Groves filled her lungs, ready to shout again. She had a surprisingly loud voice for such a small woman.

Stokes beat her to it.

'Midshipman Windette!' They both listened, holding their breath. Nothing but seagulls, and the lapping of the waves against the hull.

Groves frowned. 'Did you hear that?'

'What?' Stokes strained his ears. Groves looked puzzled.

'I thought I heard a splash.'

'If he's gone overboard he'd be making a lot more noise than that.' Stokes led the way aft, towards the hatch. It hung open, creaking slightly in the wind.

'Well, he must have got this far. Give me the torch.' Stokes flashed the beam around, catching the gleam of rippling water below. 'Windette!' His voice echoed off into the darkness.

'Do you think he went down there?' A note of uncertainty crept into Groves's voice for the first time.

'He'd have to be a complete idiot.' Stokes thought

9

about it for a moment. Or young and overconfident. Same thing, really. 'In which case, probably. Stay here. Keep your radio on receive. We shouldn't have any trouble keeping in contact at this range, however much metal there is in the way.'

'Yes, Chief Petty Officer.' Groves nodded, once, looking serious. She didn't have to ask why, in that case, Windette wasn't getting through.

Stokes paused at the bottom of the companionway, getting his bearings. Cold water rose up his legs, numbing them, killing sensation. He started aft. Find the valve, and you find Windette, he thought. He called again.

'Midshipman Windette!' Nothing replied except the water he'd disturbed, lapping against the walls of the corridor.

Through here. He breasted the mounting water level, half swimming now. He fumbled the radio into his free hand.

'Midshipman Groves. Are you there? Over.'

'Receiving you, Chief.' Her voice was reassuringly loud in the narrow space.

'No sign of him. I'm just going to check the assigned objective. Then we call in the search teams. Out.'

He entered the compartment, flashing his torch around, taking in the far bulkhead.

'Groves. He was here. The valve's gone.' He swept the beam across the surface of the water. Black. Oily. Empty. 'No sign of Windette.'

He turned, ready to leave, and a faint patch of green luminescence caught the corner of his eye. He swung the torch beam towards it.

The screen of a notepad brightened as it rolled face-up in the gentle swell. Rising slowly to the surface beside it was the body of Midshipman Windette.

# « One »

Water rippled quietly outside the window. Beckett stifled a yawn, and tried to tear his attention away from the river. The river was interesting. Boats moving up and down, heavy cargo lighters riding low in the water, pleasure craft with gaudy sails teasing them as they lumbered along, swooping and turning with the wind like the gulls in the air above them. Every few minutes a riverbus glided past, skimming smoothly on its hydrofoils, leaving the little sailing boats bobbing in its wake.

The hotel exhibition hall, on the other hand, was too full, the air conditioning inadequate, and the temperature just high enough to nudge him towards sleepiness. It was hard to believe that the largest gathering of computer security experts in the country could be so dull. If it wasn't for the glass wall at the far end of the room with its panoramic view, his brain would probably have crashed by now.

The Computer Security Show had sounded a lot more exciting when Ros told him about it. All the hardware you can eat, she'd said. A chance to check out the latest developments in intrusion software, and the Ice to counter it. Meet the biggest experts in the field and pick their brains. Chat up the existing clients, trawl for new ones.

He should have known that Ros had an ulterior motive. She had disappeared almost as soon as they'd arrived, leaving him to take care of the Gizmos stand on his own.

Every now and then he caught sight of her over the sea of heads. Engaged in animated conversation with someone, no doubt, while he fielded idiot questions from questioning idiots. Some took a leaflet, but most wandered off in bovine confusion. Middle management and hobby hackers mostly. Barely capable of understanding how their off-the-peg systems worked, let alone some of Ros's more imaginative custom jobs.

He sipped dregs of cold coffee from a polystyrene cup, and put his feet up on one of the hotel's glossy coffee tables. All in all, he reflected, the day could hardly get worse.

'Hello, Beckett. Fancy seeing you here.' His former boss didn't seem in the least bit surprised. 'Working hard?' His eyes flicked briefly from Beckett's face to his exhibitor's badge.

'Hard enough.' Beckett didn't get up. Dent seated himself carefully in the chair opposite, and deposited a fresh pair of the styrene cups in the space between them.

'I noticed you seem to be stuck here.' Dent popped the lid and sipped cautiously, grimacing. 'Coffee?'

'That's what they told me when I bought it. Maybe it evolved.' Beckett took the proffered cup. 'What do you want, Dent?'

'Somewhere to sit quietly with a drink and a snack. This seems to be one of the less frenetic corners.' He stripped the packaging from a couple of sandwiches, which leaked pinkish ichor down his fingers. 'Please, take one. Prawn and mayonnaise. They're quite horrible, but it's all they had left.'

'I'll pass.' Beckett sipped at his drink, watching Dent narrowly through the haze of steam.

'A wise decision.' Dent chewed thoughtfully. 'This job you're doing for Kamen and Ross . . .'

Aha. So that was it. He wanted information. Well, he wasn't going to get it. Not for a cup of coffee and the sniff of a prawn sandwich, anyway.

'I hope you're not going to ask me to breach client confidentiality,' Beckett said.

'Of course not.' Dent looked vaguely shocked for a moment, then, more genuinely, amused. 'I hardly think you could tell us much we couldn't find out for ourselves if we wanted to anyway.'

Beckett conceded the point with a nod. That was what the Hive did, after all. Gather and process information. Their resources could turn a simple merchant bank inside out, if they had any reason to look there. Which raised the question of what possible interest they might have in Kamen and Ross.

All Beckett knew was that they were hoping to strengthen their intrusion countermeasures, and had approached Gizmos for some hardware the previous month. Ros was the one to ask. She'd had dealings with them before.

He glanced over Dent's shoulder, scanning the room. Ros was chatting to their head of security now, making notes on her palmtop. The man, Graeme Hurry, was nodding. That explained why Ros had wanted to be here, at least. As Beckett had suspected, the Gizmos trade stand was just a cover. A cover that hadn't fooled Dent.

Beckett rather liked Hurry. The man really did understand the answers to the questions he asked. And he wasn't afraid to show ignorance when he asked them.

13

'Which brings me to this.' Dent snapped open his briefcase, and pulled out a folder. Plain plastic cover. Anonymous. He dropped it on the table. 'A morsel of information we came across recently. It cropped up in the course of a Marine Command investigation.'

'Really?' Intrigued in spite of himself, Beckett opened the folder. The top sheet was a photograph. A middle-aged man, staring at the camera as though it had just spilt his drink. A brief biography followed. Military service. A subsequent career as a commercial diver. A number of brushes with the law. 'McTiernan. Never heard of him.'

'No reason why you should. But I think you'll find Mr Hurry has.' Dent snapped the briefcase closed, and returned his attention to the sandwiches. A brief expression of distaste flickered across his face as he chewed.

'According to this, he's suspected of stealing components from a naval yard.' Beckett glanced up. 'Possibly even murder.'

'The verdict at the inquest was misadventure,' said Dent. 'The deceased was foolish enough to ignore safety procedures.'

'Nothing to connect it with McTiernan. I see.' Beckett shrugged. 'And you think he might be some sort of threat to our client?'

'I wouldn't know. I'm just a civil servant. The business world is a closed book to me.'

'Quite.' As if anything was a closed book to the Hive. 'And what are you after in return?'

'Nothing.' Dent tried to look ingenuous. 'You terminated your employment with us under somewhat strained circumstances.'

'I was forced out. Because your precious toy got broken.'

'SACROS was more than a toy, Beckett. But it's not

irreplaceable. The blueprints still exist. And the software.' Dent smiled, coldly. 'Anyway, that's beside the point. Your freelance activities appear to be going well.' He glanced around, pointedly taking in the flood of clients patently failing to crowd the stand. 'I thought a little unofficial assistance might mend a few fences.'

'Oh.' Beckett thought about it. He looked for an angle. It was just possible that Dent was telling the truth. Not likely, but possible. 'Well. Thanks. And for the coffee.'

'Don't mention it.' Dent stood. 'Oh, by the way.'

Here it comes, thought Beckett.

'You must come across some interesting odds and ends on these jobs of yours.'

'From time to time.'

'If you should happen to come across a particular type of intrusion software, we'd be quite interested in hearing about it.'

'I'm sure you would.' Beckett tried to ignore the hint for a moment, before curiosity got the better of him. 'Um. Just how particular are we talking about? In this particular case.'

'You'll know it if you ever see it. If it exists. Which it probably doesn't.' Dent dismissed the subject, as though it were of little interest. 'Ah. Miss Henderson appears to be coming back. With your client, unless I'm much mistaken.' He turned his head, tracking the crowd. 'I don't see your other colleague anywhere. The excitable one.'

'Ed's not here. He's got a flying job this afternoon.' Lucky old Ed. Next time, Beckett thought, he was going to make sure he had a cast iron excuse for avoiding the show as well.

'Is he still doing that too?' Dent looked thoughtful. 'I'll bear that in mind the next time we need a pilot.'

'He might not be too keen,' Beckett reminded him.

'The last time he did a job for you, someone tried to shoot him down.' Although, knowing Ed, that would probably be an incentive.

'Oh yes. So they did. Not very successfully, as I recall. He's a resourceful young man.' Dent turned away. 'I expect I'll be seeing you.'

Not if I see you first, thought Beckett. He nodded.

'Be seeing you,' he said.

'You have control,' the woman in the left-hand seat said.

Ed nodded. 'I have control.' He moved the control column a few millimetres, experimentally, and the slim executive jet soared upwards. 'Wow. Responsive, isn't she?'

'Fly by wire.' Jerry Langford grinned.

Ed had liked her as soon as they met. Despite the decade and a half between their ages, and her exalted position as managing director of one of the country's largest airports, they had a lot in common. The same sense of humour. The same disregard for rules that could be bent or circumvented.

'I could get used to this.' Ed kept the conversation going with half his mind, relaxing, getting the feel of the controls. If you let yourself you could become attuned to a plane, feeling what it felt, adjusting the control surfaces without conscious thought, so that it became an extension of your own body. It was a talent with him, an instinct. It often surprised him that most other people couldn't do it.

'I hope so.' She turned in the pilot's seat, regarding him seriously. 'Do you think you can fly her solo?'

'Just try me.' Ed grinned, then matched her mood. 'Yes, I think so. But I thought you only wanted a co-pilot this trip?'

'I do.' Jerry regarded him levelly. 'But next week I've

16

got a meeting in Amsterdam, and then I've got to brief the board as soon as I get back. I'll be up to my ears in paperwork both legs of the trip.'

'I see. You'll need someone to handle the flying.'

'That's the idea.' She hesitated. 'And I'd rather have a pilot with a security background.'

'So you're still worried about those faxes.' Ed checked the instrumentation. Data flickered on the cockpit screens, bypassing his conscious mind. Airspeed, fuel, engine temperature. Straight and level flight. The plane was a beauty, no doubt about it. She practically flew herself.

'I'm probably just being paranoid.' Jerry shrugged. 'But we had another one yesterday.'

'You're sure it was from the same guy?'

'Well, it was signed Icarus. Just like the others. But the threats were more specific.'

'How specific?' This sounded interesting. He'd have to tell Beckett and Ros about it. Maybe put the trace back on the line. Not that it had done any good the last time he'd tried. But his colleagues should have finished the Kamen and Ross job by now, so they'd be able to work with him on it. Signal tracking was much more their area of expertise.

'He said we'd hear from him again next week. That's the first time he's mentioned any kind of timetable.'

'Yeah.' Ed shook his head slowly. 'I hate to say this, but I still think it's just some nutcase we're dealing with here. I spent the best part of a week working on it the last time you got one of these messages, and we got nowhere. I couldn't find any holes in your security.'

'It didn't stop you trying though.' Jerry smiled at the memory. 'Nigel's still seething over that bomb alert you triggered.'

'I don't see why. At least he knows his system works.' But the airport's head of security was very much a by-the-book man. He hadn't appreciated Ed's freewheeling approach at all. But then he'd probably have resented any outside consultant being called in, interpreting it as a lack of confidence in his own abilities.

Jerry nodded her agreement. 'He's very competent. Within the parameters he knows. But there's something unusual going on. Something outside the normal boundaries.' Her brow furrowed. 'I can feel it. But I can't put my finger on what. Or why. That's why I need someone around with an outsider's perspective.'

The penny dropped. 'You mean someone with a legitimate excuse for hanging around the airport. Keeping his ear to the ground.'

'Exactly.' She nodded. 'Which is why I asked you to co-pilot for me today. And fly the plane next week.'

'Say no more. You've got yourself a pilot.'

'Thanks.' She became businesslike again. 'That's assuming you check out on the systems, of course.'

'No worries there.' He swept his gaze across the instrument panel again. 'I've never known a plane so easy to fly.'

'Well.' Jerry shrugged, elaborately casual. 'That's NavCom for you.'

'NavCom?' Ed examined the data displays more carefully. 'That's real cutting edge stuff. I thought only airlines and the military could afford it.'

'That's true, if you buy it. But I know the designer.' Jerry looked smug. 'He lives near the airport.'

'That's handy.' Ed almost managed to keep the edge of envy out of his voice. 'Has he got a version for helicopters?'

'I think so. I'll ask, next time I see him.'

'And he'll just hand one over to a complete stranger? Right.' Ed laughed, incredulous.

'Quentin gives copies away to anyone who asks.' Jerry's voice took on a reflective tone. 'He's proud of it.

Lives for the day every aircraft in the world uses NavCom. And it doesn't cost him anything; he sold the patent rights for a lump sum. He'd have got ten times the money if he'd asked for a royalty.' She shook her head, sadly. 'He's a genius with software, but he's got no head for business at all.'

'I've yet to meet a genius who has. Nature's way of keeping us humble, I guess.'

'Was that who I think it was?' Ros watched Dent's retreating back, one eyebrow quirked into a puzzled frown.

Beckett nodded. 'The one and only.'

'What did he want?'

Beckett lifted the styrene cup, and grimaced.

'I think he was trying to poison me.'

'Oh. That reminds me.' Graeme Hurry held out a cup and saucer. Steam rose gently from it, freighted with the aroma of real, fresh coffee. 'We thought you could do with this.'

'You thought right.' Beckett took it gratefully. 'Where did you get it?'

'Never underestimate a head of security.' Hurry smiled. Every time Beckett met him, he wondered how someone so physically large could be so self-effacing. The young Scotsman topped him by at least six inches, but blended into a crowd as easily as Dent. Even more perfectly, if that were possible. Something about the way suits seemed to crumple as soon as he wore them, perhaps.

'They've got a percolator on the Stross Cybertek stand,' Ros explained.

'And I managed to sneak off with this while Ros kept them talking.'

'So you owe me big time, Beckett.' Ros feigned exhaustion.

'You did that for me?' Beckett played along with the joke. 'Went and talked to Charlie? On purpose?' He held out the cup. 'Here. You need this more than I do.'

'It wasn't that bad.' A trace of genuine enthusiasm entered her voice. 'He's working on some fascinating stuff. Active sound suppression, using anti-noise generators. They should have a prototype up and running by the end of the year.'

'Active sound suppression?' Beckett nodded thoughtfully. 'That could be useful. In all sorts of ways.'

'Especially if you use it on Charlie,' Ros said.

'Where did you get this from?' Hurry interrupted them. He was holding the folder Dent had left behind, his face suffused with surprise and suspicion.

'You're not the only one who can get hold of stuff, Graeme,' Beckett replied. So, Dent had been right. There was a connection between the thefts from naval yards and Kamen and Ross. Something worth killing for. 'Our source thought you might find it interesting. Care to tell us why?'

Hurry liked visiting Gizmos. He liked the sense of purposeful clutter the place exuded. He liked the air of informality. The place was a refreshing change from the ordered efficiency that surrounded him at Kamen and Ross. And he liked the people. Ros especially. She was the one he felt most comfortable with, but then he'd worked with her before. The others he was still getting the measure of.

'These are the people we're interested in,' he said. He played with the buttons on the handset, and the grainy video image froze. He zoomed in on a section. Three sets of heads and shoulders filled the screen. A tight group, standing in the middle of a public park. 'Sorry about the picture quality. It was taken at extreme range for the equipment.'

'What about sound?' Ed leaned forward, blond hair dropping across his forehead.

'Nothing.' Hurry shrugged. 'They were talking near the bandstand. We tried enhancing the tape, but we couldn't get anything usable.'

'If you've got a copy with you, I'll see what I can do.' Ros looked at him appraisingly. Hurry smiled ruefully, and pulled the DAT cassette from his pocket.

'Still reading my mind,' he said.

'You're so transparent, Graeme, I don't have to.' She smiled too, chalking up the point, and took the tape. 'I'm not making any promises, mind.'

'Your best shot's good enough for me.'

'Glad to hear it.'

Beckett was studying the freeze-frame, memorising the faces. Of the three, Hurry thought, this was the one he'd least like to try to keep secrets from. The planner. The organiser. He had a healthy respect for Ros's intellect, which he knew from experience was tempered by a strong streak of intuition. Ed, he was sure from their brief acquaintance so far, was a creature of impulse, more comfortable with action than planning. But Beckett chewed away at a problem methodically, like the intelligence analyst he used to be, extracting every last shred of meaning from the data available.

'McTiernan we know,' Beckett said. 'Who are the other two?'

Brief, and to the point. Hurry nodded approval.

'Bryan and Juliet Brody.' He indicated the statuesque redhead in the expensive designer coat. 'We don't know much about the woman. My staff are still digging, but if she's been up to anything in the past she hasn't been caught.'

Beckett nodded. The first rule of security. Absence of evidence isn't necessarily evidence of absence.

'We don't know if she's actively involved in all this,' Hurry added, 'or just coming along for the ride.'

'She doesn't look like any scrap metal dealer I've ever met before.' Ed again, cheerfully oblivious to the looks he was getting from his colleagues. 'Do we have any idea what sort of scam they're planning?'

'None,' Hurry admitted. 'We've got all the pieces. But at the moment they don't seem to fit.'

'But you're sure Kamen and Ross is the target?' asked Ros.

'It has to be,' said Hurry. 'Brody used to work in our International Department. Computer services manager. He knew the system inside out.'

'Used to?' Beckett said.

'We fired him. I found out he'd been using other employees' passwords to gain unauthorised access to sensitive parts of the network.' Hurry smiled at Ros. 'One of your deep cover security programs caught him out. He'd been using an Icebreaker on the visible stuff, but he hadn't noticed the lurker in the hidden files.'

Ed looked impressed. 'So when this guy Brody tried to hack into the system at Kamen and Ross, your program blew the whistle on him. Torpedoed his Icebreaker, as it were.'

'Nicely put,' Hurry said. 'That's exactly what happened. We've kept an eye on him ever since, but there's nothing so far to indicate what he's planning.'

'Well, he'd be a fool to try hacking into the system directly,' Beckett said. 'You caught him before. And I take it you've beefed up the system since then?'

'Yes,' Hurry said. 'The stuff you provided us with was just icing on the cake.'

'So assuming the Icebreaker he used before was his best shot, the current system is way beyond his capabilities.' Beckett looked directly at him. 'I don't see why you're so worried.'

'Because it's my job to be,' Hurry said.

'Well, if you've had the Brodys under surveillance this long without getting any leads, I think McTiernan's our best bet,' Ros said. Hurry nodded.

'If you only knew how much time and effort we'd expended trying to identify him. This source of yours must have some impressive resources.'

'As good as they get.' Beckett's tone was light, but

the undercurrent was unmistakable. End of conversation on that subject. Hurry didn't push it.

'According to the file, he lives in a mobile home. Down by the new railway.' Ed was flicking through the dossier. Either he'd seen it before, or his reading speed was phenomenal. Hurry would have bet on the latter. Under that flippant exterior was another first-class mind. He looked from one to the other: Ros, Beckett, and back to Ed. For a moment he almost felt sorry for the Brodys.

'Shouldn't take long to search, then. All we need is an excuse to get him away from there.' Ros looked speculatively at Beckett and Ed. 'Which one of you looks best in a suit?'

'He does.' They spoke and pointed at one another simultaneously. Beckett reached into his pocket, producing a coin. He flipped it, caught it, and slapped it down on the back of his hand.

Ed sighed; he could guess the result.

'Heads,' he said.

'He cheated. He definitely cheated.'

'How, Beckett?' Ros pushed her headphones back and stretched. She wasn't sure how long she'd been working on Graeme's surveillance tape, but judging by how hungry she felt it must have been several hours. 'You flipped the coin, remember.'

'He wouldn't give me best out of three.' Beckett leaned back from his own workstation. 'What do you think?'

'You want tact, or honesty?' Ros walked across the room, and bent over his shoulder. She nodded approvingly. 'Hey. Pretty good.' Surprisingly good, in fact. She wondered if forgery was one of the things the Hive taught its agents, or if it was something he'd just picked up as a hobby.

'Well, if I get tired of this I guess I've always got a future in junk mail.' He looked critically at the letter on the screen. 'Do you think it sounds bland enough?'

'Don't get too carried away. After all, we want him to read it.' Something caught her eye, and she pointed. 'Nice touch. Spelling his name wrong.'

'Where? Oh, yes.' Beckett recovered fast. 'Gives it that churned out by the thousand look, don't you think?'

'It'll do.' She returned to the audio setup. Maybe if she boosted the high end a little, and took down the low frequencies into the subsonic range . . .

Blast. If she had to listen to the Radetsky March just once more she'd scream. There had to be a way of screening out the music and getting to the voices underneath. She watched the visual display of sound, rising and falling on the flickering screen. If it was a simple interference pattern she could cancel it out, but it was just too complex. No way to isolate something as tenuous as voices. If she had a matching pattern she could search for the differences, but . . .

'Of course!' She must be losing her touch. How could she have missed something that obvious? Fatigue, it had to be. She called out. 'Beckett! Is Ed back yet?'

'No.' He appeared in the doorway, carrying two mugs of coffee.

'Good.' She pinched the bridge of her nose. 'Is he wearing a headset?'

'Well, I built one into his crash helmet. I don't know if he's got it switched on, though.' Beckett shrugged. 'It's probably too late to change your order anyway. He'll be halfway here by now.'

'I'm not talking about the takeaway, Beckett.' She picked up one of the headsets lying next to the radio base station. 'Ed. Are you receiving me? Over.'

'Strength five.' A chuckle from the speaker. 'Getting a bit peckish, are we?'

'Never mind the food, Ed. There's something else I want you to bring back. Stop at a record store, and pick me up a CD of military bands. Something with the Radetsky March on it.'

'Right. No problem.' He chuckled again. 'I guess it does kind of grow on you after you've heard it the first forty or fifty times.'

'I can patch it through to your headset if you like.'

The channel went dead with almost indecent haste.

'What's the idea?' Beckett sounded curious. Ros waved him over to the console, and keyed up the display.

'Normally we'd try and isolate the frequencies we're interested in, right?'

'Right.' Beckett nodded.

'But they're swamped by the noise of the band. Which is probably why they met there in the first place.'

'It's what I'd do,' Beckett agreed.

'So if we get another recording of the same piece of music, and overlay it, then isolate the differences, we should be able to pull out some fragments of conversation.'

'It's a bit of a long shot.' Beckett frowned, dubious. 'Different band, different instruments, different tempo. Different acoustics. You'll be lucky to get much of an overlap.'

'It's worth a try.' The flash of irritation in her voice took her by surprise. Low blood sugar. She must be hungrier than she thought.

'It's more than that. It's almost brilliant.' Beckett tapped a few keys. 'Maybe we could try morphing the frequencies through a pattern recognition routine, using fuzzy parameters. Squeeze them to fit. That should force a much higher percentage of overlap.'

26

'Now you're talking.' She considered it. 'We'll end up with a higher percentage of signal drop-out too, don't forget.'

'It'll get us into the ballpark, anyway. Once we've isolated a few fragments we can refine the parameters. Build up from there by successive approximation.'

'OK. So let's get started.' She began cabling new modules into the rig. 'Where's that CD drive I was working on?'

By the time they heard footsteps on the stairs, they'd almost finished. She looked up as Ed bounded into the room, unzipping his motorcycle jacket.

'I've got your CD.' He handed it to her, a dubious eye on the new configuration of the audio equipment. 'I hate to say this, but it'll never replace rock and roll.'

'If I'm right, it won't have to.' Ros slotted it into the CD drive, and selected the track. Accessed Beckett's pattern recognition software.

'That's not good enough.' The voice broke suddenly from the speaker on the desk, hazed with static, distorted by strange, atonal squalling.

'It worked!' Her hunger forgotten, Ros turned back to the keyboard. 'We're still missing a lot, but . . .'

Another voice, higher pitched, completely unintelligible. Juliet Brody, obviously. Interrupted after a moment by more mush, deeper in tone. A few words emerged from the aural slush, like reefs from the sea. '. . . hired to do a job. We agreed . . .'

'Must be Brody. Sounds like McTiernan wants to renegotiate his contract.'

'Interesting,' said Beckett. 'Maybe we can use that. Play them off against each other.'

'Rather you than me,' said Ros. 'We know McTiernan's a killer. Probably.'

'Think about it.' The first voice again. 'You still need me . . .'

27

'. . . plenty of others . . . that kind of money . . .'

'Don't sound too pleased with each other,' said Ed.

'. . . still got the parts.' Even through the distortion, McTiernan sounded smug. '. . . get very far without . . .'

'. . . think about it.' Brody's voice trailed away. The DAT ended, and began to rewind automatically. The Radetsky March burst, uninterrupted, from the speaker.

Three index fingers stabbed simultaneously for the OFF button of the CD player.

He picked up on the third ring, cradling the phone. 'Bryan Brody.' Automatically, he scanned the screen of the PC on the desk next to it. No bugs. No traces. Line secure.

'This is Icarus.' The voice sounded amused. Sardonic. 'Don't bother sweeping the line. My Ice is more secure than yours could ever be.'

'It's not your Ice I'm interested in, Mr Icarus.' He watched Juliet sit up, instantly alert as he spoke the name. Tide charts spilled across her lap. He smiled at her. 'My wife says hello.'

'You want an Icebreaker program. Mine's the best.' Not a man for the social niceties, this Icarus.

Brody slipped into his best corporate negotiator voice. 'So you tell me. I want a demonstration first.'

'Check your bank account.'

'What?' For the first time since they started this, he felt events slipping away from him. McTiernan was getting difficult, but McTiernan could be dealt with. This anonymous voice was something else. The man who called himself Icarus seemed driven, obsessive. His motives were unclear. He had found Brody by computer link and apparently by chance.

Brody didn't like any of it.

'You have home banking facilities, through the

terminal on your desk. In your study. Where you are now sitting, talking to me.' Icarus paused. 'Access your account details now.'

'I don't see what this is supposed to prove.' Brody made the connection to the bank, blessing the foresight that had led him to run a second line through the modem. One CommEx didn't know about, or charge him for. He typed in his password. 'What the –'

'What's the matter?' Juliet walked over to the desk, stared at the screen. 'That can't be right!'

'Convinced, Mr Brody? I have removed the sum we agreed on. If you consider this a sufficient demonstration, I will download the software to your terminal now. Through the line you use to defraud the phone company.' The tone turned mocking. 'I must say, I'm surprised to find a man of such vaunting ambition stooping to petty theft.'

Brody refused to be needled. 'A penny saved is a penny earned, as my dear wife would say. Or, in this case, a penny stolen. As you so rightly point out.'

He smiled at Juliet. She scowled back. She didn't trust Icarus. But then she didn't trust anyone. Except him, of course. Which was quite good, as it happened, because he didn't trust anyone else either. Only her.

'Quite so, Mr Brody. If, on the other hand, you wish to cancel the arrangement, I will replace your funds now. I will terminate this call, and I will not contact you again.'

The line went silent. Decision time. He looked at Juliet. She inclined her head a fraction. Go for it. He concurred.

'A most impressive demonstration, Mr Icarus. I'm looking forward to seeing your program in action.'

'A word of warning.' The screen began to fill with data as the Icebreaker downloaded itself. 'The fee you have paid is for one use only. The software will erase

29

itself at the conclusion of its run. It will also erase itself if you attempt to open or modify any of the system files. Is that perfectly clear?'

'Perfectly.' Blast. He'd been hoping to find a way of duplicating it. Too risky to try that now. Oh well. One run was all they'd need. After that they'd be rich enough not to worry about repeating the hit. Or anything else, ever.

'It's been a pleasure doing business with you.' The sarcasm was unmistakable. Icarus hung up.

After a moment, the datastream stopped. Brody looked at the program he'd bought – for a surprisingly small amount.

It was beautiful.

# « Three »

'This is Romeo Delta to Control. We're ten miles from threshold. Over.'

Ed checked the instruments again, ready to make the minute adjustments to heading and trim that were always necessary this close to the runway, but there was nothing to do. The executive jet continued to slide smoothly down the optimum approach vector, losing altitude as though nailed to an escalator. No doubt about it, this NavCom stuff was something else.

'Roger, Romeo Delta. We have you on radar. You're cleared to land.'

'That's a roger, Control.' Ed scanned the instruments again. 'Romeo Delta out.' He cut the radio, and glanced back at his passenger. 'I'm surprised you needed a pilot. This thing's practically flying itself.'

'According to Quentin, it can. He thinks pilotless planes are the wave of the future.' Jerry switched off her laptop. She had her knees drawn up on the seat. Her shoes, kicked off, lay on the carpet beneath it.

'Where's the fun in that?' Ed asked, appalled at the idea.

Jerry laughed. 'My sentiments exactly.'

'Better get strapped in. We're on final approach.' He returned his attention to the instruments. Moved a hand to adjust the flaps, then withdrew it as the software beat him to it.

'There's really no need.' She complied anyway, straightening up, and snapping the seatbelt closed. 'With NavCom you'll never even notice when the wheels touch the ground.'

'I could go off this thing.' He broke off as the engine power indicator suddenly soared. Acceleration slammed his spine against the seat, and the plane started to climb.

'Ed! What are you playing at?' Jerry shouted. 'If this is supposed to prove a point –'

'I didn't do anything!'

Training and experience fought the surge of adrenalin. Think. Analyse. Stay calm. He nudged the control column forward, tried to level out. It resisted him.

'Maybe NavCom isn't quite as foolproof as everyone thinks it is,' he said, checking the instrumentation. Funny. No failure lights. No emergency displays.

'Romeo Delta, this is Control. You are deviating from your approach vector. Over.'

'I know.' Ed leaned harder against the control column. It moved, suddenly, hurtling the plane into a near-vertical spin. Jerry cried out behind him. Unsecured luggage leapt from the floor and slammed against the inner wall of the fuselage.

'We have a complete loss of control functions. I say again, we have lost all control. Prepare for emergency landing. Over.'

'Roger, Romeo Delta. Listening out.'

Good. Someone was sensible enough to leave the channel open without bothering him with stupid questions. He hauled back on the unresponsive column, while the altitude display flickered downwards with alarming rapidity. Twenty-three thousand feet. Twenty-two. Twenty-one . . .

'Disengage the NavCom,' Jerry cried.

'I'm trying.' He flicked the switch to manual. Nothing. Back to auto. Back to manual again. 'It won't release the controls.'

'This isn't good,' Jerry said.

'You're telling me.'

Eleven thousand feet. Ten. Nine.

Sudden G forces slammed him into his seat. The plane broke out of its spin at seven and a half thousand feet, and started climbing again at full power. No, not climbing . . .

'Hang on to your lunch,' Ed called back. 'We're looping!'

The plane hung, suspended, for an eternal moment, green fields and a silver thread of river wavering above his head; then it fell, powering back towards the ground.

Well, he thought wryly, you always did say you wanted to go out with a bang. Not quite this soon, though.

The altimeter flickered back downwards. The G forces increased. A faint grey fog began whispering at the edges of his vision.

And the plane levelled off. Two hundred feet from the ground. The seat harness cut into his shoulders as it corkscrewed into a barrel roll.

'If this is the wave of the future, Jerry, I'm selling the surfboard!' The plane levelled out again. Ed held his breath. Nothing happened. An old windmill, a familiar landmark, flashed past, too close to the port wing for comfort. They must be almost on top of the airport.

He pulled back on the column. The plane climbed. Flashed over the control tower, registering the shocked faces behind the plexiglass almost subliminally.

'I've got control!'

'Well done.' Jerry dropped into the right hand seat. She slipped on the co-pilot's headset with a smooth economy of motion, crushing her expensive executive hairdo in the process. The functional shoulder harness didn't do a lot for the mustard yellow jacket and skirt either, but she paid them no attention.

'I don't even know what I did,' Ed admitted.

'Who cares? It worked.' She started casting a professional eye over the instrument readings.

Ed was impressed. He didn't know anyone else who would have recovered so fast.

'Romeo Delta to Control.' He took a deep breath, quelling the faint tremor in his voice and hands. Adrenalin comedown. 'We have control again. I repeat, we have re-established control.'

'Well done, Romeo Delta.' The traffic controller sounded more shaken up than he did. 'You're cleared for immediate landing. Over.'

'Glad to hear it. Romeo Delta out.'

He tilted the control column cautiously, banking the plane round in a wide turn. Everything felt normal.

He shot a grin at Jerry. 'Looks like you'll be in time for that meeting of yours after all.'

'Let 'em wait.' Her eyes stayed glued to the airspeed indicator.

Ed lined up on the runway, and adjusted the flaps. They began to descend slowly.

'Undercarriage down.'

They were still descending smoothly. The display went green.

'Undercarriage locked.' Ed made minute adjustments to the angle of descent. An honour guard of fire engines lined the runway. As they crossed the threshold, a couple more started up, following them. 'Here we go.'

The tyres bit. Jumped. Bit again.

'Reversing engines.' He redirected the thrust forward. The plane began to slow. 'Powering down.'

Jerry applied the brakes smoothly. The plane rolled gently to a halt. The fire engines pulled up next to it, and their crews bailed out, deploying their equipment. An ambulance followed, its blue light strobing.

Jerry slumped in the co-pilot's seat. 'I'm getting too old for this. Next time I'm walking.'

'Think I'll join you.' Ed activated the radio for the last time. 'This is Romeo Delta, down and safe.'

'It's the waiting around I can't stand.'

Beckett paced the room. Ros sighed, halfway between exasperation and sympathy, and looked up from the screen of her laptop.

'Give the man a chance, Beckett. He only got our piece of junk mail this morning. He might not even have read it yet.'

'Maybe he's just not interested.' The conviction grew even as he spoke the words. 'Maybe we made it too good. I mean, who actually reads that stuff anyway? He probably never even opened the envelope.'

'He'll read it.' She was just trying to reassure him, he knew. 'You designed it specifically to hook him after all.'

They stared in unison at the newly-installed phone. It failed to ring.

Maybe that was it, Beckett thought. Maybe he'd wired it up badly. He looked speculatively at the junction box.

'If you check that wiring just one more time, I'm going to strangle you with it.' Ros looked levelly at him until he sat down again.

She was right, of course. It was simple enough; a standard telephone, connected to the modem attached to one of the desktop computers. Which, in turn, kept in touch with a simple little intrusion routine they'd inserted into the local exchange. When McTiernan dialled the non-existent number in the letter they'd sent him it would divert the call to the Gizmos account, and that particular extension.

Which meant there was no risk of anyone giving the game away by admitting who they really were when they picked up the phone. Or, for that matter, a client hanging up because they thought they were talking to the wrong company.

He'd been willing the phone to ring for so long that when it did it took him completely by surprise. He started, then hesitated as Ros picked it up.

'Millennium Financial Services. How may I help you?'

She affected the faintly bored, sing-song intonation of switchboard operators the world over. Beckett suppressed a grin. He had to sound serious, he reminded himself. As though he really wanted a slice of this man's money.

'Putting you through now.' Ros pressed a button on the phone. Beckett heard a few bars of the Radetsky March, tinnily, through the earpiece.

Well, why not. They'd had to put up with it. He counted to three, and lifted the nearest extension.

'Investments and Unit Trusts. Nick Beckett speaking.'

'Good morning.' It was the first time he'd heard McTiernan's voice undistorted. Crisper than he'd expected. Self-confident. 'My name's McTiernan. I got one of your mailshots today.'

'Thank you for calling, sir.' Might as well lay it on with a trowel. 'How can we help you?'

'Well, it's rather complicated. But I expect to be coming into a large sum of money soon. And your exserviceman's investment plan looks very attractive.'

36

So it should, Beckett thought. Any real investment broker offering that level of return would go broke within weeks.

'In that case, perhaps we should get together for a chat.' He riffled some papers next to the mouthpiece. 'I could come to your home if that would be convenient.'

Ros directed an expression of shocked surprise at him. He waved, small, calming gestures. If he knew his man at all . . .

'I'd rather not,' McTiernan cut in quickly. 'I run my business from there. Some of the equipment can be dangerous, and I prefer to minimise the possibility of any accidents.'

'I see.' Beckett hesitated, as though thinking. Ros settled again, with a sigh of relief. 'Then perhaps it would be better for you to visit us here.'

'I think so,' McTiernan agreed.

'Fine.' Beckett paused again, just long enough to be making a note. 'Perhaps you'd find our industrial accident insurance worth considering as well.'

'I'm already covered for that.' Perfect. Just the right tone of polite brush-off. He was buying the whole thing.

'Ah. Well, in that case, when would you like to come in?'

'I've one or two things to take care of. How about the day after tomorrow?'

'That would be perfect, Mr McTiernan. Any particular time?' He tied up the rest of the conversation as quickly as he could, and hung up.

'Piece of cake,' Beckett declared.

'What do you mean, piece of cake? You nearly blew it,' Ros said, a touch of asperity entering her voice.

'How?' He dropped into the sofa, sprawled out, and gazed contentedly at the ceiling.

'Offering to see him at his home. Are you out of your mind?'

37

'There was never any chance of him agreeing to that.' Beckett smiled lazily. 'Knowing what he's up to.'

'Fair enough.' She conceded the point. 'But supposing he had?'

'I'd have poked around as much as I could while I was talking to him, and if that wasn't enough we'd try something else.'

'Like industrial accident insurance? What was all that supposed to be about?'

'Extra verisimilitude.'

'Beckett.' She looked him straight in the eye. 'You can't even spell verisimilitude. Let alone explain it.'

'I was supposed to be a salesman. I tried to sell him more than he wanted. It's what salesmen do. If he was at all suspicious before, that will have convinced him I'm genuine.'

'If you say so, Beckett.'

He hadn't convinced her, that was for sure. Before he could pursue the point, the phone rang again. The main one this time.

'Gizmos.' Ros answered it, scooping up the handset in one fluid movement. 'What? You're kidding.' Her face flickered through shock to grim determination. Beckett sat up. This looked serious. 'Stay put. We'll be right there.' She replaced the handset.

'What's up?' Beckett stood, ready to move, but not entirely sure why.

'It's Ed.' Ros started collecting equipment, the set of her shoulders betraying barely suppressed anger. 'Someone's just tried to kill him.'

'They're on their way.' Ed replaced the handset.

'Good.' Jerry paced her office. She felt faintly ridiculous doing it, but she had to dissipate the nervous energy somehow. 'And in the meantime I'll get the technical people to take that plane apart.'

'Well, it's a start. We don't even know what we're looking for, though.'

'But we do know there's something.' She snatched the sheet of fax paper from the surface of her desk, crumpling it angrily in her fist. 'And someone's responsible.'

Ed perched on the edge of the desk. 'Someone's claiming to be responsible. Not necessarily the same thing. Maybe it's just some con artist trying to take advantage of the situation.'

'How would they know?' She threw the ball of paper down again.

'I don't know. But we'll find out.' He hesitated. 'I hope it is a con artist. Because if it's genuine...' he tailed off, unable to find words that wouldn't sound unduly alarmist, settled eventually on '... things could get a bit complicated around here.'

A bit complicated, Jerry thought. That was the biggest understatement she'd ever heard. She watched him smooth out the paper again. Read the words she already knew off by heart. Simple words, in stark block capitals.

NEXT TIME WE KEEP CONTROL. ICARUS.

39

## « Four »

The airport was everything Ros had expected it to be. Large. Anonymous. Wide open. Security here was bound to be a major headache.

Beckett nudged her elbow, and pointed. 'There they are.' Ed waved, and walked towards them. There was a woman with him. Blonde, looked natural. Expensive taste in clothes, but stylish and understated. Probably a good five years older than she looked, too.

'Geraldine Langford?' Ros stuck out a hand. The woman took it, shook once. Firm grip too. A formidable lady. But then she had to be, running an airport this size.

'And you must be Ros.' A welcoming smile. 'Please, call me Jerry.' She glanced at Beckett. 'And Nick, is it?'

'I prefer Beckett.' He shook hands, looking vaguely discomforted.

'Of course. Ed told me. Old service habits die hard.'

She was good with people, Ros thought. An asset in this job. She found herself warming to her.

'It doesn't sound like we've got much to go on,' Beckett said.

Ed nodded his agreement. 'The way I see it, we've

got two possibilities. Either we're dealing with deliberate sabotage, or there's a really sick hoaxer out there somewhere.'

That sounded reasonable. Except for one minor flaw. 'How would a hoaxer know what had happened, though?'

'I've been thinking about that, ever since Ed first suggested it.' Jerry looked thoughtful. 'We were in contact with Air Traffic Control throughout the incident. Anyone with a shortwave radio could have listened in to our transmissions.'

'Well, that narrows it down to just about everyone within a thirty mile radius,' Beckett said. 'I think we'll need a little bit more than that to go on.'

'Our best lead's probably the fax,' Ros said. 'Did you manage to trace it?'

'No.' Jerry shook her head. 'There's no ident. Nothing to go on.'

Ah. A challenge. This could turn out to be fun.

'But you must have a call recording system,' Ros said.

'Well, yes. But I don't see how that could help.'

'If I can get a copy of the signal, I can break it down. Analyse it. Fax machines are as individual as fingerprints.'

'You can do that? From raw data?'

'You'd better believe it,' Ed assured her. 'There isn't an electronic signal on the planet that won't roll over and beg for a biscuit when Ros gets to work on it.'

'He's exaggerating a bit,' Ros conceded. 'But it's worth a try.'

'Right. Then let's try it.'

Beckett looked at Ros. 'And while you're doing that, Ed and I can start going through the technical reports on the plane.' He turned back to Jerry. 'I assume they'll be ready for us?'

'Any time now, I hope. I've got my technical director working on it personally.'

'Does he know his stuff?' Nice one, Beckett, Ros thought. Tactful as always.

Ed cut in. 'I reckon so. And his people are thorough. If there's anything there, they'll find it.'

'I'd still like to go over the system ourselves.' He glanced at Jerry, a belated thread of tact kicking in. 'Get a fresh perspective. And have your people check our results too. See if anything strikes them as odd.'

'That sounds reasonable,' she agreed.

She broke off, waving to someone on the mezzanine floor above them. 'This way,' she said, ushering them towards an escalator.

Ros looked down as they were carried upwards. Across heads, and luggage, and confusion. So many people, she thought. So many lives. Outside, through the glass wall, airliners rose into a flawless blue void, dappled with wisps of cumulus. More lives, cocooned in aluminium, suspended. Vulnerable.

And if someone can really jam flight controls, none of them are safe. She shuddered.

'Ah. Nigel.' Jerry stepped off the escalator, just ahead of her. The man she'd waved to from the concourse was waiting for them. A thin grey man in a thin grey suit. He took in the three of them in a single glance. Evaluating. Unease, some way short of outright hostility, but undeniably present. His voice was flat, as though it were afraid of betraying any emotion.

'Ms Langford.' He nodded, stiffly. 'These are your experts, I take it.'

'That's right.' Jerry waved an introductory hand. 'This is Nigel Todd, our head of security. Nick Beckett, Ros Henderson. Ed you already know, of course.'

'Of course.' Todd's eyes rested a fraction longer on Ed than on anyone else.

Ros found herself wondering what their previous dealings had been. If she knew Ed, he wouldn't have been able to resist winding the man up in some way.

'They'll need airside passes,' Todd said stiffly.

'Of course.' Jerry nodded her agreement, effectively handing the matter over to him.

'If you'll come to my office?' Todd ushered them through a door marked AUTHORISED PERSONNEL ONLY. As it thudded closed behind them, the hubbub of the concourse disappeared.

'Nice view.' Ed glanced approvingly out of the glass-walled corridor, with its panorama of the airport.

'It's useful,' Todd conceded. He fell into step with Jerry. 'I hope you know what you're doing. Calling in outside consultants is highly irregular.'

'So are the circumstances.'

'I'm not disputing that. We could have had a major incident this morning.'

'It felt major enough from where I was sitting.'

'That wasn't what I meant.' Todd waved his hands for emphasis. An oddly forlorn gesture, of a man out of his depth. Ros felt sorry for him. He was obviously doing the best he could, but it just wasn't enough. 'Suppose your plane had come down on the school. Or the ringroad.'

'Then it wouldn't be my problem any more.' An edge of irritation entered the woman's voice. 'Which it is at the moment. And in my judgement we need expert advice, which these people can provide. I'll expect you to co-operate with them.'

'Of course.' Todd nodded. 'But I'm sure there's a simple explanation for all of this.'

'Well it wasn't pilot error,' Ed said, flatly. 'Something affected the controls. Believe me. It was systems failure or sabotage.'

'Well who stands to gain if it was sabotage?' Beckett

asked. 'Do you have any enemies?'

Jerry's jaw dropped. 'You think this was a murder attempt?'

'You were nearly killed,' Beckett pointed out mildly.

'Well, so was Ed. You might as well ask who'd want to kill him.'

'Who wouldn't?' Ros said.

Ed grinned, turning to fire off a verbal riposte, then stopped, his attention caught by something outside the window.

'Who's the guy being shown the exit?' he asked. Everyone turned. Ros tiptoed a view over Beckett's shoulder.

A middle-aged man in a battered trilby and a fraying green cardigan was being politely but firmly escorted away from the terminal building by a couple of uniformed security guards. He was waving his arms vehemently, and his unbuttoned mackintosh was flapping in the breeze.

Todd groaned audibly. 'Kirkby. Our resident plane-spotter. A real pain in the neck.'

Jerry nodded agreement. 'He keeps wandering out of the public areas, trying to get a better view. We just can't get it into his head how dangerous it is out there for unauthorised personnel.'

'He even managed to get airside the other day.' Todd shook his head. 'I found him wandering around in one of the hangars.'

'Really.' Beckett considered the implications. 'I think one of us ought to go and have a word with Mr Kirkby.'

'Well, I've already got a date with Mr Fax Machine,' Ros said hastily. 'Could take hours.'

Unfortunately, Beckett wasn't falling for that one.

'Not as long as checking out the plane's going to take,' he said. 'And we definitely need Ed here for that.'

'Then you go and talk to Kirkby.'

'I was planning to give the security systems the once over. But I suppose that could wait.' Beckett nodded thoughtfully, weighing the options. 'There's only one way to settle this.' He pulled a coin from his pocket, flipped it, and covered the back of his hand. 'Call.'

'Tails,' she said. Beckett lifted his hand.

Blast. 'Best out of three?' she suggested. Beckett hastily re-pocketed the coin. 'Cheat.'

He shrugged, unabashed. 'Look on the bright side,' he said. 'At least you won't have to wear a suit.'

'These are your passes. Wear them at all times.'

Todd held the three slivers of plastic out as though he was about to do a card trick with them. Ed resisted the impulse to take one, examine it, and return it to the deck, although his mouth quirked involuntarily at the image. The man was so pompous it was laughable.

Satisfied that everyone had had time to take them in, Todd slipped the first pass into a slot on his desk terminal, and typed a quick password.

'I'm giving you level two access,' he said. 'That'll get you in everywhere your presence won't compromise safety. If you need to enter any restricted areas, Ms Langford or I will come down to escort you in.'

'What sort of areas might those be?' Beckett asked.

Ed could almost see the lightbulb come on above Beckett's head. Something weird is going on. There's somewhere we're not supposed to go. Therefore that's the obvious place to start looking. Todd could see it too; he was going to enjoy explaining it.

Ed cut in before he could speak. Making Beckett look like an idiot was supposed to be his job. 'Air Traffic Control, for one.' He noted the flicker of annoyance from both men, and chalked up the point. 'Not a good idea to start breathing down their necks while they're juggling the stack.'

'Quite.' Todd returned his attention to the terminal, repeating the process for the remaining two cards. 'Use these as swipe cards on the security locks everywhere else. They'll log you in and out automatically.'

'So you have an automatic record of which passes were used to enter a restricted area?' Ros asked, with apparently casual interest. Ed knew that tone better; she thought she was on to something.

'That's right.' Todd nodded, unbending a little as he turned to speak to her. A touch of gallantry. How unexpected.

'So you must have a record of whose pass was last used to get into the hangar where you found Kirkby.'

'Yes. But it doesn't help.' Todd looked vaguely embarrassed. 'It was mine.'

'You mean you lost your own pass?' Beckett asked, sounding incredulous.

Ed laughed. 'Some head of security you are.'

'It was only gone for a few minutes.' At least Todd was professional enough not to deny it. 'The clip broke. It was a warm day, and I had the jacket slung over my shoulder. I hadn't even noticed it was gone until Richard brought it into the office.'

'Richard?' Ros asked.

'Richard Wyman. Our technical director. He'd stayed on after the meeting to have a word with Ms Langford. He said he'd found it lying in the corridor, outside the conference suite.'

'And you didn't change the codes?' Beckett asked. He clearly found that hard to believe.

'I know, I should have done. But Richard found it in a secure area. It didn't seem urgent.' He spread his hands. 'It never occurred to me that someone might have cloned it.'

'But you've changed them now,' Ed prompted.

'Oh yes.' Todd nodded. 'We've plugged that little leak.'

'I'd like to see the forged card,' Ros said. 'If we can get some idea of how the cloning was done, it might lead us to the perpetrator.'

'Unfortunately, we don't have it. It wasn't on Kirkby when I apprehended him, and he gave me some cock and bull story about the hangar already being unsecured when he wandered inside.' Todd shrugged. 'You're probably going to laugh, but I believe him. He's a fool but he wouldn't put innocent lives at risk. Not on purpose, anyway.'

'Well, maybe we'll find out more when I have a word with him,' Ros suggested.

'Fine.' Beckett picked up one of the passes, and clipped it to his jacket. He handed another one to Ed. 'And while you're sorting that one out, we'll go and check out the plane.'

'Well, that business with your pass proves something at least.'

Ros glanced at Todd's reflection in the workstation screen. The airport communications centre was cramped, stuffed with the miniature electronic exchange that regulated traffic from eight hundred phones, fax lines, and modems. The diagnostic routines were slow and cumbersome, off-the-shelf software a generation old, into which someone had tried to patch new subroutines to cope with the up-to-date hardware. False economy, Ros thought.

'What's that?' Todd watched her work with the fascinated incomprehension of the non-specialist kibbitzing on something only half-understood.

'Whether or not you've got a genuine saboteur on your hands, somebody's compromised your security. Aha.'

Got it. The datastream started downloading to the DAT recorder she'd spliced into the system under Todd's watchful eye. There had been three previous faxes containing vague, but unspecified, threats. Better get those too. Verify they'd all come from the same machine.

'Someone with a fair degree of technical sophistication,' Ros added.

'I was groping towards the same conclusion,' Todd said dryly. 'But I'm still not convinced they're related.'

'It's a working hypothesis, though.' Gotcha! Ros isolated the second signal. One more to go.

'I'm not denying that.' Todd hesitated. 'But I'm not ruling out any other possibilities either.'

Something about the way he said it rang alarm bells in her mind. She looked him directly in the eye.

'What exactly are you trying to say, Todd?'

'Your colleague was involved in the incident this morning.' He chose his words carefully. 'And now here you are. All three of you. Promising to save us from the mysterious Icarus. For the right fee, of course.' He let his words hang. 'As I say, I'm not ruling anything out at this stage. Anything at all.'

'How very open-minded of you.' Ros returned to work.

In spite of himself, Ed found his breath catching as he stepped inside the hangar. The slim executive jet stood at its centre, highlights ricocheting from the curving metal skin. The plane that had tried to kill him, crouched beneath the lights. Expectant. Waiting.

He breathed deeply. Familiar scents. Metal. The sickly sweet tang of aviation fuel. Calming. Comforting.

At least their new passes had worked. The locks had clicked open as Beckett ran his card through the reader, and now here they were.

48

A sudden shaft of daylight stabbed across the floor in front of them. Ed turned. Jerry stood silhouetted in the doorway, gradually taking on substance as the door swung closed behind her.

'Well,' she said. 'There she is.' She joined the two men. Their footsteps rang loudly on the concrete floor as they walked forward in unison. 'Any ideas?'

'A few,' Ed said. 'We were flying by NavCom, so that's the obvious place to start. Look for a glitch in the software.'

'What kind of a glitch?' Jerry asked.

'A bug, or a virus,' Beckett said. 'If we find one of those, we determine once and for all whether it was accident or sabotage.'

'I'm not sure I grasp the distinction,' Jerry said.

'If it's a bug, it's an accident,' Ed explained. 'But a virus would have to have been introduced deliberately. The question is, how?'

'It needn't have been recent,' Beckett said. 'It could have been introduced during routine maintenance, and remained dormant until something set it off.' He frowned. 'But it's an incredibly complicated program. Checking it thoroughly could take days. Weeks even.'

'Maybe we should talk to that friend of yours,' Ed suggested. 'I mean, he wrote the thing.'

Jerry nodded. 'Good idea,' she said. 'I'm sure he'd be pleased to help out.'

Beckett stopped dead in his tracks. 'You mean you can get hold of the designer?'

'Quentin Elverson. Bit of a hermit, but he's amiable enough. He'll probably relish the challenge.' A frown clouded her forehead. 'Unless he thinks you're casting aspersions on his baby, of course.'

'He's a bit obsessed with this software of his,' Ed explained, noticing Beckett's puzzled look. 'Apparently.'

'Obsessed is hardly the word,' Jerry confirmed. 'Any other ideas?'

'We'd like to set up some monitoring equipment,' Beckett said. 'It's possible the system was jammed by some high-frequency signals, maybe up in the microwave bands. Accidentally or on purpose.'

'If you say so.' Jerry sounded unconvinced. She continued to talk technicalities to Beckett. Ed left them to it, and began to walk around the plane. One of the ground crew, anonymous in his company coveralls, was just stepping from the access ladder at the far end of the plane.

'How's it going?' Ed called.

The man broke suddenly into a sprint, his footfalls on the concrete ricocheting from the enclosing walls like machine gun fire. Ed dropped the shoulder bag full of diagnostic equipment he was carrying and took off in pursuit. The man had a fair turn of speed, accelerated by the adrenalin rush of fear, but Ed was younger and fitter. He closed the gap rapidly.

His quarry reached a personnel door in the far wall, fumbling for something in the pocket of the coveralls; a swipe card, like the one Todd had issued him with less than an hour ago. Ed smiled, grimly. No worries. He'd be on him before he could get the door open.

The man must have thought of that. He turned, grabbing a wrench from a nearby workbench, and threw it hard at his head. Ed ducked, instinctively, the spinning metal missing him by inches.

The moment's hesitation was enough. The door swung closed, his quarry behind it.

You don't lose me that easily, Ed thought. He shoulder charged the door, bursting it open again. He hurdled a pile of fallen boxes, obviously knocked over by the fleeing man. He stopped, looking around, his ears straining for the faintest sound.

Nothing. A large, enclosed space, full of bundles and boxes, disassembled aircraft parts. The place was a maze. He held his breath, trying to still the thudding of his heart. Nothing. No movement. No sound.

A faint scraping, over to his right. He moved cautiously towards it, his senses taut. Could be nothing. Could be an ambush. He rounded the tarpaulin-shrouded bulk of some large, unidentifiable engine component.

There. A flicker of movement in the shadows. He began to move a little faster, closing the distance. Maybe they'd start to get some answers now.

A faint rattling overhead. He glanced up, catching movement in his peripheral vision. Something huge and heavy was dropping towards him.

'What was that?' Jerry swung her head, searching for the source of the noise.

'Nothing good.' Beckett did the same. It was hopeless; the impact rang like an explosion in the confined space, echoes bouncing everywhere. The concrete floor vibrated under their feet.

'This way,' Jerry pointed, decisively. 'The middle hoist shouldn't be empty.'

Beckett followed her through the maze of machinery. No doubt about it, he thought, she knew her territory. This was hands-on management taken just about as far as it would go. She vanished around the corner of what looked like an airliner engine, lying broken and distorted on the floor. Stress fractures in the concrete radiated out around it like lunar rills.

'Over here!' Jerry called. Beckett rounded the heap of mangled machinery, apprehension knotting his stomach. If Ed had been under that when it fell . . .

'Are you all right?' Jerry was leaning over Ed, helping him to his feet. The sudden surge of relief left

Beckett breathless. Ed seemed winded, and unnaturally subdued, but neither state of affairs was likely to last for long.

'Yeah.' Ed started brushing himself down. 'But it was a bit too close for comfort.'

'What happened?' Beckett asked.

'Just the usual. Someone trying to kill me. It's starting to get tedious.'

'Did you get a look at his face?' Beckett asked.

Ed shook his head. 'No. But I'd recognise that engine again in a line-up.'

'Big help that'll be.' Beckett turned back to Jerry. 'Looks like we lost him.'

'Maybe not.' She looked speculative. 'He used a pass card to get in here. The computer will have logged it.'

'Good. Where's the nearest terminal?'

'Technical Support. This way.' She led them towards another door at the far end of the room.

A middle-aged man in a well-fitting suit, with a lurid yellow tie incongruous against it, glanced up from a workstation as they entered. Behind him, overalled technicians were working on stripped-down components, diagnostic equipment, and terminals of their own. Beckett saw Ed's eyes flicker over them, failing to spark with recognition. 'Ms Langford. I was about to call your office. We've got the preliminary report ready,' the man said.

'Good.' Jerry flicked a hand between the three men. 'Richard Wyman, our technical director. Beckett. Ed.'

'So you're the security consultants.' Wyman stood, proffered a hand. Beckett shook it. Soft, perfunctory. 'I hope you're not putting Nigel's nose too far out of joint.'

'He's been very helpful,' Beckett said. 'So far. May I borrow your terminal?'

'Be my guest.'

Wyman stood aside to make room for him, and watched with barely concealed interest as he logged into the security system.

'Bingo,' Beckett said. 'The last card used in those locks, before ours was . . .' He tapped a few keys. 'Todd's.'

'It can't have been Todd.' Ed shook his head. 'He's with Ros.' He hesitated. 'Isn't he?'

'One way to find out.' Jerry picked up a nearby phone, dialled a three digit number. She waited for a moment. 'He's out of his office . . . Ah. Nigel. I was about to hang up.' She listened for a moment. 'Is Miss Henderson with you? I see. Yes. We've had another security breach. It looks like your ghost pass is still haunting us.' She listened again. 'No excuses, Nigel. I don't care what you thought you'd done, I want that code cancelled right now. Definitely and for good.' She hung up.

'Well?' Beckett asked.

'Ros left to talk to Kirkby twenty minutes ago. He's got no alibi.'

'It still leaves a pretty tight margin.' Ed sounded dubious.

Beckett agreed with him. But still. Admitting someone had copied his security code would be the perfect cover for misusing it himself. And he had said he'd changed the codes.

'You can't be serious.' Wyman didn't seem sure whether to be amused or outraged at the idea. 'Nigel's a bit of a plodder, but he's totally dedicated. And you know someone copied his pass card. The idea that he could be mixed up in anything shady is utterly ridiculous.'

'Oh yes.' Beckett turned to face him. 'You're the one who found the pass, and handed it back to him.'

'That's right. Ms Langford was with me.' He turned to Jerry for support.

She nodded.

'I hadn't even noticed it myself. But we were discussing some complicated issues,' she explained.

So Wyman wouldn't have had the chance to duplicate the card. On the face of it. But he did have all the equipment he'd need right here. Interesting. And why would a thief plant it somewhere so obvious, unless they wanted to make sure it was found quickly? Before Todd had a chance to alter his authorisation codes, and torpedo the scam.

'So what's our next move?' Ed asked.

'You go through the technical reports, and make a start on scanning the plane,' Beckett said, rubbing his chin thoughtfully. 'I think I'd better go and have a chat with this Elverson.'

'And the best of luck.' Wyman seemed amused at the idea. 'It's as big a waste of time as talking to Kirkby. I mean, they're both nice guys, but barking mad the pair of them.'

Beckett glanced at Jerry to see how she was taking this. After all, Elverson was supposed to be a friend of hers. But she didn't seem to disagree with Wyman's assessment. Terrific.

'Well then,' he said. 'It sounds like I'm in for an interesting afternoon.'

# « Five »

'Good afternoon.' Ros directed an ingratiating smile at the middle-aged man as he opened the front door of his house. It had been harder to find than she'd bargained for, tucked away down a farm track leading off from a little-used lane. It was almost an hour since she'd left the airport. Todd had told her the trip would only take a few minutes. That was the last time she'd trust anyone who said you can't miss it. 'Mr Kirkby?'

'Yes.' Mild blue eyes scrutinised her, blinking with vague puzzlement. Close to, Kirkby was shorter and chubbier than she'd expected after her brief glimpse of him earlier in the day. He didn't look dangerous. He didn't look guilty. If anything, Ros thought, he looked like a prematurely balding teddy bear. 'Can I help you?'

'I hope so.' Ros turned Bright And Eager up a notch, and held out the press credentials Beckett had made up for her in an idle moment a few weeks before. It was the first time she'd used them. Kirkby glanced at them with vague incomprehension. 'I'm doing an article on the effects an airport has on the local community, and I wondered if you could spare me a few minutes? I gather you're something of an expert.'

'I wouldn't say that, exactly.' Kirkby's brow furrowed for a minute, then cleared as some sort of penny dropped. 'Oh. Because I'm on the parish council, you mean?'

'Precisely,' Ros said, as though she'd known that all along. Kirkby stepped aside, and ushered her in.

'Well, I'll do my best. The living room's the most comfortable.' He opened a door off the hall. 'Sorry about the mess. I don't get many visitors out here.'

The room was immaculate. Bright sunlight spilled in through leaded light windows, dappling the carpet and the three piece suite. Bookshelves filled most of one wall, crammed with books on aviation. A lower shelf was stuffed with back issues of aircraft magazines, and a few more recent copies lay on the coffee table in the middle of the room.

Every other flat surface was covered with miniature aeroplanes. Airliners, mostly. A large, radio controlled Spitfire was on the desk in one corner, partly disassembled and surrounded by tools. Ros took a couple of steps towards it, feigning interest, while her eyes took in the fax machine and the modem, linked to the desktop computer, which had been shunted to one side to make room for it.

'I really need a proper workbench,' Kirkby said. 'It's a bit of a nuisance having to pack everything away when I need to do paperwork.'

'You're certainly equipped to do that,' Ros said. 'That's a pretty impressive computer.' It was top of the range, less than a year old, and ridiculously overpowered for simple home use.

'One of Quentin's spares,' Kirkby explained. 'Quentin Elverson, that is. One of my neighbours. You ought to talk to him too. Fascinating chap. He's in the business. Writes aviation software. Always upgrading his system and selling off the old stuff.' He patted the hard drive affectionately. 'A real collector's item this. The original workstation the second edition updates for the NavCom system were bench tested on.'

'I've heard of that.' Ros tried not to show too much interest. 'I don't suppose you've still got a copy on there?'

'Of course not.' Kirkby looked slightly disappointed. 'Quentin wiped the hard disk before he donated it.'

'Donated?' Ros asked. 'To the parish council you mean?'

'Partly. I'm secretary of the local flying club too. He thought it might help with some of the paperwork.'

'Flying club?' Ros considered the implications. Kirkby was beginning to look more convincing as a suspect by the minute. 'So you're a pilot yourself?'

Kirkby's face crumpled, an expression of forlorn yearning flickering across it. The sheer rawness of the visible emotion shocked her. He looked like an overgrown child locked out of the sweetshop. He shook his head.

'I'm afraid not. I have – used to have – epilepsy. I haven't had an episode in years, but the regulations are ridiculously inflexible. I can never hold a pilot's licence of my own.'

'I'm . . . sorry.'

Kirkby shook himself free of his introspective mood. 'Well, it can't be helped. Some of the other members take me up. And I like to visit the airport most days. Watch the airliners.'

'Yes, I know.' Ros watched him carefully, wondering how he'd react. 'I've already spoken to Mr Todd.'

A mischievous grin spread across his face. 'Poor old Nigel. He's a bit of a stuffed shirt, isn't he?'

'Yes, he is rather,' Ros agreed.

'Salt of the earth, mind you. Works awfully hard for

57

the parish council. Very civic minded. A sound man on drains. Get him in the pub afterwards, and he's perfectly amiable.'

'So you'd consider him a friend?' Ros asked.

'Not a friend, exactly. More of a pleasant acquaintance. Except when he's throwing me out of the airport, of course.'

He thinks it's all a game, Ros thought. Todd was right. He really has no conception of the trouble he could cause. Or get into.

'Do you know any of the other airport staff?' she asked.

'Well, there's Richard Wyman. Turns up at the flying club occasionally. Seems nice enough, but we don't see a lot of him. He's a busy man.' He certainly is today, Ros thought. 'And he lives on the other side of Hunsford, so Collington's a fair distance for him to come.'

'Collington? So the club isn't attached to the airport?'

'No. Too much commercial traffic. Look.' Kirkby called up a map on the computer screen. 'These are the flight paths in and out of the airport. And here's Collington. Well out of the way. It's an old Air Command station. We lease part of it from the ministry.'

'What do they do with the rest of it?' Ros asked. This was getting weirder by the moment.

Kirkby shrugged. 'Nothing. That's the whole point. They use it as a dumping ground for obsolete aircraft. Once they've stripped out anything worth salvaging, of course.'

'Of course,' Ros echoed. Coincidence. It had to be. But ... 'There haven't been any accidents there recently, have there?'

'Accidents? Of course not.' Kirkby bristled slightly. 'Our safety record is second to none.'

'I'm glad to hear it.'

Kirkby relaxed again. 'But I'm forgetting my manners,' he said. 'Would you care for a cup of tea?'

Elverson's home had been easy to find. Just look for the windmill, Jerry had said, and turn left. Then second right. Piece of cake. Beckett hadn't even had to use the automap software. He slammed the door of his four by four, and looked around.

The cottage was isolated, screened from the road by a line of trees and a meticulously maintained hedge. A garage, its door closed, stood to one side of the house. The gravel of the turning circle crunched under his feet as he walked towards the front door.

A small video camera, mounted on a bracket inside the porch, tracked him as he moved. No sign of a knocker or a bell.

Well, at least he was expected. Jerry had phoned from the airport to warn Elverson he was coming. Faxed him a photograph too. Beckett stared into the camera, feeling slightly foolish, waiting to be identified. There was an audio pickup below the lens. He cleared his throat.

'Mr Elverson? It's Mr Beckett. I believe you're expecting me.'

The door clicked, and swung open. Beckett stepped forward, his hand outstretched. He'd already begun to mumble an automatic greeting before he realised he was alone. He stepped cautiously into the front hall.

'Mr Beckett. Please come in.' Elverson appeared in a doorway at the far end of the corridor. 'I think you'll find my study the most comfortable.' The front door swung silently closed.

'It's good of you to see me at such short notice,' Beckett said.

He followed the man into a room full of computer equipment. A workstation in one corner was humming quietly to itself, evidently abandoned in mid-task. A small window in the corner of the screen overlaid the video image of a panoramic view of the front garden, obviously piped through from the camera in the porch. His own face was spilling from the output slot of a fax machine, the sheet of paper hanging down from it like a diseased tongue.

Elverson waved him to an easy chair, and settled into another one opposite. With his neatly-clipped white beard and receding hairline, he reminded Beckett of a gently reproving Santa Claus.

'When it's a question of defending my work from baseless scaremongering, I can always find the time,' he said. Wyman had been right, Beckett thought; he was fiercely protective of his precious program. He'd have to choose his words with great care.

'It's just one of a range of possibilities we're investigating,' he said. 'But you must appreciate, in a matter this serious, we have to consider every potential cause. Even the most unlikely one.'

That seemed to mollify the old boy; he relaxed a little in his seat, and nodded judiciously. 'I suppose so. But it's a complete waste of time.'

'That's why I wanted to talk to you,' Beckett said. It felt uncannily like trying to persuade McTiernan to buy a non-existent investment plan. Had that really only been this morning? 'The sooner we can eliminate NavCom from the enquiry, the sooner we can start narrowing down the other possibilities.'

'The likely possibilities,' Elverson said. 'I'm sure it'll turn out to be pilot error. These things usually do.'

Lucky Ed was back at the airport, safely out of earshot, Beckett thought.

Elverson leaned forward in his seat, his enthusiasm growing. 'Information overload, you see. The faster, more sophisticated aircraft become, the quicker pilots have to react to changes in circumstance. And the more information they have to assimilate. We're already at the limits of human adaptability. And the next generation of aircraft will be even more complex.'

'Hence the need for NavCom,' Beckett put in.

'That's right.' Elverson nodded. 'It takes all the decisions itself. Eases the burden. One day it'll replace human pilots completely.'

'According to the pilot this morning, the problem began while the aircraft was under NavCom's control. When he tried to disengage it, the system locked him out. Refused to switch the controls back to manual.'

'I don't see how that's possible,' Elverson said. 'Unless there was some sort of problem with the aircraft's own systems. If NavCom was trying to compensate for a glitch in the fly by wire software, it might not release the controls if it diagnosed a fault in the manual interface. Not until it had restored straight and level flight, anyway.'

'That ties in with the pilot's report,' Beckett said. 'The controls went back to manual once the plane had levelled out.'

'There you are, then.' Elverson smiled triumphantly. 'Check out the manual interface and you're home and dry.'

'I wish I shared your confidence,' Beckett said. 'But we have other evidence that points to deliberate sabotage.'

Elverson's eyebrows shot upwards. 'Then NavCom undoubtedly prevented a terrible accident.'

'Unless it was NavCom itself that was sabotaged.' Beckett struggled on. 'Can you think of any way that someone might have found to tamper with the software? However unlikely?'

'None at all.' Elverson was positive. 'It has the most

61

rigorous anti-virus protection of any commercial aviation package. After all, when it's piloting an airliner, hundreds of lives are at stake.'

'Precisely,' Beckett said.

Elverson stood, and walked over to the workstation. He ejected a CD from the drive.

'Here.' He slipped it into a case, and handed it to Beckett. 'The latest version. Just as it would have been originally installed. Compare them. If there is a bug or a virus in your aircraft's system, there'll be an obvious discrepancy. But I'm sure you won't find one.'

'Thank you.' Beckett slipped the disk into his pocket. 'You've been a great help.'

'Don't mention it.' Elverson ushered him to the front door, and raised a hand in farewell.

As Beckett unlocked his car, Elverson called out. 'Oh. Mr Beckett. If you do discover an anomaly, please let me know.' A hint of a smile. 'After all, it's not every day I get to see the impossible.'

Kirkby was taking an awfully long time with the tea. Ros checked her watch again. Too long.

At first she'd been grateful for his absence. The moment he'd disappeared she'd made for the phone on the desk, dialled the airport, and activated the fax's test routine. When she got back she'd have a signal to compare with the faxes from Icarus.

It didn't make sense, though. Kirkby wasn't the type to be involved in anything like that. Unless someone was using him. He'd be easy to manipulate. An overgrown schoolboy, obsessed with aviation, who thought dodging Todd's security guards was a game of tag. All Icarus would have to do was tell him he was playing some kind of practical joke, and Kirkby would do whatever he was asked without a thought for the consequences.

Icarus. He wasn't a hoaxer, Ros was sure. He was someone with a definite plan. Someone dangerous.

The house was too quiet. She stood, walked to the door, and nudged it ajar. It creaked. She took a step into the hall.

'Mr Kirkby?' No reply. No sound or movement from the top of the stairs. 'Mr Kirkby. Are you all right?'

Silence. She padded down the corridor, all but silent on the carpet. A grandfather clock ticked loudly, the pendulum syncopating with the thudding of her heart. Something was definitely wrong.

She tried a door. It led to a dining room, the table covered with model aircraft parts, neatly laid out on sheets of newspaper. Pictures of aeroplanes hung on the walls, but there were signs of earlier decoration too, farming scenes and horsebrasses. He obviously spent a lot less time in here. She returned to the hall.

The door at the end must be the kitchen. As she moved towards it, an eddy of vapour edged out, hugging the ceiling. Steam. She pushed the door open.

The room was full of steam, issuing from a kettle on the old-fashioned cooking range. It must have all but boiled dry by now. She hurried towards it, plucking it from the heat, dropping it again hastily as the metal scorched her fingers. The hot, moist air began to clear, dispersed by a cooler draught.

The back door was ajar. Odd. He must have stepped out for a moment. She walked around the kitchen table.

'Oh no.'

Kirkby was lying on the floor, a cup and saucer near his outstretched hand. A neat, unmistakable bullet hole in the back of his head. She knelt, already knowing it was useless, and laid a hand across his carotid artery.

No pulse. Big surprise.

She looked around the kitchen. As she'd expected, it

was clean and neat. No obvious clues. The door didn't seem forced, but then it might have been open anyway. This was the countryside after all. Two cups and saucers were standing ready on the table. A teapot. A caddy of Earl Grey tea standing next to it, the lid already off. A plate with a neat circle of biscuits arranged around the rim. A jug of milk, still frosted from the fridge. And a sugar bowl. He'd been taken completely by surprise.

Wait a minute. Two cups and saucers on the table. A third set on the floor. The implication was obvious.

Kirkby had known his killer. Well enough not to be surprised when he turned up unannounced at his back door. She could reconstruct the conversation as vividly as if she'd bugged the room.

Hello. Come in. This is a surprise. You're just in time for tea. Then he'd turned his back to get another cup out, and the killer had shot him. A silenced automatic at point-blank range.

Her knees went weak. If the assassin had realised the significance of the extra cup on the table . . .

She approached the back door cautiously and peered out across the farmyard. Nothing. She edged along the wall, her back pressed tight against the cold stone, expecting to feel the impact of a bullet at any moment. Stupid, her rational mind said. He's long gone, whoever he was. If he knew I was there he'd have killed me too, while he had the chance.

Nevertheless she crouched low, keeping to the cover of the garden wall. Maybe that's what he wants me to think. Just because you're paranoid, it doesn't mean they're not out to get you.

The drive turned here, a dogleg round to the front of the house. Round that corner was her car. Safety. A way out of here. She froze. If the killer had seen her car he'd have known for sure she was there.

Wait. Fresh tyre tracks, coming and going. Turning in the entrance to the yard. He hadn't gone far enough to see her car after all.

She let out her breath in a long, relieved sigh. And started to run.

She let out her breath in a long, relieved sigh. And

# « Six »

'Well, that's it then.' Beckett sat back in the swivel
chair, and pushed it away from the terminal. 'Someone's got into the computer security system.'

'Are you sure?' Ed scooted his own chair across the
narrow room. Wyman had found them a corner of his
department to work in, but it was far from ideal.
The three workstations were almost on top of one
another, and there was barely enough room to patch in
the specialised equipment he and Ros had brought
with them. Just as well Ed had already been here, he
thought. If they'd had a third car load of kit, they
would have spilled out into the corridor.

'Positive. Look.' He called up the data.

Ros leaned in across his shoulder for a better view.
'So that's how they did it,' she said.

'Did what?' Ed looked baffled. But then Icebreakers
weren't really his field of expertise.

'Kept the ghost pass active when Todd changed the
codes,' Ros explained.

'They've inserted a lurker program,' Beckett explained. 'Normally it hides itself, pretending to be part
of the communications interface. When Todd changes

66

his codes it activates, copies the new authorisations, and holds the duplicate data. All our ghost has to do is download it back to his own card.'

'Clever,' Ed said.

'It was. I'm about to delete it.' Beckett's fingers hovered over the keyboard.

'Wait a minute,' Ros said. 'Can't you follow it back? If we can find which terminal the duplicate data was downloaded from . . .'

'Already thought of that. It cleans up after itself. Automatically erases any traces of access.' He shrugged. 'It may not be any of the terminals here at all. For all we know, it could be someone hacking in from outside.'

'That would need some pretty sophisticated intrusion routines,' Ros said doubtfully.

'Yes. It would.'

Like the one Dent was so interested in, perhaps? If it even existed, he'd said. You'll know it if you see it. Well, there was nothing here to see. Which might be significant in itself. He pushed the idea to the back of his mind, and deleted the program. Let's just wait and see what develops.

'How are you two getting on?' he asked.

'Well, NavCom looks clean,' Ed replied, sounding as though he took it as a personal insult. 'I've compared everything from the plane with the CD ROM Elverson gave you. A perfect match.' He shook his head. 'But I still don't buy it.'

'Pride a bit bruised, is it?' Beckett couldn't resist teasing him a little. 'Must be galling to be outflown by a computer.'

'You weren't there. I know what happened. It wasn't just a random failure, whatever Elverson says. The manoeuvres were textbook. Too perfect. It felt like someone was flying the plane.'

'Well, NavCom's supposed to be an expert system,'

Ros pointed out. 'It ought to fly like a real pilot.'

'It's not the same.' Ed shook his head, evidently frustrated at his inability to explain in words. 'It just didn't feel right, that's all.'

'Go over it again, then,' Beckett said. He trusted Ed's instincts a lot more than a bundle of software, however good it was supposed to be. 'Look for traces of data erasure. If it was a one-time virus it would have deleted itself after running, but it might still have left a hole behind.'

'Gotcha.' Ed turned back to his own workstation, looking a lot happier.

Beckett looked up at Ros. 'Getting anywhere with the fax signals?'

'I think so.' She hit a few keys on her terminal. A digital waveform appeared across the top of the screen. 'This is the signature of the Icarus faxes. All from the same machine. And this . . .' She called up another waveform. ' . . . is from Kirkby's. They're identical. No doubt about it.'

'So Kirkby was Icarus?' It didn't feel right. Ros obviously shared his doubts.

'I don't see it, Beckett. I really don't. I think he was being set up as the fall guy. And when we got too close . . .'

'Icarus popped him. In case he gave the game away.' It sounded more likely than any of the other hypotheses he'd come up with. Ros nodded.

'And there's something else. He had a modem on his phone line. So someone could have phreaked in and bounced the signal through his fax. Just made it look as though it came from Kirkby's.'

'Better and better.' They couldn't even narrow the list of suspects down to people he'd known, then. Not for certain. But it was a place to start. 'Who knew about his computer system?'

'Everyone on the parish council. Which includes our friend Todd, by the way. At least some of the members of the Collington Flying Club. Which might include Wyman. And Quentin Elverson. He set it up for him in the first place.'

'Quite a cosy little community, isn't it?'

'That's village life for you, Beckett. Everyone knows everyone else.'

'How very convenient.' Not to mention confusing.

'So much for that.' Ed pushed back from his terminal, frustration colouring his voice. 'The software's clean.'

'Which brings us back to outside interference,' Ros concluded.

Beckett nodded. It had to be. Luckily they'd managed to squeeze the monitoring equipment into the back of his off-roader.

'Ed, my boy.' Beckett stood, clapping him on the shoulder. 'You're looking peaky.' Ed looked up, suspicious.

'Definitely peaky,' Ros agreed. 'Too much time cooped up indoors.'

'Staring at computer screens,' Beckett added. 'It isn't healthy.'

'You need some fresh air.'

'Fresh air and exercise.' They nodded agreement at one another.

'What sort of exercise?' Ed asked.

'You'll love it,' Beckett assured him. 'After all, you like climbing things. Don't you?'

It was cold at the top of the radio mast. Ed shivered, and zipped his jacket up to the neck. The thin metal structure swayed gently in the wind.

'Be careful, Ed.' Ros's voice sounded in his earpiece. He grinned, turning his face to the wind, feeling it ripple through his hair.

'You were right,' he said. 'Fresh air and exercise. I feel like a new man.'

'Put a foot wrong up there and you'll become one.' Beckett. Always worrying about nothing.

'I'm fine.' He swung himself on to a narrow inspection platform. 'Great view from up here.' He looked down, waved to his colleagues on the rooftop below. Ros waved back, a tiny hand two hundred feet below. He unslung the microwave aerial from his back, and unfolded it. Slot that in here, and that in there, and we're ready to go. Assuming he could find somewhere to put it.

'Deploying the aerial now.'

That would do. A narrow gap, between two of the communications antennae. He took the spanner and the retaining brackets out of his pocket. Clamped the assembly to a convenient girder, and tightened the nuts. Plugged the cable in.

'Look out below. I'm dropping the cable.' He let the other end fall, unreeling as it went, to smack on to the roof at the feet of his colleagues. Beckett picked up the other end and attached it to the monitoring equipment laid out at the base of the mast.

'Fine,' Beckett said. 'It's working.'

Great. He took a last look round before descending. The view was spectacular from up here. He could see the entire airport; beyond that, the windmill, and still further away, the village of Hunsford itself. In the middle distance an airliner was taxiing out on to the runway. Glancing down he could see the terminal building, and closer than that . . .

'Uh oh.'

'Uh oh what?' Ros asked.

'Todd. He's heading this way. And he doesn't look happy.' He started down.

He arrived back on the rooftop a moment or two

70

before Todd erupted through the doorway leading down into the building. He was, indeed, unhappy.

'What on earth do you think you're doing up here?' He looked from one to the other, his gaze lingering longest on Ed. Then a suspicious glare at the equipment. 'And what's all this?'

'Monitoring equipment,' Beckett explained. 'We're scanning for any signals that shouldn't be here. It's beginning to look as though whatever affected the aircraft this morning was jamming the system from the outside.' This was clearly lost on Todd.

Ed affected his most helpful expression. 'We're scanning mainly in the microwave and UHF bands. We think they're the most plausible candidates for a trojan signal.'

Todd's air of bafflement grew. 'This is a restricted area,' he said.

'But you gave us level two access,' Beckett said. 'Which reminds me. You'll have to change your pass codes again.'

'What?' Todd was beginning to get angry now. 'What have you done this time?'

'Saved your bacon, we think,' Ros explained. 'Someone's got into your security system. They've already copied your current codes.'

'But we deleted their ferret program,' Beckett assured him. 'So the next time you change them they should stay secure.'

'I see.' He obviously didn't. 'So what's to stop them hacking in again and replacing it?'

'Well, we've put in some tripwires.' Even Beckett sounded less confident than usual. 'If they try again, we should know about it. Maybe even get a look at the intrusion systems they're using.'

'But you can't keep them out. I see.' Todd jumped on the unspoken implication.

'It's not as easy as all that,' Ed said. 'After all, you didn't even know they were there.' Ros glared at him. Well, maybe it hadn't been too tactful to point that out. Too late to worry about it now, though.

'You still haven't answered my question.' Todd refused to be diverted. 'You were told to check with me or Ms Langford before entering any areas where safety might be compromised.'

'We didn't think that applied here,' Ros said. 'We're all thoroughly familiar with communications systems.'

'These aren't just phone lines you can tap into whenever you feel like it!' Todd was outraged. 'These are vital links between planes and Air Traffic Control! One slip here could cost hundreds of lives . . .'

'We really do know what we're doing, Todd.' Ed tried to play the diplomat. 'And Wyman said . . .'

'Oh great. Now Wyman's going behind my back too.' Todd held his temper with a visible effort. 'Understand this. I'm head of security. That makes me responsible for questions of safety, not Richard Wyman. If he approves a course of action on technical grounds, you still have to bring it to me or Ms Langford to make a final decision. Is that clear?'

'Perfectly clear. Thank you.' Beckett nodded, curtly. It seemed polite enough, but Ed knew that tone. He was losing patience rapidly.

Without warning, a klaxon mounted on a corner of the roof began howling. Talk about saved by the bell, Ed thought. Ros raised her voice, barely audible over the skull-splitting noise.

'Emergency drill?' she shouted.

'There's none scheduled.' Todd made for the stairs at a run, his irritation forgotten. 'This one's for real!'

Ed followed without a thought. The others rattled down the staircase behind him.

* * *

72

'Mayday, mayday, mayday.'

Captain Roger Kramer spoke as calmly as he could. This was the moment every pilot tried not to think about, but couldn't help wondering every time they practised the emergency drills in the simulator; how would I react if it happened for real? But when it did, the training took over. There'd be time to panic later. He hoped.

'This is Hotel Lima Six Four Seven. We have complete failure of all control systems. I say again, complete failure. Please stand by for an emergency landing. Over.'

'Any sort of landing would do.' His co-pilot, Monica Trent, wrestled with the control column. 'She's still locked into straight and level flight. At this rate we won't be coming down till we run out of fuel.' Only the angle of her shoulders betrayed her tension.

'Well, that gives us a good few hours yet.' Which might be something of a mixed blessing. It gave them longer to regain control. But in an emergency landing the tanks could rupture. It would only take a spark on the runway to send them up in a fireball.

The implications weren't lost on Trent. 'Shall I vent the tanks?' she asked.

'Not yet,' Kramer decided. Once they did that, they were committed. Land or die. And if the controls were still frozen, they wouldn't have a cat in hell's chance of gliding her in.

'Roger, Hotel Lima Six Four Seven.' The traffic controller's voice was reassuringly calm. 'Emergency services are standing by. Over.'

'Thank you control.' Kramer ran a practised eye over the cockpit monitor screens. 'All systems are reading normal. But we still have no control. Over.'

'Stand by, Hotel Lima Six Four Seven.' The channel went dead for a moment. Out of the corner of his eye, he could see Trent running diagnostic routines. Check, check, check. Green lights all the way. So why wasn't anything working? The voice came back. 'We have a pilot here who experienced a similar systems failure this morning. We're putting him on now.'

'Good.' Kramer felt a surge of relief. If he was there in Air Traffic Control, he must have got his own plane down safely. 'We're open to suggestions up here.'

'Hi there.' A new voice came on, the cheery tone belying the underlying tension in it. An Australian accent. 'Look, when it happened to me this morning, the controls went back to manual spontaneously.'

'Well they're not doing that now,' Trent said. 'We're still locked out.' The engine note rose in pitch, and the nose tilted. Kramer leaned hard on the column. It wouldn't move.

'We've started climbing,' he said.

'Get everyone strapped in. Now.' The Australian dropped any pretence of relaxation. 'If I'm right, you're about to experience some drastic manoeuvres.'

Trent hit the button for the seat belt sign. Kramer activated the intercom.

'Ladies and Gentlemen. This is your captain speaking. Please fasten your seatbelts immediately. We are about to enter a region of extreme turbulence . . .'

The bottom dropped out of the world. The plane tilted forward, diving suddenly. His stomach lurched. Through the windshield, Kramer gaped at the pattern of fields now pinwheeling furiously. Trent hauled back futilely on the control column.

'Hotel Lima Six Four Seven.' The air traffic controller's voice was tense. 'You're descending too fast. Pull up!'

'We're trying,' Kramer said. He pulled back on the unresponsive column, his muscles cracking. 'We still have no control.'

'We believe the problem may be in the manual interface.' The Australian again. 'Can you override it? Over.'

'Negative, Control.' Trent was dabbing frantically at the touch screen in front of her. 'We're still locked out.'

No help for it, then. Kramer re-activated the intercom.

'Ladies and Gentlemen. We are experiencing problems with our computerised control functions. We are still trying to clear the fault. In the meantime, purely as a precaution, please take up your emergency positions.'

Trent flashed him an ironic grin. 'Nicely put. I'm glad I'm not one of the cabin staff right now.'

The altimeter plummeted.

'Oh no.' Kramer's blood turned to ice. 'Control. We're heading straight for the housing estate. Can you evacuate?'

'Negative, Hotel Lima.' The controller's helpless horror was evident in his voice, even over the radio. 'There's no time. Two minutes to impact.'

A strange, almost supernatural calm came over Kramer. No fear. No regrets. So this is it, he thought dispassionately. I'm going to die. The analytical part of his mind seemed to take over entirely. He activated the intercom for the last time.

'Brace! Brace!' he said, wondering how many of the passengers would have been listening to the stewardess at the start of the flight, and would realise that meant a crash was imminent. Houses filled the windshield, model railway people staring up at him in horrified expectation.

*Beep!* The status display on the screen suddenly changed. *Manual Control Selected.*

'We have control!' He hauled back on the stick.

Beside him, Trent did the same. The horizon beyond the nose began to tilt, dropping away again. Slowly. Too slowly?

'We're climbing,' Trent said, a faint catch in her voice. 'Two hundred feet. Two hundred and fifty . . .'

'Good.' Reaction hit suddenly, leaving him trembling. 'Then let's get this thing on the ground before anything else has a chance to go wrong.'

'They're down.' The air traffic controller let out a sigh of relief. He turned to Ed. 'Thanks for coming in.'

'I wish I could feel I'd done something to help,' Ed said. But he hadn't. Just sat and listened, while another pilot had repeated his own ordeal. And just like his own experience, the fault had cleared as mysteriously as it had begun. If it really was a fault.

He turned to pick up his jacket, hung over the back of a nearby chair. Glanced at the computer screen beyond it. And froze.

'Look at this.' No doubt about it. Not any more. Both incidents had been sabotage. Deliberate.

I WANT FIFTY MILLION POUNDS BY EIGHT AM TOMORROW, the screen said, in lurid block capitals. ICARUS.

# « Seven »

'It's come up on every screen in the airport,' Jerry said. Behind her, through the window, the complex seemed eerie in the gathering twilight. No movement. No aircraft. No people. Weird. It was only in their absence, Ros thought, that they became noticeable. 'Can you trace the source?'

'Beckett's working on it now,' she said. 'But it's not easy. We know Icarus is using some highly sophisticated intrusion software. Until we manage to isolate it, and devise some specific protection, he can hack in and out virtually at will.'

'Some experts you are,' Todd said scathingly. 'I thought you said you'd put some protection in place.'

'Not protection. Just tripwires,' Ros said. 'We can analyse the effect Icarus's Icebreaker had on them, and try reconstructing the code. We may even be able to follow the traces back. But it'll take time.'

'Time we don't have.' Todd looked at each face around the conference table in turn. Jerry. Wyman. Ed. And back to Ros. 'I think it's time to get some professionals in. You've had your chance.'

'We're the best chance you've got, Todd.' Ed rose to

the bait. 'And you've been down on us ever since we first got involved.'

'Well, that's just it.' Todd looked thoughtful. Insinuating. 'You've been involved right from the start, haven't you?'

'Are you suggesting we're Icarus?' Ed looked as though he wasn't sure whether to laugh or lose his temper. Ros was pretty sure which reaction Todd was hoping for. She glanced at Jerry, hoping to see some sign of support. She looked sceptical, but was still listening.

'I haven't entirely discounted the possibility,' Todd said. 'But I doubt it.'

Well, thanks for nothing, Ros thought.

The security chief went on. 'The point is, you were almost killed this morning, and in my opinion that's affecting your judgement. You and your colleagues have been treating this like a personal vendetta. In the course of which you've blundered into restricted areas, flouted safety procedures, and put innocent lives at risk.' He turned to Jerry. 'This cannot be allowed to continue.'

'How have we put innocent lives at risk?' Ros asked.

'You mean apart from interfering with the communications system?' Todd shot back.

'We didn't interfere with anything. We just installed some monitoring equipment.'

'Which you've already admitted failed to monitor anything during the incident this afternoon.'

'If we hadn't been interrupted before we could finish setting it up, it might have done.'

'And for all we know your precious microwave gadgets might well have caused the problem in the first place.'

'For all you know,' Ed said scornfully, 'it might have been the battery in your watch.' Wyman trapped an

78

incipient laugh behind the bridge of his nose, and coughed loudly. Jerry suppressed a smile.

'Ms Langford.' Todd tried to regain the initiative. 'However well-intentioned these people are, they're loose cannons. And we simply can't afford any more complications at the moment.'

This argument seemed to be having some effect. Ros watched Jerry consider it, a sinking feeling in the pit of her stomach.

'Yes. You're right, of course.' Jerry nodded. 'But we can't afford to lose their expertise now either.' She turned to Ros and Ed. 'I'm asking Nigel to rescind your security clearances. From now on, you'll need an escort to enter any of the restricted areas.' Well, it could be worse. At least she hadn't fired them outright.

'Whatever you think best,' Ros said, her resignation evident. But she took some small satisfaction in watching Todd deflate, having braced himself for an argument that hadn't happened.

'I hate to drag the meeting back to the point,' Wyman said. 'But what are we going to do about all this?'

'We've evacuated the airport. Diverted all the incoming flights. But that's purely a stopgap.' Jerry was back in control of the briefing. 'As soon as they resume, Icarus can start playing his little games again.'

'Not to mention the loss of revenue while we're shut down.' Wyman worked the keys of a scientific calculator, and whistled softly. 'As much as that?'

'Exactly.' Jerry nodded, incisively. 'I'm doing my best to get the money. But it's a considerable sum to get together at such short notice.'

'We may be able to help you there,' Ros said. 'We have high level contacts in several merchant banks. Kamen and Ross, Yamada Global . . .'

'Thank you.' Jerry smiled gratefully. 'That would be a great help.'

'Are you serious?' Todd interrupted. 'You know the industry guidelines are quite specific about non-payment of ransom demands.'

'I also know that lives are in danger if we don't.' Jerry closed the subject. 'I trust you'll make all the necessary arrangements?'

'Of course.' Todd stood. 'Just don't expect me to like it. If you'll excuse me?' He stomped out of the room.

Ros wondered how Beckett was getting on.

Icarus was a genius, Beckett thought. He downloaded fragments of coding from his lobster traps. This was the most sophisticated Icebreaker he'd ever seen. It had penetrated the existing security systems without leaving a trace. Only the tripwires he'd installed that afternoon had registered it, and then just barely.

It was like being a palaeontologist, he thought. Trying to reconstruct a fossil from the imprint it had left behind in the surrounding soil. But at least a palaeontologist usually had some idea of what he was working with.

Let's see now. Animal, vegetable, or mineral? He glanced up as Ed entered the narrow workroom.

'How's it going?' Ed asked.

'Slowly,' Beckett said. He shifted the fragments of computer code around the screen, trying to get them to form a pattern. Some vague impression of recognition hovered frustratingly on the fringes of his subconscious, slipping away every time he tried to focus on it. What was it Dent had said? You'll know it when you see it?

His conviction that this was the Icebreaker the Hive was interested in grew stronger with every minute he studied it. The question was, why? And who had written it?

'How's it going upstairs?'

'All over bar the shouting.' Ed shrugged. 'Mainly from Todd. If you can't trace that signal back, Jerry's going to pay.'

'No chance of that. It's too well protected.' Maybe if he inverted it? Nah. Worth a try, though.

'Oh yes. Mr Personality has just pulled our security clearance,' Ed added.

'Terrific.' Beckett barely glanced up from the screen. 'You know, this is a beautiful piece of coding. The best I've ever seen.'

'Yeah.' Ed pulled up one of the swivel chairs. 'Don't take this the wrong way, Beckett. But coming from an ex-signals intelligence spook, that really worries me.'

'Me too,' Beckett said. 'If anyone else has managed to get hold of a copy, then we could all be in serious trouble.'

'Maybe.' Ed tried to lighten his mood. 'But this Icarus is a pretty secretive guy, right? Who else would he have passed a copy on to?'

'How much longer is this going to take?' Juliet Brody asked. Bryan stopped fiddling with the cables hanging from the back of his computer, and smiled at her. She smiled back, her flash of petulance dissipating as it always did in the warmth of his approval. Him and his gadgets, she thought. He loves them almost as much as he does me.

'A day or two.' He waved her over to the desk.

That long. That was too long. Almost as long as the original plan would have taken. She didn't like waiting. For Juliet, wanting something meant wanting it now. Her disappointment must have shown on her face.

Bryan reached up and brushed her cheek. 'We're only going to get one shot at this, remember. Better make sure it works.'

'I don't see why it should take so long.' She sat on his lap, watched him tapping on the keyboard. 'All you've got to do is run the program.'

'I need to configure it first. If I get that wrong, we can kiss our money goodbye.'

'Assuming it works anyway. Do you trust Icarus?'

'Of course not.' He laughed at the absurdity of the idea. 'But he's not as anonymous as he thought. I might not be able to get into the program and see how it works, but I did manage to slip a tracer routine past him. When he thought I was sweeping the line for taps.'

'So you know who he is?' Good old Bryan. Didn't miss a trick.

'Not exactly.' He beamed proudly at her. 'But I know where he lives. Somewhere in Hunsford. It's a start.'

'Who's a clever boy then? So if it doesn't work . . .'

'We pay him a visit. And ask for a refund.'

'He might not be too keen on the idea.'

'I'm sure he'll see reason.' He began massaging her shoulders. 'You can be very persuasive when you put your mind to it.'

'Flatterer,' she said.

# « Eight »

'Are you sure this is a good idea?' Ros asked. She drew closer into the shadow of the hangar.

Beckett's silhouette nodded. 'Of course it is.' He sounded less sure than he was trying to. 'Look, everyone's running around like headless chickens getting the money together. By the time we get permission, it could be too late.'

'But we don't know what we're looking for,' she reminded him.

'Ah, come on.' Ed was positively enjoying himself. But then breaking and entering had always been one of his favourite games. 'We'll know it when we see it.'

Beckett started, briefly, then recovered his composure. Ros wondered what was eating him.

'Well if we can't get inside the hangar, it's academic,' she said. She blew on her hands. Now night had fallen the air was growing chilly.

'No problem.' Beckett sounded smug. 'Our passes are time coded. They won't expire until midnight.' He swiped his through the security lock. It beeped. Access denied. He tried again.

'On the other hand, Todd might have cancelled them,' Ros pointed out.

'Not quite as stupid as he looks, is he?' Ed said. He started checking the side of the building for handholds. 'Don't worry. There's an open window up there.'

'Ed,' Beckett said.

Ed ignored him. 'Sit tight. I'll be right back.' He started swinging himself up the wall.

'Ed . . .' Beckett gave up. Slithering sounds and muffled cursing drifted down to them. He pulled something out of his pocket, and smiled at Ros.

'Coming?'

'Coming where? Oh. I see.' She watched him swipe a second card through the lock. It clicked open. 'You downloaded your own copy of Todd's authorisation before you deleted the ferret.' Well, why not. It was what she would have done.

'It seemed like a good idea at the time.' Beckett pushed the door open.

Ros followed him into a narrow hallway. Offices led off from it on either side. A staircase rose up into darkened silence. She paused, getting her bearings.

'This way, I think.' A metallic clatter upstairs, and more muffled swearing. 'Sounds like Ed's found the broom cupboard.'

Ed appeared at the top of the stairs, massaging his shin. His jaw dropped.

'How did . . .' He glanced at Beckett. 'Why didn't you . . .'

'We tried. But you were having so much fun we didn't have the heart to stop you.'

'Thanks a bunch.' He came down to join them. 'So what now, oh fearless leader?'

'I think,' Ros said, 'we have a plane to catch.' She slipped the lock on the access door, and stepped inside the hangar.

Close up, the plane was bigger than she'd expected. It loomed over her, its sleek lines softened by the moonlight falling through the skylights. The blue and silver highlights, the soft indigo shadows, made it seem somehow insubstantial. She caught her breath.

'Beauty, isn't she?' It was only when Ed nudged her shoulder that she realised she'd stopped in her tracks.

'It's just a pile of machinery, Ed.' She spoke a little too vehemently, and he smiled. He pulled his headset from his pocket, and put it on. Beckett did the same. Ros rummaged through her shoulder bag for a third one. They ran a quick radio check. Everything functioning.

'OK. So where do we start?' Beckett asked.

'NavCom's the obvious place. I'll run a diagnostic on the software.' Ros started towards the stairway leading up into the airliner.

'Sounds good to me.' Beckett's voice followed her, attenuated in her earpiece. 'We'll start sweeping the exterior.'

The darkness folded itself around her as she stepped inside the airliner. She stopped for a moment, waiting for her eyes to adjust. Dim shapes swam up out of the gloom, gradually solidifying into seats and luggage racks. She pulled a low light vision enhancer from the bag, and slipped it on. Everything took on solid form, limned in softly-glowing green.

That was better. She stepped through into the cockpit. Took a moment to orientate herself, and approached the flight engineer's station. The on-board computers ought to be here.

She took out her laptop, and some interface cable. Patched it in. Loaded the diagnostic software, and ran it.

'Nothing so far,' Beckett's voice said.

'Me neither,' Ed agreed. They both sounded discouraged.

'And the software seems clean,' she added. Not that

there was any reason to expect otherwise. Nothing had shown up on the executive jet either. She let her breath out in a sigh of frustration. There had to be something, damn it. Maybe they were just looking in the wrong place.

The light enhancers overloaded, suddenly, blanking out in a flare of photons. She snatched them off, blinking. Harsh white light flooded the cockpit, spilling in from the hangar outside.

'We've got company,' Beckett said. Ros peered cautiously over the rim of the windshield. The overhead lights had come on. Todd, backed up by a squad of security guards, was standing by the personnel door. He looked angrier than she'd ever seen him.

'And just what do you think you're playing at this time?' His voice carried easily to Beckett's headset.

'Plane spotting?' Ed suggested.

'Come out. All three of you.' Beckett and Ed appeared beneath the nose of the aircraft. Todd swung his head from side to side. 'Where's the other one?'

'She went home,' Beckett said. 'It's her turn to cook.'

'I'll get you for that later, Beckett.' She slipped down out of sight.

Todd's footsteps were echoing on the concrete floor. She scooped up her equipment, stuffing it behind the inspection panel. Somewhere to hide.

'Walked back to London, did she?' Todd was climbing the stairway. 'Her car's still in the parking lot.'

'She's an exercise freak,' Ed said, unconvincingly. 'Runner, gymnast . . .'

'Thank you, Ed.' She swung herself up into one of the overhead luggage lockers, bracing herself like a rock climber in a chimney, supporting her weight on her shoulders and feet. Her legs bent almost double, her knees brushing the ceiling. She reached down to grab the door, tugging it up, and holding it closed. It was heavier than she'd expected, the weight threatening to unbalance her. The tension across her shoulders grew almost unbearable. Not cramp. Please, not now.

Feet scuffed the carpet below her. Walked the length of the plane. Began to descend the staircase at the tail end.

'She's not there.' Todd sounded surprised. She let the locker door fall open, and stepped down. Bliss. She started to work the cramps out of her shoulder blades. The argument continued in her earpiece.

'As for you two comedians, I want you off this airport right now.'

'I think you'd better run that past Ms Langford first, Todd. She hired us, not you.'

Attaboy, Beckett. Keep him talking. Play for time. Ros returned to the cockpit, and retrieved her equipment. The interior lights came on. Damn, she thought. What did I do? Outside, the argument stopped suddenly.

'What on earth? She must be in there after all!' Something about Todd's tone convinced her that he wasn't likely to take being fooled as anything other than a personal insult. As she watched, other systems started to come on line. A servo whined, and a dull, metallic boom echoed through the fuselage. That didn't sound good. She hurried back into the cabin.

'Ros. What's happening?' Beckett had dropped all pretence.

'I don't know. The systems just started activating themselves.' The stairway was retracting; as she reached it, the door closed in her face. 'The door just closed!' She tugged the handle. It wouldn't budge.

'Get out of there!' Ed cut in. 'The rear hatch is still open.'

'You don't have to tell me twice.' She turned, and sprinted down the narrow aisle. Another servo whined ahead of her. 'Oh no!' The door swung closed as she reached it.

Another whine, deeper in pitch, rising rapidly in volume.

'Ed. The engines are starting!'

'Yeah. I know.' He tried to sound reassuring. 'Get back to the cockpit. Disengage the NavCom.'

'Lot of good that's going to do. It didn't work either of the other times, did it?' She ran back to the cockpit anyway. 'Ed. Everything's coming on line!' She dropped into the pilot's seat. 'OK, I'm here. What do I do?'

'Look for the autopilot. NavCom ought to be interfaced through it. Shut up, Todd!' His voice came back, a little calmer. 'Can you see it?'

'No.' She swept her vision across the array of screens. Every one of them showed status checks on a different system. As near as she could tell, all four engines were powering up. This really didn't look good. She banished the picture of the plane accelerating inexorably into the hangar wall from her mind. 'Where is it?'

'It's yellow.' Ed hesitated. 'Or orange. One or the other. It should be next to the throttles. On the left . . .'

'You mean the one with the label on it, saying Autopilot?' She dabbed at the touch screen. 'Nothing. I'm locked out. Just like before.'

'OK.' Beckett's voice. 'I'm trying to get up on the wing. Maybe we can spring the emergency exit from the outside.'

She looked out of the cockpit window. Beckett and Todd were standing next to the starboard wing. The head of security had his hands cupped together, ready to give Beckett a boost up. Looked like a truce, at least until the situation was resolved.

The plane lurched. The hangar walls began to slide past the windshield. Both men went sprawling.

'Ros! You're moving!'

'Tell me something I don't know, Ed.'

The nose of the plane lined itself up on the main hangar doors. They started to slide open.

'Have you still got the laptop patched in to the on board computer?' Beckett asked.

'Yes.' Of course. She might be able to override it through the keyboard. She climbed out of the seat, and went to pick it up.

'Why are the hangar doors opening?' Ed asked.

'Icarus must be hacking into the security system again,' Beckett said. 'Overriding the locks.'

'In which case you might be able to trace him this time.' Ros opened the laptop. Data cascaded down the screen. 'Nope. Whatever's got into NavCom's locking out any external override commands too.'

'Can you crack it?' Beckett asked.

'Not quickly enough.' The airliner started to taxi forwards, out of the hangar. The uniformed security guards scattered. Ed and Beckett ran forwards, pacing it. After a moment they started to fall behind.

'Taxi!' Beckett stepped in front of an approaching fire engine, waving his arms.

It slowed, its blue light flashing. Then Ros's view was blocked by the starboard wing. Only the voices in her ear kept her abreast of the situation. The sound of the door being wrenched open, and Beckett's voice again. 'Security. There's a woman trapped aboard that plane. Follow it.'

'Right.' Another voice, presumably the driver. A slamming door. 'What about your mate?'

'He's riding outside. Try to get alongside the wing.'

'You've got it.' Whoever the driver was, he was quick on the uptake.

'Ros.' Ed's voice again, distorted by the wind. 'Can you hear me?'

'Yes.' She swallowed. 'Be careful, Ed.'

'I'm always careful.' He sounded as though he was enjoying himself. 'Can you get to the emergency exit above the wing?'

'I'm on my way.' She hurried down the aisle. The plane was out on the taxiway now, heading for the main runway. Not much time.

Blue light strobed through the starboard windows. She dropped into the seat next to the emergency exit, and tugged at the handle. Nothing happened. Of course. Disengage the safety locks and try again. She tugged harder. Nothing.

'It won't move!'

'Relax.' The fire engine appeared behind the wing. Ed was crouched on top of it, clinging to the ladder. His hair danced in the slipstream. 'We're going with Beckett's plan. I'll pop it from the outside.'

'It sounds dangerous, Ed.'

'More dangerous than staying where you are?'

'Since you put it like that.' She watched, her breath frozen, as Ed balanced carefully on his feet. He shifted his weight easily, compensating for the motion of the fire engine. He caught her eye, and waved.

'Easier than riding a surfboard.'

'But a lot more painful if you fall off.' Ros watched him inch forward. He was six feet from the wing now. Five. Three. He jumped.

Slipped. Went down hard on the upper surface of the wing. Started sliding towards the trailing edge.

'Beckett! He's fallen!'

'Not yet.'

The soles of his sneakers got a grip. He grinned, and flashed her a thumbs up.

'If you ever do that to me again, Ed.' She exhaled,

90

releasing the tension that had knotted her muscles.

'We're running out of time here.' Beckett cut in.

'No worries. I'm on it.' Ed began to inch forward, toes and elbows, minimising the wind resistance. He rounded the bulge of the inner engine. 'Almost there.'

His hand smacked against the glass. A moment later his face appeared. He grinned at Ros through the window.

'Cab for Ms Henderson?'

'Get on with it, Ed!'

'I'm trying.' He tugged at the external release lever. Tugged harder. His expression grew grimmer. 'It won't budge.'

'It's got to!' Ros lowered the pitch of her voice with a conscious effort. 'Look for the safety latch.'

'It should have disengaged.' Ed tugged again. 'Nothing. That's not going to shift without a crowbar.'

The plane turned again.

'We're on the runway!' Beckett cut in again. 'We're out of time. Jump, Ed!'

'I can do this!' Ed's face contorted with the effort.

'Getting yourself killed won't help me,' Ros said. 'Jump!'

'Hotel Lima Six Four Seven, you are not cleared for takeoff. Repeat, you do not have clearance for takeoff.' The air traffic controller's voice burst from the cockpit radio, tight with tension.

'Thanks. I'd never have guessed.' The whine of the engines rose in pitch. 'Jump, Ed!'

He hesitated another instant, meeting her eyes; then he waved, and ran down the wing. The fire engine was right alongside now, going flat out. It began to slip astern. Ed jumped for it, teetered for a moment on the ladder, and vanished.

'Ed! Ed, are you all right?'

'When was I ever all right?' The sound of his voice brought a surge of relief. And then there was a surge of acceleration, and the familiar dropping away of her stomach.

She was airborne.

# « Nine »

'How's she coping?' Jerry asked.

Ed shrugged. Well enough, if he knew Ros. She'd keep a level head. Work something out.

He wished he was up there with her, though, instead of sitting around a table in a conference room. He wasn't good at this sort of thing. He preferred to leave client liaison to the other two. But Beckett was back with the computers, trying to trace the mysterious Icarus, and Ros was going round in circles at twelve thousand feet.

'The plane's in a holding pattern,' Wyman said. He called up a display on his laptop, and turned it so everyone could see. 'Circling with a constant ten mile radius, centred on the airfield.'

'Not quite.' Ed reached over, and enlarged part of the map. 'The exact centre's offset by about half a mile. Right over Hunsford.'

'Whatever.' Wyman shrugged. 'I don't see that half a mile one way or the other makes all that much difference.'

'It might,' Ed said. 'If someone's controlling it from the ground, the centre of the circle's the best place to look.'

'I'm still not convinced that's technically possible,' Wyman said.

'It's the only explanation that fits.'

'But there would have to be a receiver of some kind to pick up the signal,' Wyman objected. 'We didn't find anything like that when we took your plane apart this morning.'

'Which explains what the guy who tried to flatten me was after. He was there to remove it.' He glared at Todd. 'And if you'd let us finish examining the airliner tonight we'd probably have found it, and Ros wouldn't be stuck up there now.'

'And if you people had stuck to proper security procedures, she would never have been aboard the plane in the first place!' Todd shot back.

'This is not helping.' Jerry reasserted control over the meeting. 'The money will be arriving within the hour. Unless anyone can come up with a better course of action, we'll be making the drop at eight.'

'I'm still against it,' Todd said firmly. 'Give in once, and every lunatic in the country will think they've got a blank cheque with us.'

'I'm with Nigel on this one,' said Wyman. 'It's setting a dangerous precedent.' Todd looked surprised, then grateful for the unexpected support.

'I'm well aware of that.' Jerry nodded, curtly. 'And I'm also aware that Ros's life depends on it. Not to mention any number of others.'

'What do you mean, others?' Wyman asked. 'She is alone up there, isn't she?'

'Yes. But the last time Icarus took control, he nearly crashed the plane on a housing estate. He could do that again.'

'I see.' Even Todd looked visibly shaken at the idea. 'Then I suppose you must do whatever you think best.'

'Don't worry, Nigel.' Her voice was hard. 'I fully intend to.'

Beckett reached for the cup of vending machine coffee next to the workstation. It had gone cold while he worked. He put it back down again. The screen seemed to ripple. He rubbed his eyes.

Icarus was good. Very good. But he was better. One of his tripwires had caught the signal which had opened the hangar doors. Caught and tagged it, so he could trace the line. Let him deploy his own intrusion routine.

The system on the other end was heavily protected. He launched an Icebreaker. It started to ease its way through Icarus's defences.

CONGRATULATIONS. The message appeared in the familiar block capitals. IF YOU HAVE MANAGED TO PENETRATE THIS SYSTEM, YOU ARE UNUSUALLY TALENTED. NOT TO MENTION UNSCRUPULOUS. Beckett frowned in confusion. What was this? NO DOUBT YOU FOLLOWED ONE OF THE HINTS I PLANTED AROUND THE NET, EXPECTING TO FIND SOMETHING OF VALUE HERE. YOU HAVE DONE SO, BUT NOT IN THE MANNER YOU ANTICIPATED. Uh oh. His hand hovered over the keyboard, ready to disengage, but curiosity made him hesitate. I HAVE A PROGRAM FOR SALE WHICH CAN PENETRATE ANY PRIVATE SECURITY SYSTEM, AND MOST GOVERNMENT ONES. The screen cleared. THE LOCATION OF YOUR TERMINAL HAS BEEN LOGGED. I WILL CONTACT YOU SOON. ICARUS.

No wonder the Hive were stirred up. And desperate enough to ask for his help. He already knew how good Icarus's Icebreaker was.

Like Ed had said. This was really worrying.

But if Icarus knew where he was, it worked both ways. His Ice was good enough to have prevented Beckett from getting a precise location, but he couldn't hide the fact that he'd hacked in on a local line. A grin spread slowly across his face. There was only one man in Hunsford with the computer expertise to have written that program.

'Elverson. Gotcha.' Now all he needed was the evidence. He cross-referenced the line he'd traced with the CommEx database.

'What?'

That couldn't be right. The signal had been relayed through Elverson's modem, but it had originated somewhere else. He remembered Ros's doubts about the faxes that had appeared to come from Kirkby. Icarus could have played the same trick on Elverson.

No doubt about it. Icarus was good. But he was better. He stood, and reached for his jacket. Either way, it was time to have another little word with Quentin Elverson. If the man was innocent, they'd still be able to trace Icarus through his modem. And if not . . .

His jaw tightened. If anything happened to Ros, he was going to see to it personally that melting wings would be the least of Icarus's problems.

Ros had never appreciated before just how boring being scared out of your mind could be. After the first few minutes, when it had become obvious that nothing terrible was going to happen immediately, she'd started working methodically through the diagnostic routines. The activity was calming, let her feel as though she could help herself. The gnawing panic that had consumed her as she left the ground was now subsiding. It never quite went away, but at least she could control it – a victory of sorts.

'Hello, Ros. Are you there?' Ed's voice in her headset, as cheerful as ever. Stupid question.

'No. I got tired of waiting and went out for a curry.'

Ed laughed. 'Sensible move. I wouldn't trust the airline food either.' His tone became more businesslike.

'We're all agreed down here that there must be a transceiver of some sort patched into the system.'

'I'd worked that one out for myself,' Ros said dryly. 'I've been running every diagnostic I can think of, but it's obviously hiding itself.'

'You'll have to make a physical sweep, then.'

Well of course. I'm not a complete idiot. I had figured that one out too . . . She left the words unsaid. There was no need to take her frustration out on Ed.

'Just one slight problem with that. You and Beckett had the bug detectors, remember? They're back on the ground with you. Where is Beckett anyway?'

'He went to talk to Elverson again. He thinks he might be Icarus.'

'Elverson?' It made sense. He knew NavCom inside out. Had been cheated out of the financial rewards due to him. Was a programming genius.

'Even if he isn't, we could use his advice,' Ed said. That was true too. 'But in the meantime we need to find that bug.'

'I wouldn't know where to start,' Ros said. 'There must be miles of wiring in a system this complex.'

'Literally,' Ed agreed. 'But we can narrow it down. It must be somewhere in the navigation or flight control systems.'

'Sounds logical,' Ros agreed. She looked around the cockpit. That still left a lot of possibilities.

OK, she told herself. Let's take a step back from this. If I wanted to override the system, where would I start? She called up the system specs on the laptop. There were still too many possibilities. Check them out one at a time, then.

'Don't take too long,' Ed said. 'You haven't got unlimited fuel, you know.'

'Thanks Ed.' Among his many virtues, she thought, tact was not the one he most frequently displayed.

She removed the inspection panel from one of the consoles. No damage to the wiring. Nothing attached where it shouldn't be. That unit was clean. She moved on to the next.

'Don't these things have an ejector seat or something?'

'I'm afraid not,' Ed said. 'And they don't carry parachutes either.'

'Why not?' After all, they carried life jackets, even on internal flights.

'Because nothing can possibly go wrong.' Ed's voice was heavy with irony.

'Yeah,' Ros said. 'Isn't that what they said about the *Titanic*?' She prised the next inspection panel off.

'The meteorologist down here tells me that icebergs are comparatively rare at that altitude,' Ed said.

'One less thing to worry about then.' She started examining the system. It seemed conventional enough. One computer was much like another. And you accessed a computer . . .

'Got it.' She looked at the device slotted into one of the input ports. It looked like a miniaturised modem, attached to an integral transceiver. Despite herself, she felt a pang of admiration for the quality of the workmanship.

'Don't touch it yet,' Ed warned. Her hand fell away. 'The moment you disengage it, you'll have manual control.'

'Ah.' A knot of apprehension twisted in her guts. 'I can't fly a plane, Ed!' There had to be another way. 'Are you sure there aren't any parachutes aboard?'

'Positive.' He was trying to sound reassuring, but the underlying tension was still evident in his voice. 'Don't worry, though. We've got Captain Kramer here, from the airline. He knows that plane inside out.'

Which is how he'll find it if anything goes wrong, she thought.

'He's going to talk you down,' Ed reassured her.

'Hello, Ros.' A new voice took over, calm and authoritative. 'I'm Roger Kramer. Before we do anything else, I want to run through the controls with you, all right?'

'Fine.' She sat in the pilot's seat. Fastened the seatbelt. 'I'm ready.'

'Good. Now the control column's in front of you. The NavCom screens should be showing normal in-flight status ...'

He ran through the systems quickly and concisely, answering her questions in the same way. A thread of confidence began to cut through her nervousness, transmuting it into an edgy excitement. She found herself growing impatient to begin.

'OK. I think I've got all that.'

'Good.' Kramer still sounded calm and confident. 'Ready when you are.' She looked at the bug, still attached to the flight control system. 'Remember, the moment you disengage the bug, take hold of the control column. Hold it as steady as you can.'

'Right.' Her fingers closed on the gadget. 'Here goes nothing.'

She pulled it out. Immediately, the plane tilted, and she was thrown forward, the seatbelt cutting painfully into her waist. The transceiver flew out of her fingers, rattling away out of her field of vision.

'It's diving!' She grabbed the control column, pulling it back as hard as she could. It refused to move. 'And the controls have gone dead!' All the NavCom screens had gone blank.

'It must be tamper-proof.' Ed spoke rapidly, trying to keep up with his racing thoughts. 'Replace the bug. When the system reboots, you should level out.'

'I can't see it!' She hit the quick release button on the seatbelt. It must be on the floor somewhere. The plane lurched; she fell to her knees. Where the hell was it? There! She grabbed for it. The plane jolted again, and it skittered away from her fingers.

'Ros! You're dropping too fast!'

'I know!' She almost snarled the words. Scrabbled frantically after the errant gadget. Almost there . . . Got it! It dropped into her hand as the plane lurched once more, throwing her hard against the bulkhead. Ignoring the flare of pain in her shoulder she struggled to her feet. Fell heavily against the flight computer console.

'I'm there.' She fumbled it against the input slot. It wouldn't fit. She tried again, struggling to suppress the trembling in her fingers. 'Get in there, damn you!' It gave suddenly, slotting home with a faint click.

She was thrown back against the pilot's seat as the nose came up. The cockpit display screens flickered into life. She gasped for breath, numb with the shock of such a near miss.

'You did it!' Ed sounded elated. Ros looked out and down. The lights of Hunsford village were terrifyingly close. Gradually, the altimeter rose to quadruple figures.

'I think . . .' Her voice folded. She took a deep breath and tried again. 'I think we're going to have to try something else.'

Elverson's cottage was in darkness as Beckett drew up outside and killed the engine. Well, it was the middle of the night, he supposed. The driver's door echoed like a gunshot as he slammed it. Bright moonlight spilled through the surrounding trees.

The garage door was open. Ominous. If Elverson wasn't here.

'What the –' The rogue airliner screamed overhead, low enough to lacerate his eardrums, powering out of the night from nowhere in a matter of seconds. She shouldn't be that low. He hurried across the driveway to the front door.

The camera tracked him, its servo whining. He banged on the door.

'Elverson!' He banged again. No answer. 'Elverson!' He hesitated. No time to lose. If Elverson was innocent, he could apologise later. He took a scanner out of his pocket, and ran it briefly over the electronic doorlock. Found the right frequency. Pressed a few keys.

The lock clicked, and the door swung open. He entered the hall cautiously, scanning for burglar alarms, but overriding the door lock appeared to have deactivated them.

The house was quiet. He called out again, more for form's sake than in expectation of an answer. This was the silence of an empty house. He hurried to the study at the end of the corridor. Here, the silence was broken by the humming of Elverson's computers, the darkness pierced by the glare of their screens. Screen saver patterns unfolded across them at random. Beckett switched on the light and sat at the terminal Elverson had been working on during his previous visit. Activated it.

ENTER PASSWORD.

Beckett shrugged. ICARUS, he typed.

The terminal considered it. PASSWORD NOT RECOGNISED.

Rats. But then, he hadn't really expected it to be that easy. He thought for a minute, then typed DAEDALUS.

The system opened. Beckett grinned. Daedalus. The father of Icarus. Of course. He scanned the contents of the hard disk, sifting them as he went.

Lots of stuff on NavCom, but that was only to be expected. Standard commercial word processing and spreadsheet software. And a couple of gigabytes of encrypted stuff. Now that looked interesting. He selected a writable CD from the freshly-opened box on the desk, and took a copy of it all. Slipped the copy carefully into his pocket. Then he went back to the files on the hard disk, and accessed them. Scanned the largest block of data.

Even through the fog of encryption the shape of it was unmistakable, matching the fragments of coding he'd recovered before.

'Bingo.' It was the Icebreaker. Had to be. The match was too close for coincidence. He frowned as the tenuous sense of recognition returned, stronger than the last time. He'd seen something like this before, he was sure of it. But the memory continued to elude him.

The screen blanked. Damn. He must have triggered an intrusion alarm he hadn't noticed.

CONGRATULATIONS, MR BECKETT. The familiar block capitals began scrolling up the screen. I UNDER-ESTIMATED YOU. Of course. The camera by the front door. Elverson must have been watching him all the time. BUT I STILL HAVE THE INITIATIVE. I HAVE CONTROL OF THE AIRCRAFT. UNLESS THE MONEY IS DELIVERED TO THE CAR PARK OF THE MOLETRAP BY EIGHT O'CLOCK THIS MORNING, I WILL CRASH IT. AND BE ASSURED THAT YOUR COLLEAGUE WILL NOT BE THE ONLY CASUALTY.

Beckett felt his jaw knot. He hammered the keyboard.

GET HER DOWN SAFELY, ELVERSON, OR THERE'S NO-WHERE ON EARTH YOU CAN HIDE.

I HARDLY THINK YOU'RE IN A POSITION TO MAKE THREATS.

The screen went dead.

# « Ten »

'The Moletrap?' Ed asked, baffled. It didn't mean anything to him.

Jerry nodded thoughtfully. 'It's a local pub,' she explained. 'Bit of a landmark. Everyone around here knows it.'

'Well, that makes sense,' Ed conceded. 'They wouldn't want the courier driving round in circles looking for the rendezvous.'

They were back in the boardroom, but at least this time he had Beckett to handle the tricky stuff. Beckett nodded his agreement.

'I'll make the drop,' he said. Jerry looked dubious.

'I was planning to do it myself. After all, it's my responsibility.'

'No. It's mine,' Todd cut in. 'With all due respect, Ms Langford, this is a security matter. I should handle it personally.'

'Yes. Of course you're right.' She accepted the logic of it reluctantly. 'But I don't think you should go alone.'

'Neither do I,' Beckett agreed.

Todd stiffened in his seat. Ed waited for the inevitable argument to start.

'Then I'll go too.' Wyman looked almost as startled as everyone else at the sound of his own voice. The tension dissipated.

'Are you sure about this?' Todd asked.

Wyman hesitated. 'Not really, no. But someone's got to do it.'

'Thank you, Richard.' Jerry looked genuinely relieved. 'We all appreciate what you're doing. But are you sure you understand the risks?'

'Elverson's a killer, don't forget,' Ed reminded him.

Wyman looked as though he was on the verge of second thoughts.

'We don't know that,' Todd said.

'Someone killed Kirkby,' Beckett said. 'If it wasn't Elverson, it must have been an associate of his.'

'But surely that was to conceal his identity?' Wyman asked. 'Now we already know it, what reason would he have for violence?'

'Precisely,' Todd said. 'And there will be two of us, after all.'

It still sounded dodgy to Ed. But then it wasn't really his problem. He was far more concerned with something else.

'In the meantime,' he said, 'what do we do about Ros? That plane must be getting pretty near the limit of its endurance by now.'

'I think our best bet is to try and track down the control system Elverson's using,' Beckett suggested. 'Turn it off from the ground, or use it to land the plane.' He looked at Ed. 'That's your department.'

'Sounds good to me,' Ed agreed. 'What are you going to be doing?'

'I'm going to rig up a case for the money,' Beckett said, glancing at Jerry for approval. 'One we can trace.' She nodded slightly. 'When Elverson picks it up, it should lead us right to him. And his control system, with a bit of luck.'

'Fine. Then I'm out of here.' Ed stood. 'Any further developments, you can call me on the headset.' He left them to it with a sense of intense relief, and headed for the car park at a run.

'Hello, Ros.' He spoke as he slipped the crash helmet on, the inbuilt headset activating automatically at the sound of his voice. 'How's it going up there?'

'Well, the sunrise is pretty spectacular.'

Sunrise? As he left the terminal building he was surprised to see the soft grey light of early dawn already beginning to fade. Lurid orange was staining the sky to the east. It was later than he'd thought. In every sense. He sprinted for the bike.

'How far have you got with examining the control device?' He extracted the tracking gear from the panniers, and slotted the frequency scanner into its mounting. Ran the cable to the jack in his helmet. The head-up display activated, painting data on the inside of his visor.

'About as far as I can without taking it to pieces,' Ros said. 'Which isn't really advisable under the circumstances.'

'Have you managed to work out what frequency it's using?' He swung his leg over the bike, kicked the engine into life. Accelerated through the deserted parking lot like a fire and forget missile. Slalomed through the raised and unmanned barriers.

'My best guess is somewhere between one fifty and one sixty megahertz,' Ros said. Ed let the scanner browse through the signal traffic.

'Got it!' he said. 'A data stream, up around one fifty-nine. It's faint, but I'm locked on to it.' An icon appeared in the corner of his visor, indicating signal strength and approximate direction. West.

'I don't want to pressure you or anything,' Ros said. A disturbing undercurrent of unease had entered her voice. 'But if this fuel gauge works the same way as the one in my car, I could really use a filling station.'

'Don't worry. Those things have an emergency fuel reserve.' Which ought to be seriously depleted by now. He forced the doubt from his voice. 'You'll be down in no time.'

'That's what I'm afraid of, Ed.'

He opened the throttle, and followed the tenuous signal as fast as he dared on the twisting rural roads, racing the sun towards the west.

'Well, this is it. Bit of a rough job, but it's the best I could do in the time.' Beckett hefted the suitcase on to Jerry's desk. It wasn't easy. Most of the surface was covered with banknotes. Five thousand inch-thick bundles of them, worth ten thousand pounds apiece.

He dislodged a few, as though by accident. 'Oops. Sorry.' He bent down to retrieve them, palming his little piece of insurance. It was a long shot, but still worth taking.

'Don't worry about it.' Jerry was leaning forwards to examine the case. While her eyes were off him, Beckett removed one of the notes.

'That's got it. Rats.' He pretended to fumble picking up the errant bundles, nudging them further under the desk. Replaced the note he'd taken, in the middle of the stack, and smoothed the creases. Perfect. To the casual eye, the bundle would never look disturbed. He rose to his feet, and replaced the small fortune on the desktop. He flashed an apologetic grin, being careful not to overdo it. 'I must be more nervous than I thought.'

'We're all nervous,' Jerry said, still examining the case.

Good. She hadn't noticed a thing. He supposed he could have confided in her, but what she didn't know she couldn't give away by accident. And the same went for Wyman and Todd. Especially Wyman and Todd, who already knew about the tracker he'd put in the suitcase.

'How does this work, exactly?' Jerry asked.

'Well, the tracker's pretty standard.' Beckett pointed it out, concealed behind one of the hinges. 'It's got a twenty mile range, and I'm going to be a lot closer than that. Plus, I've added an audio pickup, just to be on the safe side. Microphone in the catch here, transmitter and battery in the handle. The aerial's wired into the frame.' He shrugged. 'It's a lot less reliable than the homing device, and the range is much shorter, but it could make all the difference to Wyman and Todd. I'll be listening in the whole time. If they run into any trouble I can be there in a couple of minutes.'

'You're expecting trouble, then.' It was a statement, not a question.

'We're dealing with ruthless people. They've killed once already. And if I have anything to do with it, they're not getting another chance.'

'Quite.' Jerry regarded him soberly. 'You realise you're putting yourself in danger too.' Another statement. She could read him too easily for comfort.

'Ros would do the same for me.' It was the only explanation necessary.

Wyman breezed into the office. 'Here we are then. Ready for the off,' he said, his forced cheerfulness failing dismally to conceal his trepidation, even from himself.

Beckett smiled encouragingly at him. 'You'll be fine.' He picked up a bundle of cash, and stowed it in the suitcase.

'I hope so.' Wyman seemed to shrink inside his overcoat.

'It's not too late to back out,' Todd said, appearing in the door behind him. He strode to the desk, and began stowing the money himself. 'I'll do that.'

'Be my guest. You're signing for it,' Beckett stood aside to let him get on with it.

'No, I'll come along.' Wyman forced a smile. 'Wouldn't want you getting lost with all that money, would we?'

'It's all there.' Todd ignored the feeble joke. That was his way of dealing with the situation, Beckett thought. Hide behind his professional persona. Well, a lot of good that's done us up to now. What was it Kirkby had told Ros? Meet him in the pub and he's a completely different man? He tried to picture a convivial Todd. It wasn't easy.

Todd snapped the catches closed. 'Might as well be going then.'

He lifted the suitcase, struggling with the weight. Wyman hovered uncertainly next to his elbow.

'Do you need a hand?'

'No. Thank you.' He hesitated, looking for something else to say, and gave up. 'Coming?' He left the office.

'Yes. Well. Goodbye then.' Wyman hurried after him.

Beckett sat on the edge of Jerry's desk. She looked appraisingly at him.

'Aren't you going too?'

'I want to give them a couple of minutes head start. If Elverson or his associates are watching, I'd rather not give the game away too easily.'

'Very sensible.'

She stood, stretched, and walked to the window. Outside, the first long shadows of dawn were beginning to stretch across the eerily deserted airport. In the distance an actinic light flashed, suspended in the opalescent sky. Ros's aircraft.

'We don't have much time,' she said quietly.

'You're telling me.' Beckett glanced at his watch. Time to move. 'But it'll be enough.'

'I hope so.' She turned to watch him go.

Beckett felt her eyes on his back all the way down the corridor.

'Ed?' Ros watched the landscape gradually resolving itself beneath the circling plane. Details grew sharper moment by moment as the daylight grew stronger. 'How are you doing down there?'

'I'm getting close.' His voice was full of confidence. 'The signal strength is increasing by the second.'

'That's good.' She leaned forward in the pilot's seat, tried to sound unconcerned. 'Because this display's just come up. It says "Fuel Level Critical". Is that as bad as it sounds?'

'Well.' She could hear him picking his words with care. 'It's not as good as it might be. But we've still got a fair margin for error.'

'How fair a margin, Ed?'

'A very fair half hour. At least. Maybe more.'

And maybe not. And there was something else about his voice. A tone she knew well.

'What aren't you telling me, Ed?'

'Ah.'

In the silence she could hear him debating how much to conceal. Deciding to be honest.

'I'm having trouble pinpointing the source of the signal. It's on a very tight beam. I keep running into dead spots.'

'Well, you do say you like a challenge.'

I can't believe I'm joking about this, she thought. I don't even know whose morale I'm trying to boost, his or mine. Both, probably.

'It's not that big a problem,' Ed assured her. 'I got a

good line on it from the hill above Hunsford. As soon as I get another positive lock, I can triangulate. Pin it down to within yards.' His voice changed, became triumphant. 'Got it! I was right! It's somewhere down in the village.'

'Well done, Ed.' She slumped in the seat, relief flooding through her. They weren't home and dry yet, but at least they had the umbrella up.

'I'll call again when I hit Hunsford. Should be a piece of cake narrowing it down then.'

'I hope so.' The landscape looked beautiful from up here, she thought. Green. Vibrant. Full of life.

And hard. Very, very hard.

The rising sun was warm on Beckett's neck. A horizontal shaft through the rear window of the off-roader. He glanced at the automap screen, and the small, illuminated dot crawling down one of the back lanes. They were almost at the Moletrap, clearly delineated by the standard icon for a pub. He slowed the car a little. Mustn't get too close, he reminded himself. He turned up the volume of the dashboard speaker a little.

'I think you're enjoying this,' Wyman's voice said.

The two men in the car ahead hadn't spoken much since leaving the airport. What little conversation they'd had had been desultory, an attempt to relieve the tension rather than communicate.

'I am a bit,' Todd admitted.

His voice was the more relaxed of the two. Still guarded, but more expansive than he'd been back at the airport. 'It's like being back in the service.' An edge of animation entered his voice. 'Going out on patrol. Knowing the enemy's out there somewhere. It sharpens your senses. Makes you feel more alive.'

'Unless they find you first, I suppose.'

'You'll never understand. You have to live it to know it.' Todd laughed. 'I suppose the nearest you ever get to excitement is pottering around the sky in a light aircraft with that flying club of yours.'

'Well, I think it's fun.' Wyman refused to be drawn.

'Sounds too much like a busman's holiday for me,' Todd said. 'I'm only too glad to get away from aircraft in my time off.'

'Of course,' Wyman said dryly. 'So much more exciting listening to Kirkby droning on at parish council meetings.'

'Touché.' Todd laughed again, conceding the point. 'Well, here we are.' There was a short pause, followed by a squeaking brake.

Beckett looked at the automap screen. The blip from the suitcase was stationary, superimposed on the pub icon. He pulled off the road, into a convenient farm gateway, and killed the engine.

'No sign of anyone.' Todd's voice again, followed by the click of the car door opening.

'Where are you going?' Wyman's voice. Nervous.

Beckett frowned. They were supposed to stick together. That had been the plan all along. Of course whether or not to stay in the car had been left to their discretion.

'Just a quick recce.' Todd's old soldier's instincts had obviously come to the fore with a vengeance. But it made sense. It was what Beckett would have done. He began to relax.

'We're supposed to stick together,' Wyman reminded him, a hint of querulousness entering his voice.

'I'm not stopping you.' The scrape of shoes on tarmac. 'Or would you rather stay put?'

'I'm not letting the money out of my sight,' Wyman insisted stubbornly.

'Suit yourself.' Todd sounded faintly regretful. His

footsteps receded a short way. 'Oh. By the way . . .' His voice grew louder as he turned back towards the car, and the concealed microphone.

There was a dull thud. A moment later, the transmission ceased. The blip vanished from the automap display.

Beckett's fingers convulsed on the wheel. He knew that sound. A silenced automatic, at point blank range. He'd heard it before, on the other end of a telephone, the day Ballantyne had been shot, and his career with the Hive had started its nose-dive into the shredder.

He slammed the off-roader into gear, and floored the accelerator.

I can be there in two minutes, he'd told Jerry. He made it, too. But as he skidded to a halt in the Moletrap's car park, he knew he was too late. Todd's old station wagon was gone, and the money with it.

Something was huddled in the middle of the open expanse of asphalt. A man. Beckett bailed out of the car at a run, grabbing the first aid kit, knowing it was probably futile. He approached the recumbent body. It didn't move.

He knelt, felt for the pulse in the neck. Nothing. The front of the overcoat was sodden with blood, adhering to the tarmac for a moment as he turned the body over.

It was Todd.

'There you are.' Elverson looked up from his screens as Wyman entered the control room. He looked agitated. 'Where on Earth have you been?'

'I had some loose ends to tie up,' Wyman explained. The gun was heavy in his pocket. Shame about Todd, but he hadn't been expecting him to turn back. And once he'd seen Wyman deactivating the tracker those so-called security experts had put in the money case he'd had no choice.

112

'Do you realise the aircraft is almost out of fuel?' Elverson turned back to his precious consoles. 'There's barely time to get it down before it crashes.'

'So?' Wyman didn't get it. 'The money's in the car. Come on.'

'I have to land it,' Elverson insisted. 'Prove it can be done.'

'Who cares?' They didn't have time for this. Beckett would have found Todd's body by now, be putting two and two together. 'We've got the money. Let's move!'

'It's not about the money, Richard. It was never about the money.' Elverson looked pityingly at him for a moment, then returned his attention to the glorified video game in front of him. 'The ransom demand was just to get everyone's attention. While I proved that NavCom *can* fly a plane without a pilot. Well I've done that. Oh yes. And once I get it down again in one piece they'll have to eat their words. All the so-called experts who called me a crank.'

'You're certainly not a crank, Quentin.' Naive, obsessed, yes. But not a crank. Wyman made one final appeal to reason. As if the old fool was capable of reason in the first place. 'But we're running out of time.'

'And so's that poor girl up there.' Elverson shook his head stubbornly. 'I'm not having another death on my conscience, Richard.'

So that was it. He was still complaining about Kirkby. Anyone would have thought he'd pulled the trigger himself.

'I didn't want to kill Kirkby either,' Wyman told him. Or Todd. Better not mention Todd, at least for the time being. 'But you know how irresponsible he was. I mean, that's why he got involved in all this in the first place. It was just a chance to play with bigger and

113

better toys so far as he was concerned. When the security people went to talk to him, he was bound to let something slip. It was bad enough they'd worked out that he was the one who'd sent our faxes to the airport.'

'Yes. They do seem very resourceful.' Elverson's eyes never left the screen. 'Do sit down, Richard. It's very distracting, having you hovering there. This will only take a few minutes.'

A few minutes they didn't have, Wyman thought. He reached for the gun. Felt his fingers close around the cold metal. Elverson worked on, oblivious.

'Take as long as you like,' he said.

Elverson grunted something that might have been thanks.

Wyman shot him. It was funny how much easier it got, the more people you killed. Elverson jerked in his seat as the bullet struck. He slumped forward, his head hitting the edge of the console in front of him with a loud thud.

It wasn't supposed to be like this, Wyman thought. No one was supposed to get hurt. Everyone was supposed to get rich. Twenty million apiece for him and Elverson, and ten for Kirkby, just for running a few errands and keeping Todd busy.

Still. He supposed an extra thirty million pounds might go some way towards easing his conscience.

# « Eleven »

Hunsford was still sleeping peacefully as Ed roared into the market-place in the centre of the village.

'I'm right on top of it.' Too close to get any kind of directional fix. He killed the engine. Coasted to a stop. He glanced around at his surroundings.

Let's think, he told himself. I must be able to see it from here. He turned his head slowly. It was a typical market square. Houses on three sides. Post Office, general store, and a couple of pubs. An open green of the fourth side, next to the war memorial, leading down to the river. Ducks. Swans. Very picture postcard. A stone bridge, carrying the westernmost road to the other bank. Beyond that, the churchyard.

Aha! He looked up at the spire. Elverson would need an aerial. Which would need to be high up, to avoid interference from the ground clutter. Something like the church steeple, for instance . . .

No. He dismissed the idea. Too many people around. It would have to be somewhere private. His gaze moved on.

'Got it!' The windmill. It had to be. He pulled a pair of binoculars from the bike's pannier, and focused on it. It was half hidden by the trees, but he could still see enough. The heavy duty dish antenna attached to the upper balcony wasn't just for picking up satellite television, that was for sure.

'Nice one, Ed.' Ros sounded relieved. Well, he supposed he would be too, if he was in her shoes.

'It's the windmill, on the outskirts of Hunsford.' He kicked the bike into life again. 'I'll be there in two minutes.'

'I should have known,' Ros said. She sounded angry with herself. 'It's on Kirkby's land. It should have been obvious.'

'We've all got twenty-twenty hindsight,' Ed said. He swung off the road, down an access track leading towards the mill. 'Blast.' The track curved away, revealing a drainage ditch between him and his objective. Well he wasn't about to turn back now. He opened the throttle wider.

'Ed. What's wrong?' Ros asked.

He ignored the voice in his ear. Felt the shock through the forks as he boosted off, hauling back on the handlebars.

'Oof! Nothing,' he reassured her as the rear wheel touched down, followed an instant later by the front. 'Just a bit of an obstacle course down here, that's all.'

He slewed to a halt beside the weatherboarded structure. No sign of life, but there were fresh tyre tracks in the mud. Coming and going. This didn't look good.

'The door's open,' he said. 'I'm going inside.'

'Be careful.' Beckett's voice cut in. 'Wyman's working with him. And he's armed. He's just killed Todd.'

'So if he's with Elverson . . .' Ros let the sentence hang.

'All right, I get it,' Ed said. 'Tippy-toes all the way.'

116

As if anyone inside wouldn't have heard the bike anyway. After a moment's thought he removed the helmet. It was good, but it wasn't bullet-proof. And it muffled the ambient sound too badly. He'd rather be able to hear if anyone was sneaking up on him. He collected a regular headset from the pannier, and slipped it on.

'I've switched headsets. Can you guys still hear me?'

'Loud and clear,' Ros said.

'Yes.' Beckett answered curtly.

Ed wondered for a moment what was keeping him so busy, then forced the thought aside. He had enough of his own to worry about.

'I'm going in now.'

He stepped up to the door. Poked a cautious head inside. The musty smell of old timber overwhelmed him. There was a staircase to his right. He started up it, increasing his weight gradually on each tread, to minimise any giveaway creaking.

Artificial light spilled from a door at the top of the stairs. Ed climbed towards it, breathing as quietly as he could, his heart pounding. His mouth felt dry.

He reached the door. Flattened himself against the frame. Listened.

Nothing. No voices. No footsteps. Not even the creak of a chair. Just the faint, familiar humming of computer equipment.

Well he couldn't stay there forever, he told himself. Ros was counting on him. Whatever the risks. He pushed the door open.

'I've definitely found it.' He took in the range of equipment confronting him. 'It looks like a functioning flight simulator.'

Fascinated, he walked towards it. A dozen screens were arranged in a horseshoe configuration, around what looked like a couple of pilot's seats scavenged from an old military transport plane. From the grave-yard at Collington, presumably. They all showed different status displays from various aircraft systems.

NavCom software, without a doubt. Relaying the data back from Ros's airliner.

He couldn't suppress his admiration. 'This is brilliant.'

'Be impressed later,' Ros snapped.

Ed's eyes fell on the fuel gauge. She was right. No time to lose. He walked around the pilot's seats. Froze.

'We may have a slight problem,' he said. Elverson was slumped forward, half out of the chair, a neat bullet hole through his back.

'What sort of a problem?' Ros's voice was edgy.

'Elverson's dead.' He spoke slowly, digesting the implications. 'And he's the only one who knew how to work this thing.'

'Gotcha!'

Beckett nodded with quiet satisfaction. His insurance was paying off after all. Wyman had deactivated the bugs he knew about, but the one he'd put in with the money was still functioning. He'd set it on a timer, in case Icarus had swept the ransom to be on the safe side, and it had just kicked in. He looked at the blip which had suddenly appeared on the automap screen. He compared it to his current position, and started the engine.

Gravel rattled against the bottom of the four by four as he accelerated away from the Moletrap's car park, following the blip. His quarry had a good lead, but it wasn't going to be good enough. He scanned the map, trying to second-guess his destination.

Collington. The flying club. Of course. He changed radio frequencies. Called the airport.

'Wyman?' Jerry was incredulous. 'I don't believe it.'

'Neither did Todd. And look where that got him.'

Beckett kept an eye on the fleeing blip. He was closing the gap too slowly. 'He's got the money, and deactivated the tracking device. But I managed to slip another bug into the case. One he doesn't know about.' No doubt about it. He was definitely making for Collington. 'Can you get some security people over to the flying club? It looks like he's planning to escape by air.'

'They'll be there in half an hour,' Jerry said.

'We haven't got that long,' Beckett said. By that time Wyman would be long gone. He calculated times and distances. He'd have to take a short cut.

'I'll hurry them up as much as I can,' Jerry said.

'Thanks.' And a lot of good that was going to do. Beckett's jaw clenched. It looked like it was up to him.

He spun the wheel, heading down a farm track leading off in the right direction. The four by four shuddered, bouncing on its off-road suspension. Beckett began to wonder if this had been such a good idea.

'Right.' Ed seated himself carefully in front of the bank of monitor screens, humming hard drives, and a massive spiderweb of cabling. Glanced from one to the other in bewilderment. 'How do I switch this thing off?'

'You don't,' Ros said. 'I can't fly a plane, remember? You're going to have to bring this thing down from there.'

'But I don't know where to begin.' He fought down a rising sense of panic. 'I fly planes, not computers. That's supposed to be your job.'

'It shouldn't be too hard,' Ros said. This was ridiculous. He should be reassuring her, not the other way round. 'You've been in simulators before.'

'That's true.'

So let's start by getting the feel of the system, Ed told

119

himself. Status checks. Altitude. Attitude. All looking normal, so far as he could tell. But there was only one way to be sure. He took a deep breath. Took hold of the joystick on the desktop in front of him. Just like a video game, he thought. You've played with one of these hundreds of times.

But not with a friend's life at stake.

'OK.' He tilted it gently. The artificial horizon rolled in response. 'You should be banking to port.'

'Yes.' Ros sounded slightly breathless. 'You have control.'

'Good.' He levelled off again. Dabbed at the touch screen to his left. Adjusted the angle of the flaps. 'You should start to descend slowly now.' The altimeter started counting slowly downwards.

'It's working!' Ros sounded elated. Ed began to feel slightly more confident. So far so good. But . . .

'Landing's going to be the tricky bit,' he said. 'Can you patch us in to Air Traffic Control?'

'No problem. They've been talking to me ever since I got up here.'

'Good. They should have you on radar by now. You're six miles from the runway.' He checked the instruments again. 'And right in the slot.'

'Glad to hear it.'

'Confirming that.' A new voice cut in. 'This is Air Traffic Control to Hotel Lima Six Four Seven. Your approach looks good. And we have all the emergency teams standing by.'

'Oh good,' Ros said, with unmistakable sarcasm.

Ed chuckled, despite the growing dampness of his palms. She was still holding it together.

Her voice changed, became charged with urgency. 'I can see it! Runway dead ahead.'

'OK.' Ed took a deep breath. Nice choice of words, he thought. And she thinks I'm tactless. 'Here we go.'

Power down on the throttles. Watch the speed of descent. He'd landed on instruments before, he told himself. This was no different. It didn't matter that there was no cockpit to look out of. You didn't need to see the ground to know it was there.

'Undercarriage down and locked.' The status display turned green. Good. One less thing to worry about. No point venting fuel, either, not with the tanks so dry already. At least, if the worst happened, they wouldn't have to worry about fire.

He watched the altimeter. Less than a hundred feet now.

'Brace yourself,' he advised.

'If I was braced any more I'd be part of the fuselage.'

Eighty feet. Fifty. Twenty. Ten . . .

'Contact! I'm down!'

Reverse thrust. He looked round the consoles. The status displays flickered and changed. Reconfiguring themselves for movement on the ground. He hadn't counted on that. He searched frantically for the throttle controls.

'Ed.' A thread of alarm entered Ros's voice. 'I'm running out of runway here . . .'

'I can't engage reverse thrust. The whole system's reconfigured itself.'

'Check the diagnostic screen. It should give you an overview.'

'Right.'

Of course. He tapped the touch screen, bringing up the engine systems. 'Reverse thrust selected.'

The ground speed indicator started dropping. He applied the brakes. The speed fell gradually to zero.

'Thanks, Ed.' Ros sounded limp with relief. He sprawled back in the seat, feeling the tension dissipate from his muscles.

'Piece of cake,' he said. 'But I'd pull that override

121

chip from the computer right now if I were you.'

'I'm way ahead of you, Ed.' She paused. 'But first, if you wouldn't mind?'

'Mind what?' Had he missed something?

'The doors, Ed.'

'Oh. Oh, right.' He found the subsystem for the cabin doors, selected the open option. 'You know, this is a really amazing setup. Beckett's going to love taking it to bits to see how it runs.'

'I'm sure he is.' The same thought occurred to both of them simultaneously.

'Where is Beckett anyway?'

Beckett rocked violently in his seat as the off-roader bounced and snarled its way across a freshly-ploughed field, throwing up mud in its wake. At least he hoped it was mud; judging by the smell the field had been recently manured as well.

The twin blips on the automap screen were closing rapidly now. Wyman was there, approaching the flying club from the east, and he was here, about to hit the road. The four by four burst through a hedgerow, lurched across a drainage ditch, and crawled up on to the carriageway.

Beckett sighed with relief. Much more of that, he thought, and his fillings would have fallen out. He triggered the windscreen washers, restoring the glass to transparency. Well, almost. Thin arcs of mud still trailed across it, but at least he could see where he was going now.

He approached a junction and slowed a little, confirming the automap's assertion that this was the road to Collington. A hand-lettered sign had been fixed to the finger post. FLYING CLUB it said, above an oversized arrow. Beckett put his foot down harder.

A chain link fence appeared round the next bend,

enclosing a bleak expanse of windblown grass. In the far distance he could see a huddle of aircraft, ancient military transports for the most part. The Air Command graveyard. A little nearer were a set of sheds and some old concrete buildings.

They must be the flying club facilities, he thought. A couple of light aircraft stood next to them.

'I've reached the airfield.' So had Wyman. The blip was approaching fast, on the other side of the facility. 'I'm on the south perimeter, following the fence towards the east. Where's the gate?'

'South?' Jerry's voice sounded puzzled. 'How did you . . .' She dismissed it as unimportant. 'The gate's on the east side of the perimeter fence. There's a lifting barrier there, but it's only manned on flying days.'

'Will Wyman be able to open it?'

'Probably. He is a member.'

Beckett glanced at the automap again. The blip was inside the boundaries of the airfield now. But the scale of the display was too small for a more accurate fix.

'He's there already.' Beckett flung the off-roader round the angle of the edge of the airfield. The gate was visible about a hundred yards further on. He braked, shifting the gears down. Coasted to a halt. 'The barrier's down.'

He examined it. It was a simple affair, with a swipe card slot in it. It looked flimsy enough . . .

He backed up the four by four as far as he could, selected first gear, and kicked down hard on the accelerator. He was flung back in his seat by the sudden surge of power. Up into second . . .

The impact rocked the car, but it kept going. Beckett ducked instinctively as the barrier pole kicked up over the bonnet, buckling under the assault from its bull bars, swinging wildly towards the windscreen. Then it fell away to the left. The suspension jolted as he ran

123

over some other part of the mechanism.

Accelerate again. Third gear. Fourth. Fifth. He homed in on the cluster of flying club buildings like a cruise missile on wheels. There was Todd's car, the driver's door open. But no sign of Wyman. He rounded the corner of the clubhouse, drifting out as he turned the wheel, his tyres skidding.

There. A plane just beginning to taxi, its propeller a blur. As he watched, the rudder flexed, lining it up on the runway. He spun the wheel again, angling to cut it off.

'He's taking off!' Frustration fought with grim determination. He'd stop him somehow . . .

Wyman's face turned towards him, his attention obviously caught by the movement; his face was a mask of astonishment. Then, without hesitation, he opened his throttle. The light aircraft rolled forward, gathering speed.

Beckett's jaw clenched. He was close. Very close.

Wyman's hand appeared through the side window of the cockpit, holding the gun. Beckett saw a puff of smoke from the muzzle. Then another. He heard a subdued pop, and a neat hole appeared in the windscreen, surrounded by starred safety glass.

Big mistake, Beckett thought. Now I'm really annoyed.

The light plane began to rise. The engine of the four by four howled in protest as Beckett tried to force another few miles an hour out of it. He swung the wheel desperately, skating in just ahead of the wingtip. It rose disdainfully behind him, skimming over the roof of the off-roader.

That was it, then. Anger and frustration burned his stomach. Nothing more he could do. Wyman was home free.

A sudden impact shook the vehicle. Beckett braked hard, fighting for control. Ahead of him now, the plane dropped back to the runway.

The plane's port wheel collapsed. Of course. The undercarriage. Just low enough to catch his roof and destabilise the aircraft. If Wyman had kept both hands on the control column he would probably have been able to recover. But he'd been shooting at Beckett.

Poetic justice, Beckett thought. The port wingtip dropped with agonising slowness, scraping the concrete of the runway. Then it was all over. The plane slewed, ran into the grass. The nose dropped, the propeller ploughing up clods of earth as it disintegrated. The plane pinwheeled, rolling end over end, the wings snapping off short like a balsawood model. The fuselage slithered and bounced, finally cracking to a halt against the engine pod of an obsolete bomber.

Beckett coasted the four by four off the runway, pulling up next to the first scattering of wreckage.

'He's crashed,' he said. He got out. The air was cold, the wind hard against his face, sickly with the tang of spilt fuel. The money case was lying at his feet. He retrieved it gingerly, placing it on the passenger seat of the car.

'Crashed?' Jerry's voice was strained. 'What do you mean, crashed?'

'His aircraft.'

Beckett started walking cautiously towards the fuselage. 'He seems to have . . . lost control of things.' He paused. Against all expectation, he could see movement. He ran back to the car for the first aid kit. 'Better send an ambulance along with your security goons. He's still alive.'

He turned back towards the crash site, the medical kit in his hand. And froze. Wyman was crawling from the wreckage. One arm was obviously useless, judging by the way he supported his weight on the elbow. The other held the gun. He gave Beckett a look of absolute hatred.

'You.' Wyman focused on him with difficulty. Raised the weapon. Beckett felt his skin crawl. The smell of spilt fuel was everywhere. It would only take one spark . . .

'No!' he shouted. 'Don't be a fool!'

Wyman smiled. And pulled the trigger.

Beckett threw himself flat behind the cover of the four by four, feeling the vehicle rock on its springs as the blastwave hit. Heated air punched him, singeing the hairs on his neck. A small, dirty mushroom cloud rose from where the downed aircraft had been.

He eyed the spreading flames, already engulfing the grass where he'd stood a moment before, and dived for the ignition key.

'Beckett! What's going on?' Jerry's voice was frantic with worry. He thought about it, as he accelerated away from the inferno.

'Well, you can cancel the ambulance,' he said at last. 'Like I said, he just lost control.'

# « Twelve »

The concourse was back to normal as they made their way through it for the final time. It was amazing, Ros thought, how soon you recovered. Breakfast, a shower, and a few hours' sleep at the airport hotel, and she felt her old self again. Watching the passengers thronging the departure hall, seeing the airliners landing and taking off outside, it was hard to believe that anything had happened to disrupt the familiar routine.

'I can't thank you enough,' Jerry said.

Ros smiled. 'It was an interesting experience. Did the money go back all right?'

'Oh yes. A bit scorched, but none the worse for wear.' She frowned, becoming serious. 'Beckett was very lucky.'

'He's got a charmed life,' Ros agreed.

She picked him out, still talking animatedly at the payphone a few yards away. Funny how he'd insisted on using a public booth, instead of one of the office phones upstairs. As the ambient noise in the concourse eddied a little, she caught a few snatches of his conversation.

'I know he's a busy man. So am I . . . Look, I haven't

127

got time for this. Just tell him I knew it when I saw it. He'll know what I mean. Yes, I will hold.' He stood idly for a moment, then his expression changed. Became alert. Businesslike. 'We need to talk.' Pause. 'This afternoon. Fine. Yes, I know it.' He hung up, and made his way back to join them.

'By the way, that reminds me.' Jerry continued their conversation, oblivious to the activity behind her. 'I think this is yours.'

She held out a fifty pound note. Curious, Ros took it. There was something stuck to the back. She turned it over.

A small bug. Her eyebrows rose.

'Using the metal strip as an aerial. That's brilliant, Beckett.'

He shrugged, smiling modestly. 'Anyone can bug a suitcase.' He glanced round. 'Where's Ed?'

'Beats me. He said he had something to take care of.'

'Right here,' a voice called behind them. They all turned. Ed looked pleased with himself. 'And I've got some good news for you.'

'Oh yes?' She knew that expression. 'What are you up to?'

'Nothing.' He directed a look of transparent innocence at her. 'But I've been talking to this guy you really ought to meet.'

'And why's that?' she asked suspiciously.

'Well, he can do you a really good deal on some flying lessons.' He took a step back. 'What? What did I say?'

'Ed.' Ros took a step towards him. Then another. Then he was running. He almost made it to the car park before she caught up.

'Pleasant view.'

Dent dropped into the seat beside Beckett. There

128

was no one else in the bow of the river bus. Below them, hydrofoils curled the water aside like earth from a farmer's plough. Beckett forced back the memory of his drive across the field a few hours before. His stomach was feeling fragile enough as it was.

'Pleasant enough,' he agreed. The sun bounced off the water. Over on the south bank he caught a glimpse of the hotel conference centre they'd held their last conversation in. He pulled out the CD he'd copied Elverson's files on to. 'I think this is what you were looking for.'

'Very probably.' Dent held his hand out.

Beckett twitched the shiny plastic disk away from him.

'You know,' he said speculatively, 'these things make really good frisbees. The only thing is, you can't get them to come back.'

'So I've heard.' Dent turned his face towards the sun. 'I was quite pleased when you phoned this morning. Gave me an excuse to avoid the most tedious meeting you could imagine. Far too pleasant an afternoon to waste indoors.'

'I'm afraid I don't have quite so much time to spare,' Beckett said. At least, not for your conniving games, he added to himself.

Ros was still trying to decrypt most of the files on the disk, but they'd cracked enough of it to know that Bryan Brody had a copy of the Icebreaker, which meant Kamen and Ross was wide open. And they didn't have time to develop a counter to it on their own. Not one they could be absolutely sure of, anyway. Which meant he'd have to trade for one. If Dent would play ball.

'Of course not. You still have a client to protect.' Dent nodded, understandingly. 'I take it you want a copy of the antibody in exchange?'

He was sharp, Beckett had to give him that. Not for the first time, he wondered just how free his decision to resign had been. Had Dent manoeuvred him out of the Hive to give himself a convenient catspaw, beyond the restrictions of official channels? Or was he just getting paranoid?

'We might find that useful.'

Too useful, and Dent must know that. There was no way he'd hand such sophisticated defences to a freelance operator, even one he thought he had some kind of control over. His doubts must have shown on his face, because Dent smiled.

'From our point of view, this is obsolete,' he explained. 'First generation stuff. You could devise your own defence against it without too much trouble. If you had the time.'

Which he knew they didn't.

'So how did Elverson get his hands on it?'

'Ah. That would be telling.' Dent pulled a CD of his own from an inside pocket. 'I think you'll find everything you need here.'

'Everything but answers.' Beckett cocked his wrist. 'Shall we try my frisbee theory?'

'Really, Beckett. There are times when I despair of you.' Dent shook his head, more in sorrow than in anger. 'It was Cottrell. Our late and unlamented colleague.'

Cottrell. Of course. The traitor. He must have compromised every aspect of the Hive's security.

'And Elverson was working for him?'

'Not directly, no. But he found a – vulnerability in our datanet. A very small one Cottrell had left behind, when he first tried to extract the information on the SACROS project. He failed, which was why he tried to steal the prototype. But Elverson was able to exploit the breach.' Dent shook his head. 'We didn't think anyone could, or we'd have plugged it straight away. But he was quite brilliant.'

'I see.' Beckett tried to contain his amusement. 'He just hacked in and stole the data.'

'Of course not.' Dent looked affronted at the very idea. 'Our Black Ice got him. All he had was fragments. He reconstructed it all by himself.' His tone mingled awe and respect. 'As I said, he was quite brilliant.'

He would have to have been, Beckett thought. It was an astonishing achievement.

'What kind of Black Ice?' he asked. Dent looked grim.

'You don't really expect me to answer that.' It was a statement, not a question. An accurate one, too. 'And I'd advise you not to try finding out. However much Miss Henderson takes it as a challenge.'

'I don't think I'll mention that to her,' Beckett agreed. Because she would, he knew.

A mental picture of her activating the Hive's data defences flashed through his mind. Black Ice didn't just keep intruders out, it fought back, tracing the line back to their terminals and dumping viruses into their systems. Wiping hard disks, trashing optical storage media, burning chips to charcoal.

Everything at Gizmos was interconnected somehow, in ways that sometimes surprised even Ros, who'd cabled most of it herself. Chaos theory in action, she called it. Beckett thought it had more to do with never getting a job finished properly before moving on to something else. If Black Ice got loose in that system, they'd lose everything.

Well, at least they understood one another. He held out the CD.

'The coding's all there. It's encrypted, but you should be able to crack it easily enough.' After all, that's what the Hive did. Minded other people's business.

Dent took the CD, and handed his over to Beckett. 'Oh, by the way. This will only work once. It'll erase itself after running, or if you try to copy it or examine the coding.'

'What?' Beckett rounded on him indignantly. Dent was unperturbed.

'You surely didn't expect us to leave an antibody to one of our own Icebreakers floating around loose?' he asked mildly. Beckett nodded ruefully.

'Not really, no,' he admitted. Well, that explained why he'd been willing to make the trade in the first place.

'After all, it's how Elverson operated,' Dent reminded him. 'One use, then the program self-destructs. Very clever.'

'I don't understand why he bothered with Brody,' Beckett said. 'The airport scam was going to net him fifty million, after all. That ought to be enough for anyone.'

'It was an expensive operation,' Dent said. 'Replacing the equipment our Black Ice destroyed would have been costly enough. Not to mention everything else he needed.'

It made sense. The river bus slowed, pulling in towards the jetty. As the hull lowered itself to touch the water, it began to roll with the swell. Beckett watched dry land approach with a growing sense of relief.

'That should do it.' Ros tapped a couple of keys. The CD Beckett had collected from Dent hummed quietly, disgorging its contents into the Kamen and Ross computer system. She watched it download, trying to follow its intricacies, but the task was beyond her.

Beckett had warned her about trying to copy or analyse it. Mind you, they still had the original

132

Icebreaker to examine, once they broke the encryption. And now she knew it had been booby-trapped, she was sure she could find some way of getting inside without it self-destructing.

'Is that all there is to it?' Graeme Hurry asked. His arm brushed her shoulder as he leaned forward for a closer look.

'Afraid so. If Brody tries to hack in directly, we've got him. This program will recognise the Icebreaker, and neutralise it. And then . . .' She spotted part of the program that could be customised by the user. '. . . we rub his nose in it.' She typed a few words, and Graeme laughed.

'I'd love to see his face when he reads that,' he said.

Beckett and Ed were still hard at work when she got back to Gizmos. Beckett looked up from his workstation as she came in.

'What do you think?' he asked. She took the brochure from his outstretched hand, and glanced through it.

'Impressive,' she said. If she hadn't known better, she would have sworn that Millennium Financial Services was a real company.

'I'm running off half a dozen through the laser printer. That should be enough if we just leave them lying around. And I've done a couple of others as well. Just to look as though we offer a range of services.'

'You have been busy,' she said.

'He's been busy.' Ed appeared in the doorway, flushed and breathless. 'He gets to sit and play with the DTP package while I shift furniture about.'

'It's all in a good cause, Ed. Tomorrow we get to see Beckett in a suit and tie.'

# « Thirteen »

'Good afternoon. May I help you?'

Ros looked up from behind the reception desk Ed had spent so much effort constructing the night before. It blocked off half the entrance hall; she pictured his face when she told him to remove it again this evening. That was something to look forward to.

'McTiernan.'

The middle-aged man across the desk inclined his head in acknowledgement of her greeting. He was stockier than he'd looked from the surveillance videos, his eyes quick and alert. While he spoke they took in everything around him. The brochures, the pot plant Ed had found somewhere, the easy chairs grouped around a coffee table. 'I have an appointment with Mr Beckett.'

'One moment please.'

She made a show of consulting an appointments book, which she'd filled out herself earlier that morning. McTiernan's eyes followed hers down. Luckily, she'd thought to use more than one pen, so the inks looked subtly different, and got Ed to fill in a few entries too, so there was more than one style of handwriting to be seen.

Verisimilitude, she thought. Beckett wasn't the only one who could do that.

She directed a smile at McTiernan, just shallow enough to be the reflex response to a steady stream of clients. 'Oh yes, here we are. Won't keep you a moment.'

'Thank you.' McTiernan's tone was neutral. No sign of suspicion. She picked up an internal phone, and dialled a two digit number. It would connect to the inner room they'd mocked up as Beckett's office whichever numbers she pressed, but two digits seemed about right for an organisation the size of the one they were pretending to be.

'Mr Beckett? There's a Mr McTiernan here to see you.'

'Oh good. Show him through, will you?' Beckett's voice was just loud enough to carry. McTiernan still didn't react. Good. He must be buying it, then.

'This way, please.' Ros ushered him through to the storeroom at the back. Ed had fixed a plaque to the door: 'Nicholas Beckett. Personal Finance Consultant.'

'Mr McTiernan. Please come in.'

Beckett stood as they entered the makeshift office, and advanced round the desk, his hand outstretched. McTiernan shook it, perfunctorily.

Beckett certainly looked the part, Ros thought. Suit and tie, neatly brushed hair swept forward to hide his earpiece. The office was convincing enough too; functionally utilitarian, with a few personal touches scattered around. Identical to a thousand others in this part of London alone.

She slipped away, closing the door quietly, and sprinted for the room upstairs where she'd set up the surveillance equipment.

Good. It was all functioning perfectly. Beckett's desk was centred in the monitor screen in front of her, the

135

fibre optic camera in the wall looking down over his shoulder, facing McTiernan. She could read every change of expression on the diver's face. And the audio pickup was functioning too. The voices kicked in as she slipped the headset on.

'You're ex-army,' McTiernan said, his gaze lingering on a photo on the desk. Beckett in uniform, looking impossibly young.

'That's right.' Beckett nodded. 'So I really appreciate the problems ex-servicemen sometimes have to face.' He launched into his sales pitch.

Ros picked up the cellphone beside her, and dialled the number of Ed's mobile. It rang twice, then clicked as he answered.

'Ed? Here's here. Get going.'

'Say again?' Ed's voice was muffled, masked by static. 'Reception's lousy around here.'

She tried again. 'McTiernan's here. Beckett's talking to him now. You've got half an hour at the outside.' This time she got through.

'Wagons roll,' Ed said, and cut the connection.

'Beckett.' She activated his earpiece. 'Ed's going in now. Keep him talking for as long as you can.' The back of Beckett's head inclined, almost imperceptibly, in acknowledgement.

'There are quite a few of us working here,' Beckett said, continuing his conversation with McTiernan. He'd taken on the inflection of someone delivering a prepared speech. 'In fact Millennium was founded by a retired admiral, who wanted to make sure his men got the best break they could.'

'Doesn't sound like any admiral I ever met.' McTiernan's voice took on a tinge of suspicion. Beckett dipped his head, conceding the point.

'Can't say I came across too many generals like that either.' That seemed to work. McTiernan lightened up.

The whole exchange baffled Ros, but it had obviously gone a long way towards convincing McTiernan that Beckett was genuine. Beckett took advantage of the point to move the conversation on to safer ground.

'I'd like to start by getting a quick overview of your current financial affairs. Then we can discuss any particular concerns you may have in more detail.'

'That sounds sensible,' McTiernan agreed.

'After that, we can examine the best options that fit in with your future plans. Then I suggest we make another appointment, so you can consider everything we've discussed at your leisure. After all, you may be making a big commitment. I'm sure you want to be absolutely positive that our scheme is the best one for you.'

'How big a commitment are we talking about, exactly?' McTiernan asked. A touch of suspicion again, but no more than she'd have expected from someone face to face with the salesman Beckett was pretending to be.

'That's entirely up to you,' Beckett riposted. 'For instance, you said on the phone the other day that you may have a large lump sum to invest in the near future.'

'True,' he conceded. 'I've been a diver for twenty-seven years now. Fifteen with Marine Command, then another twelve commercially. Freelance work, for the most part. Not a lot of security. Now I've got hold of some items I can turn into a lot of hard cash.' He paused, reflectively. 'I'm not a young man any more. It's not an opportunity I can afford to waste.'

'I see.' Beckett nodded. 'Very prudent, if I may say so. And what would these items be used for?'

McTiernan's expression changed. He'd been relaxing as they spoke, but now his face was hard. He stiffened in his seat. Ros felt a chill run down her spine.

'Careful, Beckett . . .'

'Why did you ask me that?' His voice was dangerously soft.

'I'm sorry?' Beckett was the picture of baffled innocence. 'I'm afraid I don't quite follow . . .'

'You asked me what the assets are for,' McTiernan said. 'Not what they are.'

'It's just another way of putting it,' Beckett said. 'All that's really relevant is their monetary value.'

'Exactly.' McTiernan stood abruptly. 'They put you up to this, didn't they?'

'I'm sorry?' Beckett's bafflement was unmistakably genuine. Ros felt her stomach lurch as the penny dropped. Remembered the argument on the surveillance tape she'd enhanced for Graeme a few days before.

'He thinks you're working for the Brodys,' she said. 'Trying to con him out of the salvage parts.' And he's a killer . . .

'That's it, isn't it?' McTiernan was growing angry. 'They set this up. Well it's not going to work!'

'Mr McTiernan.' Beckett was sticking doggedly to his role. He stood up himself, and walked around the desk.

'Leave it, Beckett!' Ros almost shouted the words. 'You've seen his file. He has a history of violence. Just let him go.'

'This is all just a simple misunderstanding,' Beckett said. He spread his hands, and took another step forward.

'Yeah, right. Misunderstand this.' McTiernan's hand disappeared inside his jacket, flicked back into view with a stubby revolver in it. Beckett only had an instant to register it, begin to check his stride, before McTiernan pulled the trigger.

'Aaaah!'

Ros snatched the headset off, her eardrums ringing

138

from the gunshot. On the screen in front of her, she saw Beckett slump to the floor. McTiernan turned and ran.

'Beckett!' Heedless of the danger to herself, Ros sprinted for the stairs. The front door slammed as McTiernan fled into the street. A moment later there was the sound of an engine starting up.

She skidded into the mocked-up office, grabbing the door jamb to swing herself through the gap without breaking stride. She knelt down next to him. 'Beckett. Beckett! Speak to me!'

No response.

What were you supposed to do for gunshot wounds? Stop the bleeding? She looked for an obvious wound. There was a powder burn on his shirt, but no blood. Internal bleeding, then?

Beckett groaned. One arm twitched feebly.

'Where were you hit?' He was trying to sit up. She supported his shoulders, surprised at how fast his strength was returning. He clutched at the wire of his earpiece with feeble fingers.

'Right ...' They closed, with difficulty. He started hauling on the wire. 'Right in ... the battery.' The receiver unit came free of his shirt. The front was shattered, trailing wires and chips of plastic.

'Beckett!' She started to laugh, in spite of herself, almost dropping his head. The relief was exhilarating. 'I thought you were a goner!'

Beckett struggled to a sitting position.

'Just winded.' He took a deep breath. 'Did Ed get out all right?'

'Ed!' She grabbed the nearest phone, began dialling the number of his mobile. 'I didn't warn him! I came straight down here to see how badly you were hurt.' Ed's cellphone was dead.

* * *

Half an hour, Ros had said. He'd better get started then. Ed emerged from the cover of an elevated section of the new rail system. A train rattled overhead, dulling the sound as his shoe soles scraped on the gravel underfoot. He crossed to the chain link fence, eyed the sign fixed to it.

FATHOM FIVE DIVING SERVICES, it said, in chipped and peeling paint. He pulled an electronic lockpick from his pocket, and inserted the probe into the padlock holding the gate closed. A faint click, and he was inside. He paused for a moment, getting his bearings.

He'd been expecting the mobile home, but the rest of the setup took his breath away. McTiernan had obviously been here for some time. A neat vegetable garden stood next to the caravan, and a miniature water tower loomed over everything, dwarfed only by the concrete pillars of the railway behind it.

The main structure had been welded together out of scaffolding poles, the tank atop it obviously salvaged from somewhere. Compressors, and other heavy diving equipment, stood around the compound, some in good repair, others obviously cannibalised for spare parts.

Better start inside. Although he still wasn't sure what he was looking for. He approached the caravan, inserted the probe of the lockpick into its keyhole. The lock clicked open, and he pulled the door cautiously ajar.

The living space inside was immaculate; all those years on board ship, Ed supposed. That was good news and bad news. The fact that everything had been neatly stowed meant he could complete the search faster. But it also made it much harder to cover his tracks.

Best get to it, then. He checked his watch. If Ros's count had been accurate, he had twenty-seven minutes. He set the timer for ten. If he hadn't found anything in here by then, he'd have to check the rest of the site.

Start with the largest locker. He opened it. A diving suit. No surprises there.

Move on to the fold-out table. It was down, a scattering of papers on it. Financial stuff mostly; bank statements, a bill from his credit card company, a couple of brochures from investment advisors. Ed grinned. Beckett's forgery was on top of the stack.

There was something else, too: a list of salvage parts. Grubby and grease-stained, as though it had spent some time in a workshop, or knocking around in McTiernan's pocket. There was a neat tick against each item.

Interesting, Ed thought. He pulled the miniature videodisc camera from his pocket, and shot a few frames. When he got back to Gizmos, Ros could run it through the computers and enhance the image to see if there were any impressions from writing on the other sheets that had been above it in the notepad it had obviously been torn from. They could cross-reference the parts, see if they could work out what sort of machine would require them.

Of course, if he could find the parts themselves . . . He returned the videodisc to its waterproof wallet. His watch beeped at him.

That's it. Time's up. He took a final look round. Nothing.

He stepped outside cautiously, relocking the door behind him. With luck, McTiernan would never even know anyone had been there. Now, he asked himself, if I was a piece of old warship, where would I be?

Almost anywhere around here, unfortunately. He scanned the piles of maritime junk with bewilderment. Nowhere obvious, he thought. McTiernan isn't the type to hide things in plain sight.

Then again . . . He looked up at the water tower. You couldn't get much plainer than that. And no one was likely to poke around up there by accident.

'It's got to be.' He started up the ladder. It was firmer than it looked, bracketed solidly to the main structure. Whatever else he was, McTiernan was good with his hands.

There was a ledge at the top of the ladder, running the full width of the tank, wide enough to stand on without difficulty. He stepped on to it. Metal plating rang under his feet.

Good view from up here, Ed thought. He could see all the way to the main road. He froze. An old and battered Land Rover was bouncing along the access track, too fast for safety. A Land Rover he recognised from Hurry's surveillance videos. Old, blue, military surplus, with FATHOM FIVE DIVING SERVICES painted on the side with more enthusiasm than skill.

He considered his options. The tank came up almost to his head. If he stayed crouched behind it he'd be invisible. But the ledge faced the caravan. If McTiernan looked up, he was bound to see him.

Only one thing for it, then. He jumped up, and hoisted himself over the rim of the tank.

The shock of the cold water inside took his breath away. He gasped as it hit, feeling all sensation drain away from his legs. He lifted a cautious head above the rim of the water tank.

McTiernan was examining the lock on the caravan door. Apparently satisfied, he unlocked it and disappeared inside. The door stayed open. Interesting. He wasn't planning to hang around, then. That was fine by Ed. He moved his legs, trying to keep them warm.

'Ouch!' His foot knocked against something solid. He shifted his weight cautiously. Kicked it. Something metallic. He extended his leg, sweeping it from

142

side to side like a blind man with his cane. There was another one. He crouched low, feeling the water slide up his chest, then submerge his shoulders. His fingers brushed against something. Something slick. He snatched them away, with an instinctive shudder of revulsion. Overrode the reaction. Probed again Whatever it was gave slightly under his fingers then became solid, immovable.

A picture formed in his mind. Something metallic. In a waterproof bag.

Only one way to find out. He steeled himself for a moment, then ducked below the surface.

He couldn't see much, but the murky shapes were distinct enough to be located. He grabbed the nearest one, and shot to the surface. For a moment he worried that he'd made enough noise to be overheard, but the telltale vibrations of someone climbing the ladder to investigate failed to materialise. He examined his prize.

He'd been right. It was some kind of engineering component, sealed in polythene. One of the missing salvage parts, it had to be. Why else would McTiernan go to so much trouble to hide them? He let it slide gently back beneath the surface.

McTiernan was taking a long time to do whatever he was doing. Ed decided to risk another look over the rim of the tank.

McTiernan was emerging from the mobile home, a kitbag slung across his shoulder. He locked the door, and ran towards the Land Rover. Something had spooked him. He felt a flash of concern for his colleagues. Chances were he'd seen through the subterfuge at Gizmos, and come rushing back to collect the parts.

Which meant he'd be coming up here to retrieve them. Not good. His thoughts raced. There had to be a way out of this. Maybe if he could delay McTiernan a little, it would be enough. Ros and Beckett would be on their way, he was sure; they wouldn't let him down.

Assuming they were able to, of course. McTiernan was a killer, after all. He forced the thought away.

Down below, McTiernan stopped in mid-stride, halfway to the Land Rover. Ed turned his head, following the direction of his gaze. Beckett and Ros couldn't have been that close behind him, surely?

A woman in her mid-thirties, immaculately and expensively dressed, was standing by the driver's door. Ed frowned, chasing the sense of familiarity; he knew her from somewhere, he was sure. Red hair, thin face.

Juliet Brody. The woman on Hurry's surveillance videos. This was getting very interesting indeed.

'I hope you're not in too much of a hurry,' she said. She held up the ignition keys where McTiernan could see them, and dropped them on the ground. 'But we wanted a word.'

We? Ed hoisted himself a little higher over the rim of the tank. It was a risk, but he had to get the full picture. There was a car parked across the entrance gate of the compound, glossy and black, a top of the range saloon. A man was standing next to it, opening the boot; as he turned and walked towards the woman his face came into view.

Bryan Brody. Of course. Well, that answered the question of how deeply his wife was involved in the attack on Kamen and Ross. She was a full and equal partner by the look of it.

'We've been thinking about our conversation the other day.' Brody's voice was affable. 'Thinking very hard about what you said.'

'And?' McTiernan eased the kitbag off his shoulder. Slowly. His eyes on the younger couple facing him. He stepped away from it. Ed felt a chill that had nothing to do with the frigid water in the tank. Impending violence hung over the little salvage yard like the crackle in the air before a thunderstorm.

'Well, to be honest we're far from happy.' Brody smiled ingenuously. 'We had an agreement, made in good faith. We shook hands on it.' He sighed. 'Trust is such a rare commodity these days.'

'So's honesty.' McTiernan had no intention of backing down, Ed could tell. He listened intently. With a bit of luck he'd be able to deduce how the Brodys intended ripping off the merchant bank. 'I had no idea how much you were going to get out of this.'

'That's beside the point,' Juliet cut in. 'You agreed to get us the parts for a specified fee. Now you're doubling it.'

'It's a seller's market,' McTiernan said, with a hint of smugness. 'You need the parts. I've got them. You know my price.'

'We do indeed. We were even prepared to pay it.' Brody shook his head, sadly. 'But markets change, Mr McTiernan. Investments can fall in value as well as rise.'

'What are you talking about?' McTiernan was uneasy. He looked from one to the other. They stayed poker faced.

'Since we last spoke, we've found an alternative approach. It's a good deal less complex and time consuming.' Brody permitted himself a small, triumphant smile. 'To be blunt, we don't need the parts any more.'

'You're bluffing.' McTiernan was growing angry.

'Are we?' Juliet's face was expressionless. Brody made small, placating gestures in her direction. The old sweet and sour routine, Ed thought. Corny or what? McTiernan wasn't buying it either.

'You're here, aren't you?' he said. 'Which means you still want the components.'

'Very astute.' Brody conceded the point. 'But only as insurance. We probably won't need them at all. But you did go to considerable trouble to obtain them.'

'Quite. And you know my price.' McTiernan wasn't budging.

'You really don't get it, do you, you tiresome little man.' This from Juliet. She picked something up from inside the Land Rover. 'They're surplus to requirements now. And so are you.'

'Sweetheart.' A note of warning entered Brody's voice. 'Let's not get carried away here. We still don't know if this Icarus program works. We might need the parts after all.'

So, Beckett had been right, Ed thought. They were planning to use the Icebreaker against Kamen and Ross. And much good it was going to do them, now Ros had immunised the system with Dent's countermeasures.

A slow smile began spreading across McTiernan's face. He hadn't followed the argument, but he obviously thought he'd won.

'Honestly, Bryan, you can be so spineless sometimes.' Juliet wasn't happy with that at all. McTiernan's smile spread further.

'So what's your best offer?'

'This.' Juliet stepped into his line of sight. A revolver was visible in her right hand.

McTiernan's eyes widened. His hand flashed under his jacket, and emerged empty.

'I'm afraid this is yours. You left it on the passenger seat.' Juliet pulled the trigger. McTiernan fell back. Juliet fired again. Then twice more, at point blank range. Then the hammer clicked down on an empty chamber.

Holy cow! Ed slipped down out of sight as quietly as he could. Sudden panic hit him, choking him with its

146

intensity. But not for himself.

She'd fired four shots. The gun had been in the Land Rover, as though thrown down by someone who'd just used it. McTiernan had come back from Gizmos in a tearing hurry, panicked enough to be leaving his home. Four shots in the gun. Two gone already.

Two shots. Beckett and Ros.

Not necessarily, he told himself. He might have had an empty chamber under the hammer. Most people who carried revolvers did. That would leave only one shot unaccounted for.

But either way, he couldn't count on the cavalry. He pulled the cellphone from his jacket pocket.

Useless. Water ran out of it, the power cells dead. At least the minicam was waterproofed; and he'd thought the sealed wallet was just a sales gimmick. Well, you live and learn.

He returned to the Brodys' conversation. Bryan didn't sound too happy about this turn of events.

'Not one of your brighter ideas, Lambchop.'

'Don't be so negative, Bryan. He was a loose end.'

'I'm not disputing that. I just wished you'd waited until he'd told us where the parts were.'

'Well, I'm sorry.' A little grudging, but sincere enough. Ed suppressed a shudder of revulsion. What kind of people were these? 'But he just made my skin crawl. Jumped-up little oik.'

Ed risked another quick peek over the rim of the tank, just in time to see Brody give his wife a quick, consoling hug.

'Cheer up. No real harm done. The program looks kosher. It ought to work.' He bent down to McTiernan's lifeless body. Hoisted it up on to his shoulders in a fireman's carry.

'OK. I'll take a look round anyhow. Just to be on the safe side.'

'Attagirl.' He watched her disappear into the caravan. Muffled thuds and scraping noises began inside. She wasn't being nearly as careful as Ed had been. But then she didn't need to. Brody glanced round, searching for somewhere to stash the body. Started towards the water tower.

Oh great, Ed thought. If it's not one thing it's another. He slipped back down into the water. Faint vibrations began to ripple the surface as Brody climbed the ladder. He must be stronger than he looked. But then, a lot of these city types were into pumping iron.

Ed took a deep breath, and dived below the water. A moment later something splashed next to him. A cold, limp hand brushed against his face. He fought the urge to push it away, to break for the surface. Forced himself to remain still, until the vibrations of Brody descending the ladder gave him unmistakable proof of his safety.

He broke the surface, gasping, fighting free of McTiernan's deathly embrace. The diver was floating face down. The water around him was crimson. Ed shuddered. He hauled himself up level with the tank rim again.

'Come on, Poptart. Gotta run!' Brody disappeared inside the caravan. Something had disturbed them. Ed turned, looking back towards the main highway. Movement. A small, yellow car, moving down the lane like it wanted to be formula one when it grew up. Ros.

Brody reappeared at the door of the mobile home, McTiernan's diving suit in his hands. He was still taking this plan seriously, then, whatever he'd told his wife. Juliet followed, carrying the air tanks. They sprinted for their car, dropped the diving gear in the boot, and slammed it shut. Gravel sprayed as Brody accelerated away, in the opposite direction to the approaching hot hatch.

Ros drove straight into the yard, braking to a halt just inches from the Land Rover. She and Beckett piled out, taking in the scene around them.

Ed sagged with relief. They were both all right.

'Ed!' Ros shouted. 'Ed, he's back!'

'I know!' Ed pushed McTiernan's body away again, and began to climb out of the tank. 'I don't suppose either of you thought to bring a towel with you?'

# « Fourteen »

'That ought to do it.' The screen showed the Kamen and Ross log-on display. 'They think we're a legitimate user.'

'Now what?' Juliet stepped up for a closer look. She leaned forwards, over his head, and began massaging his shoulders. He relaxed and tilted his head back.

'Now we get to see if Icarus sold us a pup.'

He called up the Icebreaker program. Hesitated. Initiated it.

'Nothing's happening.' Juliet sounded vaguely disappointed.

He wasn't sure quite what she'd been expecting; bundles of banknotes dropping out of the disk drive, like the cash dispenser at the bank, he supposed.

'We just have to wait, cupcake.' Wait while the Icebreaker did its work, feeling its way carefully through the system's defences, like a sapper probing through a minefield with a bayonet. Unfortunately, waiting wasn't something Juliet was good at.

'But for how long?' Oh dear. It sounded like she was getting ready to throw a sulk. Not to worry. She'd cheer up fast enough when they got their hands on the money.

'A few minutes, probably.' After all, he knew the system well. They were bound to have plugged most of the leaks he'd found while he was working there, but he'd compensated for that when he configured the Icebreaker. They could only have changed so much.

The screen went blank. That fast? Icarus really did know his stuff.

A new message appeared.

ICARUS WAS A BETTER SALESMAN THAN HE WAS A PROGRAMMER.

'Damn!' He slammed his fist on the desktop. All that money, gone . . .

'I told you!' Juliet was well on the way to throwing a tantrum. Which was bad news; when she got upset, someone usually got hurt. 'I told you not to trust him!'

That wasn't true, either; they'd both agreed to take a chance on the Icebreaker. Assessed the risks, and gone ahead. Jointly, the way they did everything. But now was not the time to point that out.

'Well, you were right,' he said. Luckily she'd always fall for flattery. 'Nothing gets past you.' He reached up for her hand, and squeezed it.

'Then listen to me next time.' She began to sound mollified. The terminal beeped. The message on it changed.

YOU HAVE FIVE SECONDS TO DISENGAGE BEFORE BLACK ICE ACTIVATES. FOUR. THREE . . .

He broke the connection.

'Do you think they traced it?' Juliet asked, a note of doubt entering her voice as she began to calm down. Brody shook his head.

'I doubt it.' None of his own Ice had activated. And even if they had, it wouldn't do them any good; he'd gone in over the ghost line, so the CommEx database wouldn't have a record of it to trace back in any case.

'What are we going to do now, then?' Juliet asked.

151

'Go back to the original plan, of course.' Except that she'd deleted McTiernan ahead of schedule. Which meant they had to find out what he'd done with the salvage parts.

He sighed. More complications. Fond as he was of her, he thought, there were times when her impetuous nature made her a distinct liability.

'The first thing we need to do is search McTiernan's yard,' she said. 'He must have stashed those parts nearby.'

'Right. He wasn't a very trusting little soul. He'd have wanted them where he could get his hands on them in a hurry.'

'And then,' her face hardened, 'I think we should take a little drive in the country. Somewhere up around Hunsford. I want to have a word with Mr Icarus about refunding our money.'

Oh dear. She hadn't heard. Brody turned back to the computer, and accessed the NewsNet.

'You'll need an ouija board,' he said.

'What?' She looked baffled. Brody called up the day's big story. BLACKMAILERS KILLED IN AIRPORT EXTORTION ATTEMPT. He indicated the screen.

'Icarus is no longer with us.' He watched her narrowly. Knowing Juliet, she was quite capable of taking it personally, as though Icarus had arranged his own demise for the sole purpose of annoying her. She read through the story. Called up the video clips.

'That's odd,' she said. 'No pictures of these security experts. You'd think they'd want the publicity.'

'Maybe they're modest,' Brody suggested. He rooted around the files. 'Ah. There's a long-range shot of the girl in the plane.' He called it up. It was a still photograph, taken from a long way back with a pocket camera. An airliner at the end of the runway, a small figure clambering down the stairway from the forward

152

door. One arm raised, shielding her eyes from the early morning sun. Not a lot of detail. 'I suppose her mother might recognise her from this.'

'And nothing at all on the other two. Hm.' Juliet sounded pensive. Which, in itself, was enough to worry him.

'What's on your mind, Lover?'

'Icarus. He may have kept records. Would have done, if he had any sense.' The implications weren't lost on Brody either.

'You mean they might be looking for us.' He shrugged. 'No reason why they should, though. Kamen and Ross has its own security division.' She was unconvinced, he could tell. 'But it is another reason not to hang around.'


'Beckett. This is Ed. Are you there?'

'Where else would I be?' Beckett answered the voice in his headset abstractedly. He kept an eye on the screen, firmed up the enhancement program a little. There were definite impressions on the piece of paper Ed had taken a video still of. Getting them clear enough to read was turning out to be a bit of a headache though.

'The Brodys are back. They're turning McTiernan's place upside down.'

'Have they seen you?' Ros asked anxiously. She was working at the terminal next to Beckett, running a database search of the components on the list, trying to find a single machine they could all belong to.

'No. I'm keeping well out of sight.'

This time he was watching from a signal maintenance platform on the railway viaduct. High enough for clear radio reception. Far enough away to look like an innocent railway worker if the Brodys did catch sight of him.

'Well, keep your feet dry,' Beckett said.

'Very funny.' Ed cut the connection.

'There's definitely something here.' Beckett accentuated the contrast a little more. Zoomed in on part of the image. 'Looks like letters of some kind. But I still can't get a clear enough image.'

'Try false colours,' Ros suggested.

Good idea, Beckett thought. He overlaid a filter. 'Well, that's a lot clearer. Still not much help, though.' It looked like some kind of algebraic expression. Ros scooted her chair over, and stared at the screen. 'Any ideas?' Beckett asked her.

'Nope, all Greek to me.'

Of course! Written in cursive script, in handwriting even less legible than Ed's, but if you rotated the image a little . . .

'Ros, you're brilliant.'

She looked puzzled. 'I know. But it's not like you to notice. What exactly are you on about?'

'This. It *is* Greek.' He considered it more carefully. 'Cyrillic characters, anyway. Could be Russian, I suppose. Or any one of a dozen other East European languages.'

'Greek.' Ros considered the implications. 'Don't they have a large merchant shipping fleet?'

'Yeah.' Beckett followed her chain of reasoning. 'And McTiernan was stealing salvage parts from decommissioned warships. But I suppose you could use them on a civilian vessel instead.'

'It still doesn't explain Brody's interest, though. Or the connection to Kamen and Ross. They don't have any link with the shipping industry at all.'

'Maybe if we knew what the parts were supposed to be used for, we'd have a better idea,' Beckett suggested.

Ros returned to her own terminal.

'According to this, they're all pump components.'

Well, that didn't help.

'One good thing, anyway,' Beckett said. 'While we've got the parts, they're stalled. You can tell Kamen and Ross they're safe now, at least for the time being.'

'I'm not so sure about that. The Brodys are ruthless, and they want a return on their investment. They're not going to give up.'

'Then maybe we should take the initiative,' said Beckett.

'Well that was a complete waste of time,' Juliet said.

She wanted to kick something. She wished McTiernan was still alive, so she could shoot him again. It wasn't fair. He'd spoiled everything. Hiding the parts and then making her kill him like that. If she hadn't been driving, she'd have stamped her foot.

'I think that light was red.' Bryan turned in his seat to look back, an expression of mild reproof on his face.

'What light?'

She slowed down to a hair above the legal limit. Bryan reached a hand across, tried to comfort her. 'Don't fret, Sweetiepie. We'll think of something.'

Of course they would. They always did. Good old Bryan. Always there in a crisis. She coasted into their parking space.

'Well if they weren't in the yard, where else could he have hidden them?'

The thing to do was to be logical. Methodical.

'Somewhere he had easy access to.'

He climbed out of the car, his front door key out. She followed, activating the central locking with a reassuring *thump*. The alarm light went on. The converted warehouses had their own secure parking area, but you couldn't be too careful. There were so many dishonest people around these days. It was disgusting.

She followed Bryan up the stairs to their flat.

'Could he have given them to someone else to take care of?' she suggested. The front door swung solidly closed behind her. Home. Safe.

'It's possible.' Bryan made for the desktop computer. He sounded doubtful. 'But there can't be all that many people he would have trusted.' He began to perk up. 'So it shouldn't take too long to draw up a list.'

'In the meantime, I'll go through his diary.' Juliet picked up the palmtop computer Bryan had taken from McTiernan's body before dumping it in the water tank. 'See if he visited anywhere regularly. Or soon after each acquisition.'

'That's my girl.' Bryan smiled at her. 'A mind even sharper than your dress sense.'

'Oh you.' She smiled back, the last traces of her bad mood evaporating.

Bryan's computer beeped. She knew that tone; an incoming fax. She ignored it, flipping the palmtop open. Bryan started reading the message, which had popped up in a window on his screen. Then he laughed.

'Well there's a turnup for the book. It looks like the mountain's come to us.'

'What do you mean?' Curiosity tugged her to her feet. She walked over to the terminal, peered over his shoulder at the screen. Read the message.

I HAVE WHAT YOU WANT. BAILEY. And a telephone number.

'Now there's a thing.' Bryan rubbed his chin thoughtfully. 'Isn't that convenient?'

'A bit too convenient if you ask me,' Juliet said.

'It seems McTiernan had a friend or two after all. The question is, how much did he tell them.'

'Does it matter?' Juliet didn't see the problem. 'If this Bailey has the parts, we can use him. If not, he's just another loose end to tidy up.'

'Incisive as always, my little pumpkin. One thing we do know. He's greedy.'

'How can you tell?' Sometimes his intuitive leaps left Juliet behind.

Bryan grinned, the way he always did when he was being clever.

'If he contacted us directly, he must know McTiernan is dead,' he said. 'But he's still willing to take the risk of getting involved.'

'Greedy,' she murmured. 'And not very bright.' Perfect. She felt the smile spreading across her face. Things were going to work out after all.

The boardroom at Kamen and Ross was designed to look imposing. Comfort had obviously been a lot lower on the architect's list of priorities. Ros fidgeted in the over-padded swivel chair, covertly studying the bank's board of directors. An identical row of well-cut suits, sober ties, and expressions of polite bafflement looked back at her across the polished wooden table.

Only two of them really counted, Graeme had explained. The vice-chairman, Challoner, who took board level responsibility for matters of security, and the chairman himself, Sir Norman Pettigrew, who could theoretically overrule him. The others were there mainly to keep an eye on their colleagues, and try to bend any disagreements to their own advantage in their never-ending round of inter-departmental politics.

Graeme was winding up his presentation, with an economy and precision that was probably wasted on most of the men in the room. The vice-chairman seemed to be following it well enough though. He coughed politely, and Graeme paused in his summing up of the investigation to date.

'Correct me if I'm wrong,' he said, 'but you say you

have already foiled an attempt by these people to gain unauthorised access to our computer system.'

'That's right,' Graeme said, casting Ros a questioning look. 'The countermeasures Ms Henderson supplied were able to repel their intrusion program.'

And he still wanted to know where the countermeasures had come from, thought Ros, and why they'd deleted themselves from the system as soon as they'd finished the job. Well, hard luck, she thought. Life was full of little mysteries. He'd just have to consider this one of them.

'But you're still convinced they represent a threat of some kind to us.' Challoner turned his pale grey eyes from Graeme to Ros. Consulting the visiting expert.

'There's no doubt at all that they're planning something,' Ros said.

'And they've already failed.' Sir Norman sounded even less convinced. 'Why should they stand any more of a chance next time?'

'Their attempt this afternoon was simple opportunism. They have a long-term plan of some kind, which they've already spent several weeks setting up. They might have abandoned it if the Icarus program had worked, but its failure won't have affected their primary strategy in the slightest.'

'And you still have no idea what this plan of theirs might be.'

'No, sir.' Graeme stepped in to back her up. 'But it's definitely a threat. Not just paranoia on our part.'

'On your part, Mr Hurry.' Challoner still wasn't convinced. None of them were, Ros thought. They were so secure in their narrow little world of balance sheets and petty jealousies they thought nothing outside it was of any significance. They had no idea how a computer worked, or what it did, or how totally reliant they were on the technology that surrounded them.

She might just as well have said that the Brodys were planning to steal from them by waving a magic wand. Some of these crusty old men would probably have found that more convincing.

'We don't know the details,' she said. 'But we do know that these salvage parts are vital to whatever they're planning. We intend to exploit that and find out what they're up to.'

'How, exactly, may I ask?' Sir Norman was one of the oldest men she'd ever seen. His voice rustled like autumn leaves, but his eyes were still sharp.

'We're using them as bait. My colleagues are contacting the Brodys, pretending to be friends of the late Mr McTiernan. If they're as desperate to recover them as we believe, we should get a vital lead.'

'Or a foothold in the scrap metal business.' A few of Challoner's colleagues murmured sycophantic amusement.

'With all due respect, sir.' Graeme's tone betrayed a complete absence of it. 'I don't think this is a matter for levity.' Ros noticed a flicker of interest in Sir Norman's eyes; Graeme had done himself some good there. And almost as much damage with Challoner, if she was any judge. She stepped in to back him up.

'Neither do I. I have a great deal of experience in this field, and I'm convinced Mr Hurry is right. The Brodys are well aware of what they're facing. And in my judgement they're convinced they've found a loophole in your security.'

'We're not here to discuss the delusions of disaffected former employees.' Challoner shot a venomous look at Graeme. 'Or present ones, for that matter. Unless you're trying to tell us you don't think your department's up to the job?'

'Our security is excellent.' Graeme wasn't letting that one past. 'But I'm not prepared to be complacent either. Not with this much at stake. Which is why I've called in outside assistance.'

'Very commendable,' Sir Norman said. He turned back to Ros. 'In your professional judgement, how likely are these people to succeed in their aims?'

'I can't answer that,' Ros said. 'Not until we know what their plan is. But one thing I do know.' She paused for emphasis. 'Unless we stop them, they'll certainly make the attempt. And if they're right about finding a loophole, you're going to lose an awful lot of money.'

'I see.' The chairman nodded once, incisively. 'Carry on, then. And keep me informed.'

It was like waiting for McTiernan to call all over again, Beckett thought, as he idly scanned a CD Rom of *Jane's Fighting Ships*. *Déjà Vu*. The same sense of bored frustration. The same phone, waiting for a phantom number to be diverted from the exchange. The only difference was that this time he had Ed to talk to instead of Ros.

'This is weird,' Ed said. He had the salvage parts laid out on a work surface, comparing them with schematics from the report Dent had supplied, and the screen of his laptop, which he'd also loaded with *Jane's*. 'Every single one of these is from a different kind of boat.'

'Ship,' Beckett corrected. 'Marine Command don't use boats. They use ships.'

'Oh.' Ed looked mildly puzzled. 'Then what's a gunboat?'

'It's a kind of ship,' Beckett explained.

Ed frowned. 'Then what's a gunship?'

'That's a helicopter.'

'Oh, right.' Ed nodded, unconvinced by the logic. 'Glad we could sort that one out.' He returned to the pump components, turning them over in his hands as though looking for a way to fit them all together.

The phone rang. Beckett got to it a heartbeat ahead of Ed. He grinned triumphantly as he lifted the receiver. That'll teach him to mess with my head, he thought. I picked up first, so I get to be Bailey. If we'd flipped for it he'd only have cheated.

'Yes?' he said. The voice-activated recorder kicked into life.

'I'd like to speak to Mr Bailey,' Bryan Brody said.

'That's me.' Play it taciturn, he thought. Let him fish. Behind him, Ed dropped into a workstation seat, and fired up a trace program.

'I got your message.' Brody wasn't going to waste words either.

'And I've got the stuff on your shopping list. Planning to start your own little Armada are you?'

'Never mind what my plans are. How realistic are your expectations here?'

'Let's just say I've got fewer illusions than the last owner.' Maybe he'd overdone it, he thought. The silence stretched. But Brody was only digesting what he'd said. Ed caught his eye, made a thumbs-up gesture. He'd traced the call. Good. If Brody turned them down, at least they'd have that much of a lead.

'I think we should meet,' Brody said at last.

'Sounds reasonable,' Beckett agreed. He listened carefully. 'I'll be there.' He hung up, quickly, before Brody could. Get the psychological advantage. Keep him off balance.

'I've got the location.' Ed pointed to an illuminated dot on the map currently filling his screen. 'But I don't think it'll do us much good.' It pinpointed one of the capital's busiest railway stations. 'He was using one of the cardphones in the concourse.'

'I know.' Beckett picked up his jacket. 'He wants to meet us there.'

'Suits me.' The implications weren't lost on Ed

either. 'Public space. Excellent.' Meaning much safer. 'Where, exactly?'

'That's the good bit,' Beckett told him. 'He's going to buy us dinner.'

It might have been Beckett's idea of dinner, but it certainly wasn't Ed's. Sushi was all right, he supposed, but he'd had enough of that in Japan. He looked wistfully at the spare rib and burger concessions as they hurried across the concourse. But he had to admit it was a good place to meet; the station sushi bar was quiet this late at night.

He followed Beckett through the glass door, breaking off at a tangent to help himself to a couple of bowls of green tea from the urn in the corner. When he turned back to the counter, his colleague was already in conversation with Brody.

'Mr Bailey. A pleasure.' The welcoming smile congealed on his face as Ed approached them, and sat on the next stool. He put the second bowl of tea down in front of Beckett.

'Thanks.' Beckett took it, sipped, and turned back to Brody. The banker twitched a quizzical head in Ed's direction.

'And who's this?' Suspicious, but not unduly alarmed. Ed pretended to be absorbed in the selection of dishes moving past on the countertop conveyor belt. Come to think of it, he was pretty hungry. And Japan had been a long time ago. He selected a couple. And dried salmon. That brought back a few memories.

'My insurance,' Beckett said. 'I've seen the way you do business.'

'Ah.' Brody looked mildly embarrassed, as though Beckett had caught him out in some social *faux pas*. He spread his hands. 'My wife has a temper. What can I say?'

162

Ed separated his chopsticks with a sharp crack.

'*Itadakimas.*' Funny how old habits came back to you. He lifted a sliver of raw fish to his mouth, and ate it with relish.

Beckett watched him with appalled fascination. Well, Beckett had wanted to do the talking; Ed was just supposed to look strong and silent. He could do that just as well while he was eating. Beckett took another sip of his tea.

Brody turned his attention back to business. 'I hate to broach a delicate subject. But how do I know you're who you say you are?'

'A good point.' Beckett nudged Ed in the ribs, making him drop a perfectly good rice ball. 'But my associate should be able to set your mind at rest.' His voice took on a waspish tone. 'If he can stop stuffing his face for a moment.'

Ed pulled a couple of photographs from his pocket. One of the array of parts on the workbench, and one which Beckett had spent most of the afternoon assembling on a set of image processing software of quite staggering complexity. The result was undeniably brilliant.

He handed it to Brody.

'Hm.' Brody glanced at the array of parts, but that was just a little extra to get him interested; he was already working on the assumption that they had them. He paused a little longer over the second picture. 'Photographs can be faked, you know.' It was a ritual protest.

Ed snatched it back, and looked at it critically. 'Get real. If I was going to fake a photograph I'd make a better job of it than that.'

Which was the beauty of it, of course. It was a simple enough composite, made up of library pictures, and the faces of Beckett, McTiernan and himself. All in

Naval uniform, apparently carousing with a bevy of bar girls in some Far Eastern port. The artistry came in the way Beckett had made it look like a truly terrible snapshot; bleached-out flash, red eyes, the lot.

Which made it all the more convincing, of course.

'You do have a point,' Brody said. 'And I like to think I'm a good judge of character.' He leaned forward, lowering his voice slightly. 'Now I'm prepared to pay the sum I originally agreed with McTiernan. You deliver, I pay cash, and we never see each other again.'

'Go on.' Beckett sipped his tea. Ed retrieved his errant rice ball.

'But, if you're interested, I'm willing to pay a great deal more.'

'For what?' Beckett injected just the right amount of suspicion into his voice.

'McTiernan was our marine engineer. I need to replace him too.'

'I see.' Ed nodded. 'And if we go along with it . . .'

'A simple job. And your promise of a lifetime of silence.'

'And in return?' Beckett asked.

'Ah. Now you're talking.' Brody's eyes lit up. 'A share in one of the biggest frauds the world has ever seen. And I'm talking about a truly huge piece of change.' He grinned. 'Are we interested?'

Beckett inclined his head slightly.

'I'm still listening,' he said.

'And he wasn't any more specific than that?' Hurry picked up one of the components from the workbench, and weighed it thoughtfully in his hand.

'No.' Beckett took it from him, and placed it carefully in one of the boxes Ed had scrounged from somewhere after their return to Gizmos. 'He's playing it very close to his chest.'

'But he couldn't resist bragging a little. Two hundred and fifty million, he said. Trying to impress us.'

'Well, it impressed me,' Beckett said. He'd thought Wyman and Elverson were ambitious enough, going for fifty. Brody made them look like small-time pickpockets.

'Did he give you any idea what he wants the components for?' Ros asked. Ed shook his head.

'No. But I think you're right about them being parts of a pump.' He shrugged. 'Maybe he's planning to tunnel into the vault.'

'We're a merchant bank, Ed.' Hurry tried to conceal his amusement. 'We don't deal in cash. Just credit transfers.'

'Could he intercept one?' Beckett asked. Hurry shook his head.

'I really don't see how. Our credit transfer routines are absolutely airtight.' He shrugged. 'I've tried every way I can think of to crack them from the outside. And if I can't, knowing the system as well as I do . . .'

'It probably can't be done,' Ros said. 'Not without Elverson's Icebreaker, anyway; and that's off the market for good.'

Beckett wished he was quite so sure.

'I don't see that we've got any choice,' he said. 'We're just going to have to go along with this until we find out what he's up to.'

'Two hundred and fifty million is a very specific amount,' Ros said thoughtfully. She looked at Hurry. 'Even if he's rounding it off. Do you have any transfers of around that amount scheduled in the next few days?'

'Several, probably.' Hurry looked thoughtful. 'It's worth checking, though. Might narrow the field down a bit.'

'Right. You make a start on that, then,' Beckett said.

'And in the meantime, Ed and I will follow up from the other end.'

'Go carefully,' Hurry said. 'We know they're dangerous.'

'Don't worry,' Ed assured him. 'We've got Ros for backup. She'll be tracking us the whole way.'

'Glad to hear it.'

'Do you know the rendezvous yet?' Ros asked.

'Eastgate,' Beckett said. He punched up a gazetteer entry on the nearest screen. 'Small seaside town. Very quiet. With a harbour.'

'The maritime connection again.' Ros nodded, thoughtfully. 'Nice time of year for a boat trip.'

Beckett swallowed, and tried to think about something else.

# « Fifteen »

'Smell that ozone.' Ed stuck his head out of the passenger window of the pickup truck, inflated his lungs, and sighed appreciatively. 'Sea air. Nothing like it.' The breeze carried a faint tang of salt to his tongue.

'Yes. Very nice,' Beckett said flatly.

He'd been in a subdued mood all morning. Ed couldn't work it out. He'd even been off his breakfast.

'Isn't it time you did a comms check?' Beckett asked.

If he was determined to be a grouch ... Ed turned back the lapel of his denim jacket, and checked the wiring of the concealed mike.

'Dream Team to Dream Queen. Testing. How's our signal strength?'

He turned, looking through the rear window of the cab, across the boxes of salvage parts filling the flatbed. A hundred yards behind them, Ros flashed her head-lights. Ed waved back.

'You're coming through strength five.' Her voice was attenuated by the tiny speaker. 'And the tracker's working perfectly.'

'That's good to know.'

'We're coming up to the turn-off,' Beckett said,

braking, and dropping down a gear. He swung the pickup down the access road to the quayside. Behind them, Ros carried on along the main road to the town centre. The truck bounced on its springs, wallowing down the unmade track.

'This must be it,' Beckett said. He coasted to a halt on the quayside, and killed the engine.

Ed climbed out, inhaling the sea air gratefully. It was fresher here, the wind skittering in onshore, ruffling his hair and the pennant on the Coastguard hut. Corrugated iron sheds stood around three sides of the open area, all occupied by boat builders or chandlers. A procession of beached boats followed the line of the coast, flanked by wooden pilings to the seaward side, and a gravelled roadway a few yards inland.

Only two other buildings were visible. A whitewashed pub, The Fishing Smack, stood behind a wooden picket fence. Its windows were shuttered, the sign creaking quietly as it oscillated in the wind. And facing it, equally deserted, a small, white painted kiosk, rather hopefully offering ICES, HOT DOGS, CANDY FLOSS. In the early morning chill, it was hard to imagine either of them ever opening.

'That must be it,' Beckett said. He indicated the boat riding quietly at the quayside with a flick of his head. A sea-going fishing cruiser. Large, modern and immaculate. It's engines were running, a quiet, almost subliminal, throb.

'Reckon so. Check out the reception committee.'

Juliet Brody stepped down from the deck. Despite himself, Ed felt his stomach tighten at the sight of her. Memories of the last time he'd seen her rose up; the crack of the gun in her hand, McTiernan falling back, the corpse's hand brushing against him in the water tank. Luckily, Beckett was doing most of the talking.

'Juliet Brody?'

'That's me.' She looked at both men, appraisingly, her eyes scanning them like a security camera. 'And you must be Bailey.'

'That's right,' Beckett confirmed.

'I'm afraid Bryan didn't pass on the name of your friend.'

'It didn't come up in the conversation.'

'I see.' She let it go, walked to the tail of the pickup. Ran her eyes over the boxes. 'This is it?'

'All present and accounted for.' Ed turned his gaze away from the cruiser, rocking gently at its moorings. 'Nice boat. Yours?'

'Chartered. But the skipper's reliable.'

'I hope so,' Beckett said.

'He has a somewhat flexible attitude to official paperwork,' Juliet explained. 'Customs declarations, that sort of thing.'

'That should certainly make him reliable,' Beckett said, with barely a trace of sarcasm. He lowered the tailgate.

'Seems the ideal boat for the job,' Ed said. 'Luxury model, but with a real turn of speed.' He grinned mischievously at Juliet. 'Not unlike yourself, I suspect.' It had precisely the effect he'd been hoping for.

'Just get the stuff on board.' She turned away, giving him the unmistakable cold shoulder. Now she'd written him off as an obnoxious jerk, she'd stay as far away from Beckett and himself as possible, reducing the chances of them giving themselves away. Once she was out of sight, he permitted himself a shudder.

'What was all that about?' Beckett asked. He manhandled one end of a box to the edge of the tailgate, and took the weight. Ed took hold of the other end.

'I want her at arm's length.' He didn't mind admitting it. 'She spooks me.'

'I'm not surprised.' They started towards the deck. 'But don't let it show.' They swung the crate between

169

them, hefting it up to land on the deck with an audible thud. They started back towards the truck.

'It was her face, Beckett. When she shot McTiernan, I mean. You should have seen it.'

'Why?' Beckett lifted one of the smaller boxes. 'What was it like?'

'Nothing. That's what's so scary.' Ed hefted the next one on to his shoulder. 'She had no expression, Beckett. No expression at all.'

Ros found a parking space on the seafront without any trouble. It was still too early for the holidaymakers to be out and about. She strolled across a small square, her footsteps echoing against the shuttered shopfronts, and made for the promenade. A floral clock, looking slightly windswept, ticked loudly in the early morning stillness, not quite drowned out by the crash of waves on shingle. She crossed the patch of grass surrounding it, skirting a deserted crazy golf course, and leaned on the flaking cast iron balustrade separating the promenade from the beach. Every hundred yards or so, staircases descended to the pebble-strewn sand.

She pulled the binoculars from her coat pocket, and swung them towards the quayside. Tiny servos whined as the focus adjusted, and the prisms flexed inside the barrels, compensating for the tremors of her heartbeat. The image remained rock steady, the active image compensators rendering it as clear as if she'd been using a tripod.

There was the cruiser, dead centre in the circle of her vision. Juliet Brody, her red hair unmistakable, was in the wheelhouse talking to a man Ros didn't recognise. The owner of the boat, probably. Ros sniffed, loudly. If that auburn look was natural, she'd eat the binoculars. Ed stowed one of the boxes on deck, and vaulted over the rail after it. No sign of Beckett.

She panned along the quayside, picked him up as he locked the truck, and tracked with him as he walked back to the boat. He walked slowly. Almost hesitant. Funny. The prospect of action usually perked him up more than that.

He climbed aboard the boat, Ed reaching out a hand to help him up. The man in the wheelhouse shouted something, and Ed undid the mooring lines. White foam churned at the stern of the boat, and it began to move, rocking slightly in the swell. Beckett sat down, suddenly.

The rising note of the engine drifted towards her over the water. The boat picked up speed, bouncing a little as it rounded the harbour groyne, and began to breast the waves.

Ros stood and watched it for a few more minutes, until it was too small to see anything clearly. It stayed on the same course, heading straight out to sea. Once she was sure it wasn't about to change direction, she put the binoculars away, and strolled back to the car.

The radio receiver was still activated from her brief conversation with Ed; she adjusted the gain a little, but there was nothing to hear apart from an occasional spurt of conversation between him and Beckett. The low drone of the engine was a constant background noise.

She booted a notebook computer. The screen lit up with a naval chart of the North Sea. The receiver of the tracking device was already linked to one of the serial ports. As she extended its aerial, a dot appeared on the map, marking the boat's position.

Perfect. All she had to do was wait.

Ed was enjoying himself. The sea breeze was invigorating, and the boat was a real thoroughbred, bounding through the waves like an excitable puppy. Beckett, on the other hand . . .

'Cheer up,' Ed said. 'No one ever died from sea-sickness. Just wished they could.'

'I'm watching the horizon,' Beckett said, with fragile dignity. 'They say it helps.' He swallowed, his eyes focused firmly on the middle distance. He looked distinctly greenish around the gills.

'You're supposed to be a professional sailor,' Ed reminded him. 'Lot of good it's going to do our cover if you start waving goodbye to your breakfast.'

'Nelson got seasick,' Beckett said. 'Every time he set sail.'

'Yeah,' Ed said. 'And he got killed on a boat. Don't forget that part.'

'Ship,' Beckett said. 'He died on a ship.'

'Yeah, well. Whatever.' It was no fun teasing him while he was like this. 'I'll make us some tea. Help settle your stomach.'

'I'm not sure that's such a good idea,' Beckett said.

'Trust me. Besides, it'll give me an excuse to poke around in the cabin.' He stood. Prepared a parting shot. 'In the meantime, try to think of something about as far removed from food as it's possible to get. Bacon. Chips. Lard. Anything that takes your mind off it.'

An expression of acute nausea washed across Beckett's face.

'Go make the tea, Ed,' he said. 'Or I may have to kill you.'

In the wheelhouse the skipper, who'd introduced himself as John Dobie when they came aboard, was still talking to Juliet Brody. Ed stuck his head inside.

'I'm going to make some tea. Like some?'

'No. Thank you.' Juliet barely looked up from the piece of electronic equipment in her hand.

Very interesting. A portable ground unit for the Global Positioning System. Ed had seen similar equipment in aircraft cockpits. If it worked like the systems he was familiar with, it could locate itself, or any set of co-ordinates fed into it, to within a handful of yards.

'Good idea.' Dobie grinned at him. Turned to Juliet. 'Can you take the wheel for a couple of minutes? It'll be quicker if I show him where everything is.'

'I suppose so.' She put the satellite unit down, and glowered at Ed. 'Why can't Bailey do it?'

'He's taking a bit longer to get his sea legs back than we thought.' Ed grinned at her. 'I'll ask him. But we might have to clean up in here afterwards.'

'Don't bother. I'll do it.' She took the wheel with ill grace. 'How did he ever survive in Marine Command?'

'Even Nelson got seasick,' Dobie said. 'You'd be surprised how many professional seamen suffer.' He turned to Ed. 'Galley's this way.'

He led the way down into the cabin. It was surprisingly spacious. Dobie went straight to the galley, and starting pulling mugs and teabags out of cupboards. Ed looked around, as though taking no more than a casual interest.

'You've got some interesting kit here.' Like the aqualungs, and a couple of wetsuits, stowed neatly next to a rack of spear guns. More conventional fishing gear was racked up on the opposite wall. Dobie nodded, taking the remark at face value.

'You never know what the client wants in this game. Ever been spear fishing?'

'Once or twice,' Ed admitted. 'On the Barrier Reef. Water so clear you can see for ever.'

'Not like the porridge we get in this part of the world,' Dobie agreed. 'But at least the sharks are a lot smaller. And harmless.' He nodded at the tea things, laid out neatly on the worktop. 'That ought to do you. Lapsang Souchong for me, no milk or sugar. You and your mate can please yourselves.'

'Fine.' Ed started filling the kettle.

'I'd better get back topside before her ladyship runs us into a sandbank or something.' Dobie grinned, and disappeared back up the companionway.

While the kettle boiled, Ed searched the cabin as quickly and economically as he could. There was nothing to indicate what the Brodys' plan might be, or even what they were doing out here in the first place.

He made the tea, and went back on deck.

'Lapsang Souchong. No milk or sugar.'

'Thanks.' Dobie took it without looking up, his attention on Juliet's GPS receiver. She didn't even acknowledge his presence. Hanging around would have drawn too much attention to himself, so he went back astern to join Beckett, sidestepping the salvage parts in their boxes. There were other crates on deck too, which had already been stowed by the time they'd boarded, but there was nothing on the outside to indicate their contents.

'Here you are. Get that down you.' He handed Beckett one of the mugs. Beckett took it dubiously, sipped, and swallowed.

'Did you find anything?'

'Yes and no. There's some Scuba gear aboard, but Dobie says it's just for spear fishing. He could be telling the truth.'

'Or not.' Beckett nodded. The tea did seem to be doing him some good after all.

'I think we're out here to make a rendezvous,' Ed said. 'The Brody woman's got a GPS locator.'

'Rendezvous with what, though?' Beckett indicated the heaving expanse of empty grey surrounding them with a sweep of his arm. 'There's nothing within miles of us.'

'Yeah, well. Guess we'll just have to wait and see.' Ed sipped his tea philosophically.

Up in the wheelhouse, Dobie cut the throttle. The

boat slowed, steadying. Ed tried not to smile at the expression of relief that flickered across Beckett's face.

'Tea break's over, boys.' Juliet left the wheelhouse, and came astern to join them. Ed tilted his mug.

'Why? What happens now?'

Juliet permitted herself a brief flicker of smugness. 'Now you get to admire my timing,' she said. Ed looked around. Nothing seemed to be happening, except that Beckett was beginning to look nauseous again. Funny, the tea should have fixed him up. The deck quivered slightly under Ed's feet.

The water a few yards off to starboard turned milky, then began to boil with foam. The boat rocked. Beckett's mug clattered to the deck, spilling tea, and Ed grabbed for a nearby stanchion to keep his balance.

Something huge and grey burst through the surface of the sea, rising to an impossible height in a matter of seconds, blotting out the watery sunshine. Water cascaded noisily down its flanks, booming into the sea, sending the suddenly dwarfed charter boat bobbing like a bath toy.

'I don't believe it,' Beckett said. He was so astonished he'd forgotten to be ill. Ed heard his own teeth snap together as he closed his mouth.

A submarine. Big. He took in the silhouette, tried matching it with half-remembered images from *Jane's*, but they'd been concentrating on the surface vessels the parts had come from, and he'd barely given the submarines a glance. Its blocky lines looked Russian, or East European, though. Which tied in with the cyrillic characters they'd found on McTiernan's list of parts.

Forget trying to identify it in that case. It was unmistakably old, probably obsolete, and ex-Soviet subs of that vintage had almost always been one-offs anyhow.

A hatch clanged on the conning tower. A moment later Bryan Brody appeared, looking down at them with the air of someone who had just pulled off a conjuring trick they weren't sure they could do. He was wearing a thick sweater, like a submariner in an old war movie. More for effect than practicality, Ed suspected.

'Ahoy there!' He waved to Ed and Beckett. A couple of men appeared on the forward deck, and began rigging up a transfer line. Like Brody they were wearing sweaters devoid of insignia. Unlike his, theirs were worn and grease-stained. 'Get the gear transferred as quick as you can, then come aboard yourselves. The longer we're on the surface, the more likely we are to be spotted.'

One of the sailors threw a line across to the boat; Beckett caught it by reflex, and tied it fast.

Ros was puzzled. Something was going on, but she couldn't make out what. The snatches of conversation she'd been able to pick up didn't seem to make much sense. Ed and Beckett seemed to be transferring the salvage parts to another vessel. But what, and why, continued to elude her. She tried adjusting the tuning of the radio receiver. Nothing.

Suddenly the whole system went dead. She tried retuning it, then initialising it again from scratch. Still nothing but a faint wash of static.

Ominous. She looked at the screen of the laptop. The dot marking the position of the charter boat suddenly vanished. A chill crept through her.

Don't panic, she told herself. I've lost tracking and audio. Simultaneously. It must be a fault in the bug.

She ran a quick diagnostic routine through the notebook. As she'd thought, there was nothing wrong this end. Definitely transmitter failure, then.

Which left Beckett and Ed cut off. Alone.

All she could do was wait. And try not to worry.

Try very hard not to worry.

# « Sixteen »

Beckett had been prepared for the noise, and the claustrophobia. He'd seen enough war movies to have a rough idea of how cramped conditions were aboard a submarine, especially one of that vintage. It was the smell that had really taken him by surprise.

The air inside the pressure hull was thick and humid, sickly with the aroma of diesel fuel, sharp with the ammonia tang of unwashed bodies. None of the crew looked as though they'd recognise a bar of soap without an instruction manual. Sanitation aboard the boat was obviously as rudimentary as most of the other systems he could see. He hoped desperately that he wouldn't need to use the heads.

He ducked under a run of pipework, following Brody, who seemed to know where he was going. There were pipes everywhere, some colour coded, most an anonymous grey. Control panels, and everything else he could see, were embedded in the pipes and cable runs. Even the bunks were surrounded, as though poking through the undergrowth of some eldritch metal hedgerow. His footsteps echoed on the steel mesh that made up the floor; more cabling was visible beneath it.

'Shouldn't we be leaving a trail of breadcrumbs?' Ed asked. His face was shadowed in the subdued electric lighting. The crewmen who'd ventured on deck had squinted in the daylight, Beckett recalled, even though it had been overcast. He wondered how long they'd been down here.

'Bit of a maze, isn't it?' Brody looked around, proprietorially. 'This is a real antique. I could make a fortune putting it on show after all this is over. If I didn't have other plans.'

'Like what?' Beckett asked.

'Oh, come now.' Brody looked at him in mild reproof. 'It wouldn't be much of a Houdini act if I gave out a forwarding address, would it?' He shrugged. 'And the boys would be so disappointed. I promised them they could drive it home after we've finished.'

'I've been wondering about them.' Beckett ducked, to follow him through a watertight hatchway. Brody squeezed back past him and Ed to close it. It swung into place with a solid thunk.

'They came with the boat,' Brody said. He squeezed past them again, to regain his place at the front of the group. That was fine by Beckett; Brody was the only one who knew where they were going. 'They only know a dozen words of English, but they're cheap to look after. So far as I can tell they live on diesel oil, and they don't seem to need fresh air or daylight.'

'All part of the same hard currency package deal?' Beckett suggested.

'That's right.' A messianic fervour entered Brody's voice. 'You ought to see it out there, Bailey. Everything's for sale. Absolutely everything.'

'Including the people?' Ed asked, a touch acidly.

'Especially the people. They're the cheapest thing of all.' Brody chuckled. 'God bless *peristroika* and the free market economy.'

'If you say so,' Ed said sourly.

'Sounds like a fun place to visit,' Beckett added hurriedly, diverting Brody's attention before his friend's mounting contempt became too obvious. 'I'll have to ask your advice on a few ... investment opportunities.'

'That's the spirit.' Brody clapped him on the shoulder. 'I mean, you can hardly stick your share in the building society, can you?'

'I wasn't planning to,' Beckett said truthfully.

'Is this the pump we're supposed to fix?' Ed was examining a valve assembly bolted to the nearest bulkhead. 'Because if it is, it's going to be a long job.'

'No. That's through here, in the forward compartment.' Brody indicated another hatch. 'What you're looking at is the escape system.'

'I'd hate to rely on that in an emergency,' Ed said.

'You should see the one at the back,' Brody said. 'That's completely seized up. This one still works all right, though. And I've added an inflatable boat, with a fast outboard. Rather more civilised than having to swim for it.'

'Let's hope it doesn't come to that,' Ed said. 'I'm having enough trouble adjusting to this as it is.'

'I do hope you're not going to disappoint me.' Brody's tone made it abundantly clear that that would be a very bad idea. 'I didn't make this offer lightly. You impressed me as people I could rely on.'

'I think you'll find we have all the right qualities,' Beckett said.

'I'm seldom wrong in my first impressions,' Brody agreed smugly. 'I read you the moment you walked into that sushi bar. Greed, and a willingness to take a few risks. Otherwise you'd never have contacted me. And a strong sense of self-preservation. You were bright enough to bring some back-up. I saw it at once.

You were the man for me, and no mistake.'

'Yes, well,' Ed interrupted again. 'My sense of self-preservation's telling me you can't pull two hundred and fifty million quid out of a bank without sticking your neck out. So what's the plan? Do we sail up the Thames and fire off a broadside at the front door?'

Brody laughed loudly, genuinely amused at the idea.

'I'd never thought of that. It has a certain crude elegance, I suppose. But I tend to be a little more subtle.'

'Then just how subtle, exactly?' Ed persisted. Brody eyed him speculatively.

'Just fix the pumps,' he said. 'Leave the bank to me.'

'Sounds fair enough,' Beckett agreed. 'When do we start?'

At last. Ros centred the charter boat in the binoculars' field of vision. She'd moved down to the quayside a couple of hours before. With Ed's transponder down, the only thing she could think of was to get as close as possible and wait for the boat to return. At least that way she'd be on hand to help if they needed her.

She zoomed the image. Juliet Brody and the skipper were in the wheelhouse, as they had been when the boat left. She swept the decks. No sign of Beckett and Ed. A tingle of unease, suppressed since the signal went down, fizzed back to life in her stomach.

Maybe they were in the cabin, she told herself. Somehow, she doubted it. She ran through her options.

The tracker she'd attached to the pickup truck was functioning. She glanced down inside her car, checked the automap screen. The dot was strong and steady, centred on the harbour area. She could follow it without any trouble if she had to. She picked up the charter boat again. Still no sign of her friends.

She stowed the binoculars as the boat rounded the harbour groyne. No point giving the game away. Juliet might be looking in her direction. She got back inside the car, out of sight.

She couldn't rely on Juliet taking the pickup. She ran through a quick mental inventory of the equipment she'd brought with her. She needed something simple and lightweight.

She made her selection, and palmed the tiny tracking device. No audio on this one, but it was only the size of a map pin. Smaller; the tiny aerial was barely two millimetres long. A quick glance through the windscreen. The boat was swinging round, broadside to the quay, ready to tie up. Juliet Brody was in the wheelhouse, juggling the throttle, and the skipper was in the bow, preparing the mooring lines. So why weren't Ed and Beckett doing that?

While their attention was diverted, Ros left the car and slipped down the open space between the two nearest sheds. Calculated the distance between the boat and the pickup, and the vector connecting them. Perfect. She ran behind the buildings, skirting the open space under the cover they afforded. Emerged on the opposite side, next to the pub. With any luck, Juliet would assume she'd just come from there; and the direct route back to her car intersected the line between the boat and the pickup.

She glanced again at the charter boat. The skipper had made the lines fast and gone back to the wheelhouse to cut the engines. They rumbled into silence, the lapping of the waves against the quayside suddenly audible. He exchanged a few words with Juliet. Then they walked unhurriedly down the deck and disappeared into the cabin.

Ros waited. A few moments later Juliet re-emerged,

jumping down to the quayside. She staggered a little on landing, still adjusting to the loss of her sea legs. She rummaged in her handbag, and produced a familiar set of car keys. The pickup. Excellent. Ros started forward.

She timed it perfectly, half turning and waving towards the pub, as though saying goodbye to friends inside. Still looking the other way, Ros collided with Juliet.

'Oh!' Ros turned to face the woman, looking flustered and apologetic. 'I'm terribly sorry. I should have watched where I was going.' The micro tracker slipped easily into the pocket of Juliet's overcoat. Nice material, Ros thought. But not quite that shade of russet. Not with that hair.

'Don't mention it.' Juliet accepted the apology with a perfunctory smile. 'Just one of those things.' She stepped around Ros, and kept going. Ros carried on towards her own car, listening intently. Behind her she heard the driver's door of the pickup slam, and, a moment later, the familiar cough of a diesel engine sparking into life.

The engine roared, tyres spun, and the sound diminished. Ros turned. The pickup was disappearing up the access road, the brake lights flaring for a moment as Juliet slowed to avoid a pothole.

Sure she was unobserved, Ros pulled the micro tracker's receiver unit out of her coat pocket. Good. The signal was strong, the directional display pointing firmly back towards the main highway. She put it back. Juliet would keep.

Now for the boat.

She hurried towards it. It rocked gently, tugging at the mooring lines. There was no sign of life aboard. She called out.

'Hello! Is anybody there?' What was the skipper's

182

name? She'd heard it over Ed's radio link, before it stopped working. Dobie, that was it. 'Mr Dobie?'

No answer. This didn't look good. She climbed aboard, feeling the deck shift subtly under her feet. She tried again.

'Hello?' Still nothing. She made for the cabin.

The door opened easily. She stepped inside, her eyes adjusting to the relative gloom. She called out again, her unease growing stronger with every second. Dobie couldn't have slipped ashore without her noticing, could he? 'Is anyone there?'

Again, no answer. Her gaze skipped around the enclosed space. Fishing tackle, scuba gear. A compact galley, separated from the main body of the cabin by a worktop. A small table with a spear gun on it. The string was slack. No spear in it.

'Beckett? Ed? Are you here?' The faint slap of water against the hull was the only response. 'If you can't talk, try to make some kind of noise!'

Silence. Only one place they could be. In the bunk room, beyond the door next to the galley. She pushed it open cautiously. Stopped dead in her tracks.

'Oh no!' Her breath caught. Dobie was there, half standing, but very dead. Pinned by a fishing spear to the bulkhead.

Somehow, even in death, he looked surprised.

'So, this is what all the fuss is about.'

Ed bent to examine the pump mechanism which took up a large part of the submarine's forward compartment. It had been partly dismantled, parts and tools lying around it as though abandoned in mid-job. He examined the removed components critically. Some of them were definitely shot. And most of the ones still in situ didn't look any better. He shook his head. 'No wonder you needed the spares.'

'It seems a bit over-powered for the job,' Beckett said. 'An extra margin for safety?'

Brody laughed. 'The people who built this tub didn't even know the meaning of the word. This is a seabed engineering vessel.' He indicated a rectangular metal framework, standing about waist high in the middle of the compartment. The top was hinged along both long edges, an overlapping metal seam along the middle indicating where the two lifting doors aligned. Ed had assumed it was some kind of equipment bay. Battery storage, perhaps. The overhead hoist reinforced that impression.

'What kind of engineering?' Beckett asked. 'Oil rigs, stuff like that?'

'No.' Brody paused, to make sure they realised how clever he was being. 'Telecommunications. She was built to maintain undersea telephone cables. Or, in my case, tap into them.'

'Electronic credit transfers,' Beckett said.

'Very good.' Brody smiled indulgently, as though Beckett were an unusually promising pupil. 'The bank sends the money by wire. I intercept it, and divert it. Simple.'

'Into your own account?' Ed asked.

'That's my department.' Brody clammed up, suddenly aware that he may have said too much. 'You just stick to the heavy lifting.'

'But that won't work,' Beckett said. Ed thought he was overdoing the puzzled expression a bit. 'The bank will be able to trace the transaction, won't they? And as soon as they realise it's not kosher they'll cancel it.'

'Ah. That's the clever bit.' Brody rose to the bait. 'All you have to do is get the cash out of the system fast enough. And that's all taken care of.' His expression hardened. 'And that's the end of the conversation on this subject.'

'Loose lips sink ships, eh?' Beckett asked.

'Precisely.' Brody turned, stepping aside as a couple of the crew brought the last of the boxes in. They set them down carefully, then left with curious glances at Beckett and Ed. One of them said something, and the other laughed. Ed opened the nearest box and took out the valve assembly inside. It seemed to have survived the trip intact. He replaced it carefully.

'OK,' he said. 'What's our brief here?'

Brody indicated the double doors in the top of the raised section, and the derrick above it. 'This unit pulls the cable in,' he said. 'The air pressure in here keeps the water from coming in too fast, but it isn't enough to keep it out altogether. The pump takes up the slack, otherwise the whole compartment would flood.'

'Which is why the escape hatch is right next door?' Beckett asked.

'That's right.' Brody nodded curtly. 'And the pump's just so much scrap metal at the moment. McTiernan said he could fix it, but the whole system's so obsolete you can't get the spares.'

'Which is why he was helping himself from the graveyard dock,' Ed said.

'Exactly,' Brody said. 'And when he realised how badly we needed the parts, he got greedy. Tried to double-cross us.'

'Not the most sensible idea he ever had,' Beckett said.

Ed remembered that they were supposed to have known him well. He assumed an expression of amused reminiscence. 'Did he ever have a good one? Remember that time he bet you a bottle of scotch he could get that Petty Officer's wife to –'

'A fascinating anecdote I'm sure.' Brody interrupted him hastily. He picked up the nearest spanner, and slapped it into Beckett's hand. Beckett looked at it, and raised an eyebrow. 'These were his tools. You can start any time you're ready.' He turned, and disappeared through the hatch. It closed behind him with a resonant clang.

'How's the stomach holding up?' Ed asked, the moment he was sure Brody was out of earshot. Beckett shrugged.

'Fine. Cleared up almost as soon as we got below.' He handed Ed the spanner. 'Here. Mechanical stuff is your department.'

'Thanks a lot.' Ed looked at the disembowelled pump. The job seemed more difficult than he'd expected. A lot more difficult. 'I'm not too sure I can do this.'

'Course you can,' Beckett said. He settled himself comfortably on one of the larger crates. 'You keep that bike of yours running, don't you?'

'A submarine's just a bit more complicated than that, Beckett.'

'Well then.' Beckett grinned. 'Try not to think of it as a submarine. Think of it as a motor bike in a very deep puddle.'

Ros slammed the car door and looked around. She was in an area she recognised, where high rent office blocks housed businesses with more money than many governments. Several of them had been clients of Gizmos in the past. They were a long way from Kamen and Ross, though, a mile or more at least. Even they couldn't afford the property prices around here without wincing.

She checked the hand-held tracker unit, still faithfully pointing to Juliet Brody. She had to be around here somewhere.

Ros congratulated herself silently for having had the foresight to slip the bug into the woman's coat. Juliet had abandoned the pickup in the outer suburbs, catching a train into the centre of the city. Then she'd taken a cab to this elite financial district.

'Ah ha.' In the distance she caught a glimpse of red hair, and a knee-length russet coat. She started to walk in the same direction, casually, staying well back. If Juliet saw her, put two and two together, they were all sunk.

She tried not to think about the images that brought to mind. Ed and Beckett dead, their bodies dumped overboard, sinking rapidly in the cold, grey sea. But that didn't add up. Juliet was a cold-blooded murderess, she knew, but she couldn't have overpowered both of them at once. And Dobie had been taken completely by surprise when she killed him; he would have been a lot more wary if he'd seen any violence committed.

Her colleagues were alive, she thought. They had to be.

She picked up her pace a little, closing the gap. Juliet knew where she was going. She didn't hesitate, or look behind her once. Ros slipped the tracker into her pocket.

Up ahead, Juliet was heading for the largest, most ostentatious building in the plaza. Tinted glass and subtle curves, with a large atrium at its centre. Trees inside a building, Ros thought. How ridiculous. The door slid open as Juliet approached it, then swallowed her up.

Ros slowed, looking for some clue as to the owners of the building. She could see nothing obvious. No logo. No name plate. Just the street number, in small, discreet numerals. Obviously, they expected anyone who dealt with them to know them already.

Nothing for it, then. She'd have to go inside, and hope Juliet didn't recognise her. The door hissed gently as it closed behind her.

Inside, the main impression was one of space. Afternoon sunlight, filtered through acres of glass, drifted lazily across an air-conditioned foyer larger than most firms' entire premises.

Marble clicked under her heels. She glanced around. Neatly dressed people whispered their business, appearing and vanishing through doors with palm print scanners attached to the locks. Juliet was being led away by one, someone senior judging by the quality of his suit. His attitude was deferential, as though she were a valuable client.

Interesting. She took in the far wall, where the company name was visible in plain black letters, mirroring the typography of the numerals on the wall outside. JACOBS DOYLE. Meant nothing to her.

'Good afternoon.' A male voice, close to her ear. 'Do you have an appointment?' She turned. It was impressive enough that he'd managed to approach her without her hearing. When she saw the size of him, the feat seemed astonishing. He was well over six feet tall, and stocky with it. A genetic engineering project to produce the perfect rugby player would probably come up with something like him, she thought. His immaculate suit looked somehow incongruous on him.

'Do I need one?' she asked, playing for time.

She ran through her options. If she told him the truth, exposed Juliet Brody as a criminal, it would ruin her best chance of finding out what had happened to Beckett and Ed. She couldn't take the risk. She still had the fake press credentials she'd used to fool Kirkby, but she didn't think this guy would fall for them. He was unmistakably a professional. Probably had a set of his own. Which meant he was likely to have recognised her as a security consultant the minute she set foot in the building. Better just leave with dignity, and hope Juliet hadn't noticed.

'I'm afraid so. It's company policy.' He made an almost imperceptible gesture with his hand. A uniformed security guard appeared, a holstered revolver prominent on her hip. 'Vanessa. This lady has stepped into the wrong building. Please help her to find her way out.'

'Yes, Mr Gilbey.' The guard fell into step a pace behind her, where Ros would be visible the whole time.

'Thank you.' Ros inclined her head a little, determined to be civil. She shot a last look at Juliet Brody, who was just disappearing into a lift at the far end of the foyer. She was talking to the manager and didn't notice.

Gilbey did, though. A faint frown appeared on his face, and Ros felt his eyes on her back all the way to the street.

'Excellent.' A wide grin spread across Brody's face. He gazed at the softly humming pump like a child on Christmas morning. 'I must admit I was beginning to have my doubts about you. But this is a brilliant piece of work.'

'Well, credit where it's due,' Beckett said. He nodded at Ed. 'I couldn't have done it entirely alone.'

'Thanks a lot,' Ed muttered, wiping his hands on a piece of rag.

That just about evened the balance for all those seasickness jokes, Beckett thought. 'So what happens now?' he asked.

'Now it's my turn,' Brody said. He opened one of the boxes that had already been loaded on the charter boat when Beckett and Ed had boarded it. 'I get my equipment set up.' He glanced at his watch. 'It'll be dark in a couple of hours. Then we can surface and refuel.'

'Refuel?' Beckett echoed. 'How are you going to

manage that?' Although, come to think of it, there was no reason to feel so surprised. Brody had shown himself to be formidably organised up until now. It was Juliet who was the loose cannon, whose impetuous violence had threatened the plan.

'I've stashed some diesel at a quiet little wharf I know,' Brody said. 'We can be in and out before daylight. No one will even know we were there.'

'Assuming you can find it,' Ed said doubtfully.

'Don't worry about that.' Brody produced the Global Positioning System handset they'd seen on the charter boat, and checked the reading. He nodded, with quiet satisfaction. 'Me and Mr Satellite have an excellent sense of direction.'

# « Seventeen »

The boardroom at Kamen and Ross was no more comfortable at night than it had been during the day. It was quieter, though, and more discreet than meeting in Graeme's office would have been. It wasn't entirely unfeasible that the Brodys were working with someone inside the organisation. After all, Wyman had seemed trustworthy enough, until it was almost too late.

Ros yawned, rubbed her eyes. The print of the company statement in front of her seemed to ripple like a cheap hologram. Statistics, dividends, certified accounts – they meant little to her. She needed an expert to translate the mass of raw data on Jacobs Doyle that Graeme had managed to unearth. Quickly, too. Her respect for his professional abilities had grown even stronger in the last couple of hours.

All right, then. If she was drowning in detail, go back to first principles.

'So what you're saying is that these people have no other interests at all. No subsidiaries, no stake in any other business.'

'That's right,' Graeme said. 'They're diamond traders, pure and simple. One of the biggest in the world. And they're discreet. No public profile at all.'

'So.' Ros chewed her lip thoughtfully. 'They could handle a deal on the scale of two hundred and fifty million quite easily.'

'Routinely, I'd have said,' Graeme confirmed. He shrugged. 'That's just a small bag of rocks as far as they're concerned.'

'I see.' Ros nodded, slowly. 'So all Juliet Brody has to do is pretend to be an employee of Kamen and Ross. And the next time you access their account . . .'

'They don't have an account with us,' Graeme said. His forehead furrowed. 'That's what I don't understand.'

'Well, there has to be some sort of connection,' Ros said. The frustration was back, gnawing at her gut. It was staring them in the face. Something obvious. Something they were missing.

'If there is, I can't find it.' Graeme ran a hand through his hair, as though trying to massage his brain into life. 'We've never done any business with them in the past, and we're not likely to in the future.'

'Maybe we're looking too close to home,' Ros said, tapping her teeth speculatively with a pencil. 'Maybe the connection's a bit further removed.'

'How do you mean?'

'I'm not entirely sure,' Ros admitted. 'But if we can rule out any direct connection with Jacobs Doyle, maybe there's a link with one of your clients. Or one of the other banks you do business with.'

'I see what you mean,' Graeme said. He considered the suggestion with mounting enthusiasm. He picked up his palmtop and made a note. 'I'll make a few phone calls. See what I can dig up.'

'Look for anything involving credit transfers,' Ros

said. 'Money has to be moving. Otherwise Brody can't cut himself in.'

'I know. Jacobs Doyle are the key.' Graeme shook his head in perplexity. 'But I just can't see how. We don't deal in diamonds, and they don't deal in anything else.'

'Which strikes me as rather a big hole in your argument,' a new voice said. Challoner appeared in the doorway. He glanced dismissively at the collection of papers and notebook computers covering the table top around Ros and Graeme. 'In fact, the more I examine it, the more tenuous your theories appear.' He smiled at Graeme, without humour. 'Paranoid, I believe your own phrase was?'

'It's far from that.' Graeme refused to rise to the bait. 'The threat is perfectly real. Believe it.'

'Well, that's just it, Mr Hurry. I'm afraid I don't.' Challoner radiated the unshakable self-confidence of the profoundly ignorant. 'I've spoken to our computer people. They tell me that when we transfer money electronically to another bank, the computers chat to each other to prove who they are. And the money only goes through when they're both convinced the other's genuine.'

'That's true,' Graeme said. 'But Brody got inside our computer while he was working here. He could have left a virus or a logic bomb designed specifically to get around our security procedures.'

'There's no such thing as a completely secure system,' Ros said, backing him up. Just as well, really, or she'd be out of a job.

'Correct me if I'm wrong,' Challoner said, ignoring her, 'but I was under the impression that you'd checked the system for precisely that kind of interference.'

'We did. And we found nothing. But Brody's very

resourceful. If there is a way into the system, you can be sure he's found it.'

'This is just alarmist speculation,' Challoner said. 'And unless you can show me some hard evidence, these childish spy games are going to stop here and now.'

He dropped a sheaf of spreadsheet hard copies on to the conference table. 'I've done a little checking of my own. Your department's budget has been getting completely out of control since your obsession with this Brody character started.' He paused, to add weight to his words. 'I'm not prepared to authorise any further expenditure on what's obviously a wild goose chase to everyone but you.'

'You can't be serious!' Ros rose to her feet, surprised to find her voice rising too. Challoner's patrician prissiness had raised her hackles more than she'd realised. 'People have died, for heaven's sake!' She fought for calm. Challoner, she knew, would only take anger as a sign of weakness. 'And two people I'm close to are missing. I've got no idea where they are, or what might have happened to them. You can't seriously expect me just to let this go.'

'No, I don't. But what you choose to pursue in your own time is your own business. Not mine, or the bank's.'

'I'm prepared to take this up with the Chairman,' Graeme said.

'Be my guest,' Challoner said. 'We've already spoken on the subject. I think you'll find Sir Norman agrees with my assessment.' He turned in the doorway, and glanced back at Ros. 'I hope you find your friends,' he said. 'For what it's worth.'

Ros didn't trust herself to reply.

'What do you suppose he's up to in there?' Ed asked. Beckett shrugged, and made another attempt to take a mouthful of coffee. It was easily the worst he'd ever tasted. If it was coffee at all. The outside of the enamel mug was greasy to the touch; he tried not to think about the inside.

'Setting his equipment up,' he said.

He ran a mental inventory of the stuff he'd helped unpack from Brody's boxes. A couple of high powered portable computers, a frequency sorter, lots of junction cables, a signal decoder, a couple of modems ... Enough to jack into the telephone cable, and read the traffic. And everything Brody would need to input signals of his own. He'd have to see it all assembled before he could fully assess what the system was capable of, or what Brody intended using it for, though. But Brody had insisted on being left alone to set it up.

Now Beckett and Ed were in the submarine's mess room, a cramped space roughly amidships. They sat at one end, five of the crew at the other. The submariners ignored them, talking among themselves and drinking some clear spirit from a bottle.

'I know that,' Ed said. 'What I mean is, what's he going to do?' He sniffed suspiciously at his own mug. 'I don't see why he couldn't just tap the cable back on shore. That would have been far less trouble.'

'CommEx have a computerised fault-finding system,' Beckett explained. 'The moment he tapped the cable they'd have logged it. He couldn't take the risk of a repair crew turning up before he finished.'

'I see. So what are we going to do about it?'

'I'm open to suggestions,' Beckett said. He'd been wondering the same thing himself.

'I've been keeping an eye open,' Ed said. He directed a cheesy grin at one of the submariners who had glanced in their direction. The sailor smiled back with something approaching genuine warmth, and resumed his conversation. 'I keep seeing the same faces everywhere. Apart from the guy driving.'

'The helmsman,' Beckett corrected him.

'Yeah, whatever. Him and the guy in the engine room. I reckon this is the whole crew. Certainly no more than a couple of others anyway. Less than a dozen on the whole ship.'

'Boat,' Beckett corrected him. 'Submarines are called boats.'

Ed opened his mouth. Closed it again. Blinked, slowly. Beckett kept his own face expressionless.

'Right.' Ed nodded, once. 'Anyway, I reckon if we pick our moment we can sabotage the whole operation.'

'Twelve against two. Hm.' Beckett didn't like the sound of those odds. He looked casually over towards the submariners. Two of them were playing some kind of dice game, watched by a third. He was oiling a large-bladed knife, handling it with the easy familiarity of someone for whom it wasn't so much a weapon, more of a hobby. 'We'd have to pick our moment really carefully.'

'I see what you mean,' Ed said.

The hatch behind them clanged. Beckett turned, in time to see Brody duck through it and into the compartment. He seemed pleased with himself. That expression of perpetual smugness was really beginning to irritate Beckett. Well, he thought, it would get wiped off fast enough once they got a message to Ros. Let's see how smug he looks when the authorities turn up.

'Getting on all right, are we?' Brody beamed at him, and slapped Ed on the shoulder. He turned his attention to the submariners. 'Time to surface. Surface, *comprenez-vous*?' He made an upward-sweeping gesture with his hand. The crew seemed to get the message, scattering to their posts. Brody may have missed the expressions of tolerant amusement that passed between them, but Beckett didn't.

'Gentlemen.' Brody returned his attention to Beckett and Ed. 'The countdown begins.' He gestured towards the conning tower ladder. 'Would you care to join me topside?'

On the surface it was dark, faint wisps of cloud scudding across the face of a crescent moon. Silver highlights sparked on the surface of the waves and rippled off into blackness. The chill wind cut into Beckett's lungs like pure oxygen after the stench of the submarine's interior. He inhaled it gratefully.

The darkness off to port began to solidify, resolving itself gradually into a worn wooden jetty. Oil drums were stacked at the end, ready for easy access from the sea. Muffled shouts came from the deck below, where a few of the sailors were preparing the mooring lines.

The breeze shifted slightly, bringing with it a strong whiff of body odour. Beckett stepped back a little from the submarine's captain, who was directing operations with the aid of a hand-held microphone. Unintelligible responses crackled back from the engine room.

Abruptly, the engines cut out. Looking down, Beckett could see the mooring lines tighten. The sailors on deck ran out a gangplank and disappeared down the forward hatch. The captain followed them, climbing down the ladder at his feet. They were alone with Brody.

'I'm impressed,' Ed said. 'Right up to the dock without even showing a light.'

'The miracles of modern technology,' Brody said. He hefted the GPS locator. 'What will they think of next?' His expression changed, became more businesslike. He turned to Ed.

'Get the feed line ashore, and start transferring the fuel. We haven't got long before daylight, so make it snappy.'

'I'll give you a hand, then,' Beckett said. Once they were both ashore they could slip away, get a message to Ros, and arrange to have the sub intercepted. And if they could destroy or damage the fuel dump it wouldn't get far.

'No.' Brody shook his head. 'You'll have to stay aboard to run the pump.' He turned back to Ed. 'Better wear gloves. It's nasty stuff.'

'Fine,' Beckett said, sounding unconcerned. After all, it was reasonable enough. They'd just have to think of something else.

He watched Ed clamber down the external ladder to the deck, and unship the fuel line. After a moment's rummaging, Ed pulled a pair of oversized gloves from the storage locker, picked up the end of the hose, and jogged across the gangplank.

'What about you?' Beckett asked Brody.

'I've still got a few things to set up below. Join me when you've finished.' Brody swung himself down through the hatch at his feet.

You just can't get quality help these days, Brody thought. He glared at the radio operator, who looked back at him with bovine incomprehension. He tried again, speaking as slowly as he could.

'Look.' He pointed to the external input jack on the GPS handset. 'I need a stronger signal from the satellite. The internal aerial can't pick up the signal when we're underwater. I need to patch this in to the surface antenna.'

The radioman said something. Shrugged.

OK. Back to basics here. He put the unit down on the cluttered desktop. Balled his fist and held it over the locator.

'Satellite. You know satellite?'

'Satellite. *Da*.' The man nodded.

Great. Breakthrough at last. Brody moved his other hand to it, lowered it from the fist to the locator, fluttering his fingertips like a child pantomiming rain.

'Signal. You understand signal?'

'*Da*.' The lightbulb came on. 'Signal. Satellite.' He added something incomprehensible, with the obvious intonation of a question. Then he rocked his hand over the locator, in the universal mime for water. Repeated Brody's raining gesture, but stopping at the level of his hand. Shrugged, and made a throat-cutting gesture.

'You've got it,' Brody said with a sigh. 'The first bit, at least.' He picked up the stub of pencil on the message pad, and wrote a string of numerals. 'This is the frequency. Frequency?'

'Frequency. *Da*.' The radioman's hand went to the old-fashioned tuning dial. Like everything else on the boat, it belonged in a museum. He turned it carefully, climbing the radio spectrum. Flashes of music and speech from the commercial stations, and on up into the higher frequency bands.

'Hold it.' He put a hand on the radioman's arm. There was something on a frequency that shouldn't be there. Clear and strong. Too strong. Too close. And speaking English.

'Dream Team to Dream Queen. Are you there, Ros? Over.' The voice hazed out in static as the radio operator stopped turning the dial a little too late. He looked puzzled, and pointed at the numerals Brody had written on the message pad. Asked a question.

'Not now.' Brody made a brisk chopping gesture with his hand, the universal sign for 'shut up'. He seized the dial, and turned it back. The voice grew stronger.

'. . . Not receiving. I don't know if you can hear this but our situation . . .'

The voice faded out again. The radioman took the dial, and made a minute adjustment. The voice came back, and he grinned triumphantly at Brody. The professional showing the amateur how it's done.

'... got us to the rendezvous all right. But we weren't there to meet a boat.'

The voice came through clear and strong. With an unmistakable Australian accent. Bailey's friend.

'We were just sitting there twiddling our thumbs, when this clapped-out submarine popped up out of nowhere. Which is why we haven't called in. They dived as soon as we got on board.'

And he kept saying we, not I or me, so Bailey must be a plant too. Brody's mind raced. He might not be getting through. They'd come a long way, and a transmitter small enough to have stayed concealed must be fairly low powered. But he couldn't take the chance. The Australian was still talking.

'I don't know where we are, but if the lettering on these barrels is anything to go by, my best guess would be somewhere on the Dutch coast.'

He'd heard enough. The most important thing now was to shut the man up. Fast. Even if he wasn't getting through to his contact, you never knew who else might be listening. Radio hams, the Coastguard, the whole blasted world.

Bailey was just dropping off the bottom rungs of the conning tower ladder as Brody left the radio room.

He'd keep, Brody thought. Just get him out of the way for a few minutes. There were a few questions he wanted answered before disposing of Mr Bailey. Or whatever his name was.

'How's it going?' he asked, keeping an expression of affable neutrality on his face. Bailey shrugged.

'No problem. We've just tapped the last of the barrels. We should be away from here long before dawn.'

'Excellent.' Brody forced a relaxed smile on to his face. 'I think we deserve a little treat.'

'What do you have in mind?' Bailey asked. He looked mildly curious, but not suspicious. Good.

'Some drinkable coffee. There's a small jar, packed in with the kit in the airlock chamber. A little home comfort from the wife.'

'How very thoughtful,' Bailey said, in the tone Brody could never quite be sure was sarcastic or not.

'She's an absolute treasure,' Brody agreed. 'One in a million.'

'I'll find it.' And have a good poke around the equipment too, no doubt, thought Brody. For whatever good it'll do you. He smiled. 'Mine's black. Two sugars.'

'Right.' Bailey disappeared through the hatch. As soon as he was out of sight, Brody made for the arms locker.

Security aboard the boat was shocking, he thought. It should at least have been locked. But it swung open easily. He selected a submachine gun, with a folding stock, and a couple of magazines. He slipped one into his pocket, and snapped the other one home.

That should be enough. He started up the ladder.

He emerged into the cool night air, savouring it briefly. He leaned on the lip of the conning tower, looking down to the deck. The Australian was there, just finishing stowing the fuel line.

He looked up at Brody, and waved. 'Just getting squared away. We can leave any time you like.'

'Excellent,' Brody called back. 'Any problems?'

'Nah. Quiet as the grave. There isn't a soul for miles.'

'That's why I chose the place,' Brody said. As anyone but a simpleton would realise. He had to get him back on the quay, he thought. He couldn't risk shooting him on deck. One stray round through the pressure hull and the whole plan went up in smoke.

'Better have a final look round. Make sure we haven't left any traces,' he said.

The Australian shrugged. 'If you say so. But I reckon the place is clean.'

'Apart from your gloves,' Brody reminded him. They were lying on one of the drums. He must have done it on purpose. There was probably a note inside one of them, setting out the whole plan. Well, if there was, he'd just fallen into his own trap. They were the perfect excuse to get him back on the quayside.

And if it was a genuine mistake, too bad. In that case he was just too stupid to live.

'Oops. That was careless.' The Australian grinned ingenuously. 'Be right back.' He trotted over the gangplank. Brody swung the SMG up, extending the shoulder stock. It didn't feel too different to a shotgun, he told himself. Just like shooting rabbits. Except that this one was a lot bigger.

'Got 'em.' The Australian turned, holding the gloves up. Caught sight of the gun. The lazy grin congealed on his face.

There was nothing wrong with his reactions, though. He was diving for cover behind the barrels even before Brody could pull the trigger. A trail of wood chips followed him, then the bullets started to punch into the metal drums. Ricochets whined off into the darkness, sparks dancing and flashing in their wake.

The weapon wasn't much like a shotgun at all, Brody discovered. It shuddered in his arms, pulling violently up and to the left. He forced it back on aim by sheer physical strength. He let go of the trigger.

Silence descended through his ringing ears. He scanned the quayside with his eyes. Nothing moved. Had he hit the man? He couldn't be sure. But he had to be.

He switched magazines, and sprayed the fuel dump

with bullets. The thin metal drums were chewed to shreds by the barrage of lead. Every time one hit, there was a tiny spark.

Suddenly there was a bigger, brighter flash. Brody ducked behind the protective lip of the conning tower. A second later the night erupted. A vivid orange fireball seared out, engulfing the wharf. He felt the heat. Risked a quick glance over the parapet.

The wharf was ablaze from end to end. As he watched, the mooring lines parted, the ends flaring as they dropped into the water.

He clambered down the ladder, dogging the hatch above him. If they didn't get out to sea right now, he thought, they'd all be toast. Patches of flame floated on the water, and there was bound to have been some leakage from the tanks while they were refuelling.

'Dive! Dive!' he yelled. 'Do whatever it is you do. *Right now!*' The crew were milling around like idiots. Half of them stopped what they were doing to stare at him. A couple of them were on the ball, though; someone pointed at what looked like a temperature gauge and shouted something, and they really jumped. He felt the deck plates shudder as the engines kicked into life.

Good. They weren't just moving away from physical harm. The explosion was bound to attract attention, and he wanted to be long gone before anyone arrived to investigate. The deck tilted under his feet as they began to dive.

Well, at least the Australian was dead. Even if the bullets hadn't hit him, no one could have survived that explosion.

'What's going on?' Bailey ducked through the hatch into the control room, a tray of coffee mugs in his hands. Brody felt a twinge of irritation. The idiot wasn't supposed to waste the good stuff on the crew as well. He began to swing the gun up to cover him.

'Suppose you tell me,' Brody began.

Bailey threw the tray at him, and turned to run. Hot coffee seared through his sweater as he raised an arm to fend off the tray; the mugs scattered everywhere. Furious, he brought the gun back to the firing position.

Before he could pull the trigger the captain leapt at him, grabbing the barrel, and shouting something he didn't understand. The gist of it was clear enough, though. Brody nodded, and relinquished the weapon. As common sense replaced the adrenalin rush of anger, an appalled realisation of what he'd almost done hit him in the gut. Firing the weapon inside the pressure hull would probably have killed them all. He waved an angry, frustrated hand after the now vanished Bailey.

'Well, don't just stand there like a flock of sheep!' he yelled. 'Get him!'

The metal mesh floor plates had lifted easily. Beckett slipped down beneath one, and hefted it back into place, moving awkwardly in the cramped confines of the equipment bay. Running feet clanged on it a second or two after he withdrew his fingers, and he huddled back into the shadows. Voices conferred overhead, then moved on.

He wormed his way cautiously through a tangle of equipment, catching his knees and elbows. Everything was covered in rust and grease. At least that showed nobody came down here very often. A flood of light ahead of him, as someone lifted a floor panel. A torch beam probed the undergrowth of cables, pipes, and junction boxes. He froze. It passed within inches of his face, then withdrew. The floor sections clattered back into place.

Move. Fast. He crawled forward as quickly as he

could. Now they'd searched that section it ought to be safe. He reached it, concealing himself as much as possible behind a stalagmite of valve-encrusted pipework. Just in time. The floor panel above where he'd just been was lifted, and the torch beam probed again. If he hadn't moved, he would have been caught for sure.

He let out a slow sigh of relief as the floor panel was replaced, and the search party moved on. He was behind them now. Relatively safe, at least until they started a second sweep.

'Bailey. I know you can hear me.' Brody's voice, distorted by echoes, and the boat's primitive tannoy system. He sounded really peeved.

At least I've wiped that smug grin off his face, Beckett thought. 'You can hide, but you can't run, as they don't say. It's only a matter of time before we find you.' A pause. 'You are not a king of infinite space.'

Pretentious idiot, thought Beckett. I suppose he thinks quoting Hamlet makes him sound like an intellectual. Probably memorised it at school.

'We're tracking the cable now.' The old, familiar note of cockiness was creeping back into Brody's voice. 'A few more hours and it'll all be over. I'll be rich, and you'll be sorry. Just like your friend.'

Ed. The fear he'd been trying to suppress came flooding back. What had happened to Ed? There was no sign of him on board. And something had stirred Brody up.

But Ed was resourceful, he knew. Maybe he'd got away somehow, and that was what had panicked Brody.

He forced the thought away. Whatever had happened, he was on his own now. Ed couldn't help him, wherever he was.

* * *

'Graeme. Come in.' Ros stood aside, smiling a welcome, as the security chief of Kamen and Ross stepped into the entrance hall of Gizmos. She led the way back to the main work area, vaguely surprised by how pleased she was to see him. 'Any progress?'

'Nothing substantial.' He followed, a sheaf of papers under his arm. 'I've tried talking to Jacobs Doyle, but I keep getting the runaround. No one senior enough to authorise discussion with me is available at this time of night. And it's odds on they won't anyway without contacting our board first.'

'And they're not taking the threat seriously,' Ros finished.

'Well, I am.' Graeme dropped into the sofa in the middle of the room. 'It's my job to. How are you getting on?'

'Nowhere fast,' Ros admitted. 'I've been backtracking the progress of the Elverson Icebreaker through your defensive systems, but they seem more than adequate against any conventional hacking attempt.'

'I'm not sure if that's good news or bad news,' Graeme said. 'If you had found a hole, at least we'd know what Brody was planning. As it is, we're still in the dark.'

'Which brings us back to a third party connection. Have you found any companies or institutions that deal with both you and Jacobs Doyle?'

'A few. But that's commercially sensitive information.' Graeme held up an optical disk. 'So you never got this from me, understood?'

'Loud and clear,' Ros assured him. She took the disk, and walked to the nearest workstation. Glanced at the notebook computer on the desktop beside it, and froze. 'Graeme! Look!' She pointed at the blip, overlaid on the map of the North Sea.

'What?' He joined her.

'Ed's tracker. It's reactivated.' She forced herself to calm down a little, as the surge of relief knocked her breathless. She examined the screen more carefully. 'Assuming he's still attached to it, he's somewhere on the Dutch coast.'

'Then let's hope he's all right,' Graeme said.

Ed surfaced, spitting out sea water, and flicked his head to clear his eyes of wet hair. He trod water and looked around. The wharf was still blazing, lurid orange light flickering across the water. Pieces of debris, scattered by the explosion, bobbed in the water around him. A few patches of diesel oil floated on the surface, burning fitfully.

He'd jumped just in time, running for the edge of the dock while Brody reloaded. He'd felt the heat of the explosion on his back as he'd dived, and the shock-wave rumbling through the water.

That had been cutting the deck a little too close to the ace of spades.

Well, he couldn't land on the wharfside, that was for sure. He'd have to strike out at an angle, and hit the coast a bit further down. Then head inland, look for a road, and try to find a phone.

Gradually he became aware of a new sound, louder than the crackling of the flames, and the pounding of his adrenalin-accelerated heartbeat. A low, regular throbbing, out to sea and moving closer.

The submarine? Coming back to finish him off? He dismissed the idea at once. The engine note was higher, faster, a powerful thoroughbred held in check. A lifeboat, perhaps? A searchlight stabbed out of the darkness, sweeping the sea. Behind it, in the backwash of light, he could make out a sleek, low-riding surface vessel of some kind.

'Hey!' He waved an arm. 'Over here!'

A voice called something, in a language he didn't recognise. The searchlight moved in his direction. The voice tried again.

'Are you hurt?' English this time. A woman's voice, with the unmistakable cadence of a Dutch accent. He squinted as the searchlight caught him. The boat moved closer

'I don't think so,' he called back.

'Grab the line!' A lifebelt fell into the circle of light. He struck out for it, and took hold. The line tightened. A moment later he bumped against metal; hands reached down out of the darkness, and he found himself being hauled unceremoniously aboard the vessel.

'Thanks a lot.' He staggered to his feet, supported by the men who'd hauled him in. A young woman was looking at him. Blonde, her hair tied back. Some sort of naval officer judging by her uniform.

'English?' she asked.

'Australian, actually.'

'Ah.' She nodded, as though that explained a lot. She gestured to one of the crewmen who'd helped him on board. 'We'll get you dried off and cleaned up, to start with.' Her expression hardened. 'And then, I think, we have much to discuss.'

# « Eighteen »

The contrast with the obsolete submarine could hardly have been more marked. The bridge of the Dutch coastguard cutter was ergonomically laid out, making optimum use of the space without seeming cramped. The early morning sun, slanting through the polarised windshield, struck modern, high-tech instruments. The young woman, who'd turned out to be the commanding officer, looked at him quizzically as he stepped through the door.

'That's a pretty wild story of yours,' she said. 'But it checks out. Your colleague confirms it.'

'Beckett? He got away too?' It sounded too good to be true. The young woman shook her head.

'No. The other one.' She had a radio mike in her hand. She lifted it, and spoke. 'He's here now. You can speak to him if you like.'

'Ed?' Ros's voice came from the speaker. 'Are you all right?'

'Fine.' He took the mike. 'Fed, showered, and a full change of clothes.' They even fitted properly, much to his surprise. 'The Dutch Coastguard are wonderful.' He grinned at the captain. She didn't respond.

'How did they find you so quickly?' Ros asked.

'I tried to contact you on the lapel mike. They picked it up, and started homing in on the tracker signal. And after Brody torched the wharf they could see where they were going from miles away.'

'Do you have any idea where he's heading?' Ros asked.

'Nope. But it has to be close. He only took on enough fuel for the next few hours.' He hesitated, hoping his deduction was wrong. 'I don't want to sound alarmist, but I think he's planning to scuttle the sub. Along with everyone on board. He's got McTiernan's diving gear with him, and he told me himself he's fitted a fast escape boat to the forward hatch.'

'It's one way of disposing of the witnesses,' Ros said. Even over the radio she sounded horrified at the idea. The same thought had occurred to both of them. Beckett.

'That doesn't leave us much time,' Ed said. 'Are you making any progress with Kamen and Ross?'

'Nothing good,' Ros admitted. 'We got fired last night.'

'We got what?' Ed couldn't believe it. 'Have they gone mad?'

'They don't think there's a real threat to their security,' Ros said flatly.

'Great. So we're on our own again.' He glanced at the captain. 'Apart from the Dutch Coastguard, of course.'

'Strictly speaking, this is outside our jurisdiction,' the captain said. Ed felt his heart sink. Then she smiled. 'But there is the matter of our territorial waters being violated. I have discretionary powers in that regard. Which I'm inclined to exercise. Especially since you assure me that lives may be at risk.'

'Thanks.' He smiled gratefully at her. 'Did you hear that, Ros?'

'Yes. Thank you, Captain Van Der Decken. And we have a bit of unofficial help at this end too.'

'Let me guess. Graeme, right?' Ed said.

'That's right.' Hurry's familiar Lowland burr replaced Ros's voice. 'I'm glad to hear you're OK.'

'Let's hope we can say the same for Beckett.' He replaced the handset on its rest. Turned to the captain. 'Is your name really Van Der Decken?'

'Yes.' She studied him appraisingly. 'And I've heard all the jokes. So you needn't bother. Unless you plan on walking home.'

'I wouldn't dream of it,' Ed said hastily.

'Some good news, anyway,' Graeme said. He replaced the telephone receiver.

Ros looked up from her laptop. 'I'm glad to hear it.'

Graeme leaned over to study the display. Ros had been working on it ever since she'd spoken to Ed on the radio. Factoring in tides, current directions, and the best guess she could take at the sub's performance envelope, extrapolated from the data in Beckett's CD Rom *Jane's*. Plus a modicum of inspired guesswork, she had to admit. 'What have you got?'

'I still can't get to anyone senior at Jacobs Doyle. But I've had an unofficial word with my opposite number there. A fellow called Gilbey. He's not convinced there's a problem, but at least he listened.'

'I met him, briefly.' Ros recalled the large man in the immaculate suit who'd accosted her in the foyer at Jacobs Doyle. The way he'd looked at her, and noted the interest she'd shown in Juliet Brody. 'He seems to know his stuff.'

'That's the impression I got.' Graeme nodded. 'He can't take it to his board without evidence, but at least he's keeping an eye out for anything suspicious.'

'How much did you tell him?' Ros asked.

'Nothing very specific. Just that one of our investigations had turned up the possibility that someone was planning to move against them.' He spread his hands. 'After all, that really is as much as we've got.'

'Did you mention Juliet Brody?' Ros asked.

'No. Not by name.' He hesitated. 'We've no actual proof against her. And if we do anything to scare her off, we might lose our best lead back to Beckett.'

'Thanks, Graeme.' Ros smiled at him. 'You've no idea how much I appreciate that.'

'Maybe you can tell me later. Over dinner, perhaps?'

She felt the smile broaden a little. 'Perhaps,' she agreed. She turned back to the screen.

'What are these?' Graeme leaned across her shoulder, and pointed at the thin veins branching across the map of the North Sea.

'The undersea telephone cables.' Ros tapped the keyboard, bringing up a few more icons. 'And this is the sub's last known position.' A small dot on the Dutch coast.

'Where Ed got picked up by the Coastguard cutter?'

'That's right. And the rendezvous with the charter boat was here.' Another dot, on the same side of the North Sea. 'Just about at the limit of the sub's range, assuming it's come all the way from the Baltic in one hop.'

'I see.' Graeme rubbed his chin thoughtfully. 'So it's odds on they're heading west, back in this direction. That's where most of the cables are.'

'I think so. Given that Juliet Brody's still in England, and assuming they want to link up as soon after the scam as possible.' She tapped a few more keys. 'Now if Ed's right about Brody planning to use the escape boat, its maximum range from the English coast would put them somewhere in this sector here.' A shaded area appeared on the screen.

'That's still a pretty big area to search. Can you narrow it down at all?'

'I thought you'd never ask.' Ros was beginning to enjoy herself. 'If we factor in the currents, and the amount of fuel they took on board, their most likely course is this one.' Another rattle of the keyboard. A straight line appeared, beginning at the wharf in Holland, and ending in the shaded zone. It intersected one of the cables well inside the indicated area.

'Well, I'll be.' Graeme shook his head in unconcealed admiration. 'That's amazing.'

'Simple deductive reasoning,' Ros said smugly. 'But it still leaves a pretty big area to search. That's a small scale map, don't forget.' She ported it across to the modem. 'I'll fax it over to Ed. And then . . .' Her voice trailed away.

'And then?' Graeme prompted.

'Then I'm really going to need your help,' she said.

'I'm impressed,' Van Der Decken said. She handed the chart to her navigating officer, the paper still crumpled from the fax machine. 'This ought to take some of the guesswork out of it.' Then she spoke to him in Dutch. The man nodded and went to work on a GPS ground station in the corner of the bridge. It was a lot larger and more accurate than Brody's hand held unit. But that was the difference between civil and military systems. Brody's unit was accurate to within a handful of metres; the coastguard cutter's to within centimetres.

'If we get over the cable we can follow it,' Ed suggested. 'That should narrow things down even more.'

'Of course. We know the sub will be somewhere along it.' Van Der Decken spoke to the navigator again. The only word Ed recognised was 'Sonar'. The man moved to another workstation, and activated the system. A screen flickered into life, showing a wavering line. 'The stronger the echo, the higher the peak on the screen,' Van Der Decken explained.

'We're still a long way from the search area,' he said dubiously. 'Are you sure we can get there in time?'

'Pretty sure,' Van Der Decken said.

She seemed amused at something. She picked up an intercom handset. Behind her, the navigating officer said something to the helmsman, who turned the wheel. Van Der Decken held a brief conversation in Dutch with someone Ed assumed to be in the engine room.

The deck tilted suddenly under Ed's feet. He grabbed at the edge of the navigation console for balance. The engine noise rose in pitch, as the bow of the cutter rose completely out of the sea. Looking down from the bridge, he saw hydrofoils appearing as the boat lifted out of the water. They cut into the waves like scalpels, and the faint rocking motion he'd felt since coming aboard steadied.

'Yeah,' he said, totally failing to sound blasé. 'I reckon we might get there fast enough.'

Whatever Brody was up to, he'd started, Beckett thought. He'd disappeared into the forward compartment about twenty minutes ago. The crew had gone about their duties. No one had found him. So far as he could tell they weren't even bothering to look any more.

That was ominous. It meant Brody no longer considered him a threat. Which meant his plan was all but completed.

Which left him no choice. He couldn't just skulk here forever. He had to act. And he'd thought the odds were bad while he still had Ed to back him up.

He needed a plan. He couldn't run the sub himself even if he could overpower the entire crew. He had to find a way of forcing them to the surface. After that, maybe he could get away in the escape boat.

The escape boat. Of course. There'd be breathing apparatus in the escape hatch, and an emergency radio. Once he'd surfaced he could call for help. He should have thought of that before.

He strained his ears. Nothing. No footsteps on the metal mesh above him. Just faint sounds of celebration from the mess room amidships. The vodka had obviously been broken out again.

He raised the floor panel above his head cautiously. Lifted it aside. Held his breath. Still nothing. Raised himself through the gap. Glanced around. No sound, no movement. He slid the metal mesh back into place, and padded cautiously forward. Pressed his ear to the watertight hatch. He could hear nothing beyond it, but then he hadn't really expected to.

There was nothing for it, then. He'd just have to take a chance. He opened the hatch slowly. Nothing moved beyond it. The hatch to the forward compartment, where Brody was working on his master plan, was firmly closed.

And there was the escape hatch. He unlatched it, and pulled it open. Stepped back hurriedly.

'Ah. Hello.'

One of the submariners, preceded by his pet knife, stepped out of the narrow compartment. Of course, Beckett thought. Where else would I make for? All they had to do was sit there and wait. He grinned sheepishly. 'Take me to your leader?'

'Ah, there you are.' Brody glanced up from his equipment as the submariner bundled Beckett unceremoniously through the hatch into the forward compartment. 'I was afraid you were going to miss the good bit.'

'How could I resist such a gracious invitation?' Beckett asked. The submariner prodded him forward, the tip of the knife somewhere in the vicinity of his kidneys.

'I see you went for the escape hatch.' Brody rummaged through the litter of boxes, and produced a pair of handcuffs. 'I must say, I'm a little disappointed. I thought you were more resourceful than that. A bit obvious, wasn't it?' He threw the handcuffs to the submariner.

'There aren't too many options when you're bounded by a nutshell,' Beckett said. Cool metal clicked around his wrist. The submariner passed the linking chain around a horizontal pipe run next to his head, and closed the second cuff. Undignified, Beckett thought, but at least it's not too uncomfortable. 'Another little extra from the wife?'

'She does think of everything, doesn't she?' Brody turned to the submariner. 'Well done. Very good. Now shoo.' He made little flapping motions with his hand, as though fending off an over-friendly dog. 'Run along and join the party. Drink.' He pantomimed knocking back a measure of spirits. '*Nastrovia, da?*'

'*Da.*' The submariner nodded, and vanished through the hatch with alacrity. Beckett supposed it couldn't have been much fun sitting in the escape hatch for hours, waiting for him to turn up. He tugged experimentally at the handcuffs. No give in them, or in the pipe. He'd have to think of something else.

He turned his head, taking in the assembled equipment properly for the first time. The airlock frame was open, and a loop of the underwater cable had been pulled through it. It hung from the hoist like a dead anaconda, dark, slick, and encrusted with barnacles and trailing tendrils of seaweed. A section had been opened up, the tight bundles of fibre optics inside teased apart; a few had been cut and spliced, trailing into the tangle of cabling connecting Brody's equipment.

Everything looked much as Beckett would have expected it to. Terminals, modems, signal discriminators. What he couldn't understand was why everything was duplicated. Multiple redundancy, perhaps? Brody was cautious, true, but surely not on that scale?

'Sorry to keep you hanging about.' Brody re-entered the compartment. 'Just making sure we won't be interrupted.' He was carrying a spanner. Beckett digested the implications. If he'd jammed the hatch between the escape system and the rest of the boat, the crew would be trapped. Unless they surfaced. A chill ran down his spine. Somehow, he didn't think surfacing was on Brody's agenda. 'I have been looking forward to this little chat.'

'Any topic in particular? Or do you just want to pass the time of day?' Beckett asked.

Brody grinned. 'Oh, very good. I do like a man who doesn't go to pieces under pressure.' He swung the spanner idly. 'I was really hoping for a chat about your employers. Who they are, how much they know. That sort of thing.'

'I'm working for myself,' Beckett said. It probably wasn't going to work, but it was worth a try. 'McTiernan left the parts with me for safe keeping. When he died, I decided to cut myself in. Not the most sensible decision I ever made. But you said it yourself. I was greedy, and it seemed worth the risk.'

'Oh dear.' Brody shook his head. 'You're lying to me. I do hate that.' He hefted the spanner ruminatively, testing its weight. 'Your friend had a radio. We overheard his transmission when he tried to check in. You were planted on us by somebody, and I'd rather like to know who and why.' A thought occurred to him. 'It's not the witless wonders I used to work for, is it? Dear old Graeme Hurry still sleuthing around?'

'Never heard of him,' Beckett said.

'You're not a very good liar, are you Mr Bailey? It's the eyes. They give you away.' Brody looked at him speculatively. 'If that's your real name. It isn't, is it?' His voice grew cajoling. 'Come on. What's the point of pretending any more?'

Drop dead, thought Beckett. The silence stretched. Brody swung the spanner suddenly at his head. Beckett flinched instinctively. Brody pulled the blow, grinned, and dropped the tool on a nearby shelf.

'All right, so you can't be intimidated. Not that it matters.' He turned away.

Might as well keep him talking, Beckett thought. Play for time, and see if he lets anything slip. This is too important to let pride get in the way.

'Beckett.' Anger constricted his throat. He forced the words past it. 'My name's Beckett. What happened to Ed?'

'Ed?' Brody turned back, apparently believing he'd won some sort of point. 'So he did have a name. Well, I'm afraid Ed's no longer with us. Literally or figuratively speaking.'

I don't believe it, Beckett thought. Ed can't be dead. He's lying. Or mistaken. But Brody seemed very certain.

'What happened to him?' He had to know.

'I'm really not sure.' Brody shrugged. 'I was shooting at him when the fuel dump went up. If I missed, I suppose it's a toss-up between drowning and incineration.'

Beckett felt a surge of hope, mixed with relief; he fought to keep his face neutral. If there had been a chance, he knew, however slim, Ed would have taken it. He was a natural born survivor. But Brody was turning away, back to his equipment. As Beckett watched, he made a few minor adjustments.

Get him talking, he thought. Remember what Ed said. He's a bragger. He won't be able to resist telling me how clever he is.

'I still don't see the point of all this,' he said. 'Why do you need two identical systems?'

'That's the clever bit,' Brody said, just as Beckett had known he was going to. He studied the column of letters and numerals scrolling up the two screens in front of him, both in perfect sync. 'All the traffic on this line is being diverted through these machines. And any minute now the computer at Kamen and Ross is going to make a routine call to one of the regular customers in Frankfurt.'

'But if you intercept the call it'll simply abort,' Beckett said, prompting him. He hoped he wasn't being too obvious. 'The money won't go through until the Kamen and Ross system gets the authentication codes from Frankfurt.'

'Exactly,' Brody said. 'So that's precisely what they're going to get.' The smug grin was back on his face. 'I'm using their own system against them. Which is what makes the plan so good. No one can stop it. No matter how hard they try.'

'OK. That gets us into the system.' Graeme tapped a few more keys, and the Kamen and Ross logo appeared on the workstation screen. He grimaced. 'I must say it feels a bit strange, breaking into my own bank.'

'It's quicker than leaving it to me,' Ros pointed out. Not by much, though, she thought. After all, she'd installed most of their Ice herself. The screen flashed up a password prompt. Graeme typed something, and the screen message changed. LEVEL ONE ACCESS APPROVED.

'If Challoner ever finds out about this, I'm out of a job,' Graeme said. He didn't seem terribly worried by the idea.

'If it works you'll be a hero,' Ros reassured him. 'He won't dare make a fuss about it.'

'He'll probably try and claim it was all his idea to begin with,' Graeme said. 'But I can live with that. If the bonus is big enough.' He rattled the keyboard again. Names and figures started scrolling up the screen. 'There. That's got us inside the credit transfer system. Everything coming in or going out, in real time.'

'Hm.' Ros watched the figures scrolling for a moment, then picked up the optical disk Graeme had brought over with him. She slotted it into the drive.

'What are you doing?' Graeme asked.

'I'm setting up a filter.'

She downloaded the data into a well-trusted program and set it running on a linked machine. The flow of information from the Kamen and Ross computer continued uninterrupted.

'It'll highlight any transactions with the customers on your list. Ones that have dealings with Jacobs Doyle.'

'Smart.' Graeme nodded his approval. 'There's one. Amsterdam Diamond Exchange.' The line of data in the middle of the screen was a different colour, making it easy to pick out. Ros glanced at it.

'No. The amount's wrong.' She tapped the screen. 'Only a hundred and eighty five million. Brody was very specific.'

'Two hundred and fifty million. I remember.' Graeme nodded thoughtfully. 'You think he meant that literally?'

'He probably rounded it off. But I think we can definitely discount anything under the two hundred mark. Probably under two twenty five, or two thirty.' She worked on the keyboard again, narrowing the parameters of the search. 'I've set a minimum of two hundred and twenty. Just to be on the safe side. But when it comes down to it, it's still all guesswork.'

She stared at the screen intently, bit her bottom lip hard. 'I just wish we knew precisely what he's up to.'

Brody was completely absorbed in his equipment. Beckett took full advantage of his distraction to shift position slightly. Most of the rats' nest of cabling webbing the system together was out of his reach, but a loop of it was running across the floor about a yard from his foot. If he stretched, he might just be able to reach it. One sharp tug, and he could short circuit Brody's plan for good. Literally. But he'd have to be sure. He'd only get one chance.

One of the terminals beeped. Brody rattled the keyboard, utterly absorbed. Beckett extended a leg towards the cable loop. He was a few inches short.

'Excellent.' Brody nodded in satisfaction, his eyes fixed on the screen. 'The very call I've been waiting for.'

'The credit transfer from Kamen and Ross?' Beckett asked. It was a risk, but he didn't think Brody would turn round. If anything, the mild distraction of answering questions would be enough to fix his attention even more firmly on what he was doing. If he could be bothered to answer at all.

'Got it in one.' Brody didn't move an inch. 'Which this machine is diverting. And passing on to its twin over there.'

'I still don't see the point,' Beckett said. He stretched out a leg towards the cable loop. Slowly. Carefully.

No sudden moves to attract Brody's attention. 'Without the authentication codes from Frankfurt it'll abort before any money comes through.'

'But it's going to get them.' Brody tapped a few more keys. 'The second unit's sending the signal straight on to its destination. And in a second or two –'

'– the computer in Frankfurt sends a message back saying "hello, nice to see you, come in for *Kaffe und Kutchen*",' Beckett finished. He was still a couple of inches short, the cable loop just beyond the reach of his foot. Blast. He gripped the pipe for balance, leaned out as far as he dared. The handcuffs dug into his wrists as he stretched.

Almost . . .

He dragged the toe of his shoe across the rounded surface, moving it a couple of millimetres towards him.

Come on, he thought. Nearly there . . .

He tried again.

'Precisely,' Brody said. The second terminal beeped. 'And there it is.' Now the twin streams of data on the paired screens were subtly out of sync. 'The authentication codes. Which we copy across to this machine.' Another quickfire rattle of keys. 'And kick back to Kamen and Ross.' Another beep, and the screens moved back into sync. 'There. They both think they're talking to each other. And I'm piggy in the middle, receiving everything from both of them, and no one even knows I'm here.'

'Very impressive,' Beckett said, almost meaning it. It was, he had to concede, a brilliant idea. Technically complex, too. He knew of only a few people who could have pulled it off. Ros, of course, and himself. A couple of his old associates from the Hive. And that was about it. 'But you don't seem any richer to me.'

He pulled the cable loop a little nearer. Close enough

to get his foot inside. Moved back on balance, preparing himself.

He'd only get one chance at this . . .

'Oh, I will be,' Brody said. 'In about two minutes.' He rubbed his hands together in anticipation. 'Doesn't time fly when you're having fun?'

'Is that it?' Ed asked. The sonar scope showed a definite echo. Large, lying on the seabed, almost directly beneath the Coastguard cutter. Van Der Decken had ordered the engines throttled back about twenty minutes before, the hull settling gently back into the water; since then they'd been moving methodically along the length of the cable, at what seemed to Ed to be an agonisingly slow pace.

'It could be.' She turned to the navigating officer, and exchanged a few words in Dutch. 'No. It's a known wreck. The *Callisto*.'

He remembered the name, vaguely. It had been a major news story a couple of years before. An oil tanker, holed in a collision with a Belgian ferry in a fog bank. No lives lost, but a complex salvage operation to pump the cargo out of the sunken wreck before the tanks could leak and cause an environmental disaster.

'So we just keep going?' he asked.

'We keep going,' she confirmed.

'That could be it,' Ros said. One of the transactions scrolling up the screen had been highlighted. She pulled it out of the stack for a closer look. 'Two hundred and forty seven million. Transfer to Frankfurt.'

'It's the right sum,' Graeme said. He leaned across her shoulder, studying the screen. 'But I can't see anything wrong with it. It's a routine transfer. Proceeding routinely.'

'Routine?' Ros said. Subconscious alarm bells started ringing inside her skull. 'You mean Brody would have known about it?'

'I'd have thought so,' Graeme said. An undercurrent of unease began creeping into his voice. 'You really think this is the target?'

'It has to be.' Her conviction was growing by the second. Something was wrong, she just knew it. But what? 'Of course! Look.' She pointed to the time check, a simple digital readout of hours, minutes, and seconds in the corner of the screen. Graeme looked puzzled.

'There's a time check on all the transactions.'

'Yes. But look.' Ros restored the full screen view. 'It's three seconds behind all the others.'

'Maybe the clock in Frankfurt's running slow,' Graeme suggested. But she could tell from his voice that he didn't believe that any more than she did.

'Or maybe the signal's been intercepted. Brody's reprocessing it before passing it on. Creating a second, phoney credit transfer somewhere else.'

'Jacobs Doyle. If he's bouncing it to them with the Frankfurt protocols attached, they'll just think it's a regular transfer from a regular customer. By the time they find out they're wrong . . .'

'Juliet Brody will have done a vanishing act with a pocket full of diamonds,' Ros finished. She turned back to the keyboard. 'I'll try and cut in. Suspend the transaction.' But before she could hit a key, the screen blanked in front of her.

'So you end up with a ghost transfer somewhere else,' Beckett said. He hooked the toe of his shoe under the cable again, creating a full loop around his shin. Firm. Solid. He braced himself. 'A lot of good that'll do you when the bank realises you've duplicated the signal.

They'll just cancel the transaction.'

'Let them.' Brody seemed unconcerned. 'By that time the money will be out of the system entirely. All we have to do is move fast enough.'

'I'm afraid I'm faster.' Beckett tugged hard at the cable, feeling it tighten around his leg. There was a shower of sparks from a junction box in the corner, and an almost imperceptible background hum died away. The cable hung limp now. Beckett kicked it away.

'That wasn't very clever,' Brody said, looking at him with mild reproof. Both screens remained lit and functioning.

Beckett looked at them in disbelief. Surely he must have affected something.

'I'm afraid that was the pump,' Brody informed him calmly. 'Nothing to do with the money transfer at all.' He turned back to the keyboard, and worked on it for a moment.

'There. All done,' he declared with an air of profound satisfaction at a job well done. 'And before long, my dear wife will have spent every penny on uncut diamonds. Credit, as you so rightly point out, is fleeting.' He stood, and began to don McTiernan's diving suit. 'But diamonds are forever. To coin a phrase.'

Water began welling slowly over the lip of the air-lock in the floor. Beckett stared at it. Not one of my better ideas, he thought.

'I don't suppose you'd consider reconnecting it?' he suggested.

'You're quite right. I wouldn't,' Brody agreed. He tucked the GPS handset inside the dry suit, and zipped it closed. 'Although don't think I'm not grateful to you. If I'd had to switch them off myself it would have been a terrible moral responsibility.' His insincerity was more than manifest. But Beckett seized on the opening.

225

'At least give us all a fighting chance,' he said. Even as he spoke, he knew it was hopeless. The trickle of water from the airlock had reached his feet already.

'Oh, by all means,' Brody said sarcastically. 'That would really be sensible of me, wouldn't it?' He picked up the air tanks. 'Sorry, Beckett. You're all just spam in a can, now.'

'Haven't you got any vestiges of conscience at all?' Beckett asked, trying to keep the contempt out of his voice. The only chance he and the crew had now was in an appeal to Brody's better nature. However unlikely it was that he possessed one. Brody looked genuinely surprised.

'Of course not,' he said. 'Winners do better without.' He picked up a lump hammer from McTiernan's discarded toolkit. 'But I tell you what. Just to show there are no hard feelings, I'll make it quick.' He turned, striking a stopcock attached to the pipe Beckett was shackled to. It came free, sending a fountain of water spraying out across the narrow compartment.

'That's the feed line to the ballast tanks,' Brody explained. He dropped the hammer. It splashed at his feet as he donned the facemask. 'So if it's any consolation, you'll drown long before the rest of the boys get round to suffocating.'

Now that he came to mention it, Beckett thought, it wasn't. Alarms must have gone off in the control room, because someone started banging on the sealed hatch leading back to the main body of the submarine.

'Brody,' Beckett said. He raised his voice a little over the sound of the inrushing water. But he didn't shout. He was damned if he'd give the man the satisfaction. Brody hesitated in the hatchway, a picture of polite interest.

'There's nowhere you can hide. I'll find you. Depend on it.'

Brody waved a cheerful farewell, and vanished through the hatch.

A moment later Beckett heard the unmistakable sound of the escape hatch flooding.

Well, at least I got the last word, he thought. He looked round the compartment. Now to find a way out of here.

And fast. The water was already lapping over the soles of his shoes.

# « Nineteen »

'Too late.' Ros felt her jaw clench as she stared at the message on the screen. TRANSACTION COMPLETE. If only she'd reacted a second faster.

'Don't blame yourself,' Graeme said. 'No one else I know could even have got close.' He pulled on his jacket as he spoke.

'Where are you going?' Ros asked.

'Back to the bank. I may be able to cancel the transaction from there.'

'Good idea.' Nothing to be gained by sitting around here feeling sorry for herself. Ros stood, decisively. 'And I'll take Jacobs Doyle. I might be able to head Juliet Brody off there.'

Graeme gave her a wan smile. 'Good luck.'

'Thanks.' She grabbed her coat on the fly, struggling into it as she headed for the door. Luck would have nothing to do with it, she thought. She'd stop the Brody woman, and find out where Beckett was. Somehow.

The alternative was something she simply refused to contemplate.

* * *

The handcuffs wouldn't give. And they were too small to squeeze his hand through. He'd tried both options until the flesh on his wrists was raw. And the pipe was solid. No doubt about that. He glanced along it, to where the jet of water was fountaining into the compartment.

Of course! The valve Brody had damaged. It had to have been weakened there. Maybe it was loose enough to come free entirely.

Brody's computer equipment shorted out in a shower of sparks, as the water level rose to meet it. Another graphic reminder of how rapidly time was passing.

He waded forward, the inrush of water already up to his shins. It felt awkward, his raised hands hampering his balance, but the cuffs moved freely along the metal pipe. And snagged on something.

He stopped, feeling the tug on his tender wrists, and examined the obstacle. It was a supporting bracket, secured by bolts. He tested them with his fingers. Solid. Immovable. Rusted in place, probably, judging by the condition of the rest of the sub. Maybe if he tried moving the other way.

Wait. The spanner Brody had tried to threaten him with was lying on a shelf in front of him. Out of reach of his hands, true, but there might be another way. He bent his head towards it. Strained his neck.

He could reach it. Just. He gripped it with his teeth. The metal was cold inside his mouth, and bitter with the taste of lubricants.

So far, so good. Now for the tricky part. He forced himself to be methodical, ignoring the inexorable rise of the water. It should start to rise more slowly soon, he thought, as the air in the compartment grew more compressed. No sign of that happening yet, though. It was already up over his knees.

He lifted his head slowly, clenching his jaw. The spanner was heavy and awkward, but he held it. Tilted his neck back, fumbling the tool closer to his fingertips. They brushed the metal, cold, and slick with the spray filling the compartment from the breached pipe.

He tried closing his grip, and almost dropped it. Clenched his hand convulsively. The handle dug into his palm. Got it!

He manoeuvred the spanner into position, handicapped by the awkward angle of the bolts, and the numbing of his fingers in the freezing water. It caught at last, and he began to exert some pressure.

'Yes!' It moved a few millimetres. He readjusted it, and tried again, fired by hope. There were breathing tanks in the next chamber, he thought. Even if Brody had disabled the escape hatch, he could take one and get out through the airlock in the floor.

This was going to work. If he could get all the bolts free before the water rose too much.

He forced the thought away, and concentrated on the task at hand. He couldn't afford any more distractions. Gradually, slowly, the first bolt began to come free.

'Strange.' Van Der Decken was looking at the radar, a puzzled expression on her face. 'I wonder where that came from.'

'What?' Ed moved across the bridge to join her. She pointed at a small blip, one of dozens cluttering the screen. He couldn't see anything remarkable about it.

'There's a small powerboat, back near the wreck we spotted. It wasn't there a minute ago.' Her tone became speculative. 'I suppose it could have been masked by the echo of a larger vessel.'

'Or it could be the escape boat from the submarine,' Ed finished for her.

'We could run him down easily enough,' Van Der Decken suggested. 'Find out for sure.'

'No.' It was just too obvious, Ed told himself. But still . . . 'We should turn back. There's no time to lose.'

'You think that wasn't the wreck of the *Callisto*, don't you?' Van Der Decken asked. She was quick on the uptake, Ed thought. He nodded.

'It's a reasonable deduction. If that is the escape boat.'

'That's a very big if,' Van Der Decken reminded him. 'If you're wrong, and we break off the search now.'

'I know.' Their chances of finding Beckett in time would drop from slim to virtually non-existent. But if he was right . . .

There was no way to know. He wished he could flip a coin for it. But, however much he wanted to, he couldn't avoid the decision.

'We go back,' he said.

'Mrs Brody. How nice to see you again.' The manager she'd spoken to before, whose name she'd never quite caught, stood up as she entered his office. She rather liked the decor; simple, understated, in a way that exuded wealth far more effectively than mere ostentation ever could. It was a style she looked forward to practising herself.

'Thank you.' Juliet seated herself in the slightly over-stuffed visitor's chair, and read the nameplate on the desk without appearing to. De Courcey, that was it. A large man she hadn't met before was standing next to the desk. He had an earpiece, she noticed. Something to do with security, then. De Courcey waved an introductory hand.

'I don't think you've met our Mr Gilbey. He's here to give you any advice you may wish on our security procedures.'

'As I understand it,' Juliet said, 'you guarantee my safety as far as the door. Once I set foot on the street, I'm on my own.'

'Succinctly put,' Gilbey said. 'But accurate. So we would prefer to arrange delivery ourselves. Anywhere in the world you wish, within reason. Absolute discretion guaranteed.'

'How very thoughtful,' Juliet said. Better not tell the officious oaf to mind his own business, however tempting it was. 'But my husband and I have made our own arrangements. I'm sure you'll understand if I prefer not to discuss them.' McTiernan's revolver was heavy in her handbag.

'Of course,' Gilbey said. He turned to De Courcey. 'I've authorised access to the upper parking level for Mr Brody.' He turned back to Juliet. 'I trust you'll at least allow us to see you safely to your car.'

'I will indeed,' Juliet assured him. One of the telephones on De Courcey's desk rang softly. He picked it up, and listened.

'Thank you.' He replaced the receiver. 'Our accounts department has just confirmed your credit transfer.'

Excellent, Juliet thought. Bryan had come through again, just like he always did. By now, if everything was going smoothly, he should be making his way up the river, ready to pick up the car at the backwater wharf McTiernan had used to store his boat. She resisted the impulse to look at her watch. Another half an hour and it would all be over. Nothing could go wrong now. Nothing.

De Courcey stood.

'Would you care to accompany me to the vault?'

I would indeed, Juliet thought.

'Are you sure you know how to use all this equipment?' Van Der Decken asked. Ed shouldered the air tanks of the diving suit into place.

'Sure,' he said, with a confidence he didn't entirely feel. It had been a long time since his last scuba dive, and that had been using civilian equipment; the dry suit felt clumsier than the wet suit he was used to, and there was a lot more gadgetry to assimilate. Like the sensor gear built into the helmet, for instance. But Beckett was depending on him. 'Once you've got the knack, you never lose it. Just like falling off a bike.'

'If you say so.' Van Der Decken didn't sound at all convinced. She picked up the heavy helmet, and handed it to him. 'The radio in the mask is voice activated. Keep the helmet light on at all times. You'll need it to see anyway; visibility is pretty poor down there. We'll be monitoring you through the video link, so we might be able to feed a visual enhancement through the head up display if you need it.'

'Good.' He took the helmet, and donned it. Buckled the heavy tool belt into place around his waist. Clipped the spare breather unit to it.

'If it is the *Callisto*, come straight back up,' Van Der Decken said. 'We still have time to find the submarine before the air runs out.'

She's just saying that, Ed thought. But he appreciated the gesture. He slipped the mask on, and inhaled a couple of times to test the demand valve. His breath hissed in his ears.

'All set,' he said. He glanced up at the bridge. The navigating officer made a thumbs up gesture. The radio was working.

No point hanging around then. He jumped over the side.

'You weren't kidding about the visibility,' he said, as the water closed over his head. Grey-green murk enshrouded him, scattering the beam of his helmet light just a few yards in front of his face. A dark, angular shape loomed up ahead of him. One of the hydrofoils. He trod water next to it, orientating himself.

'It should be on a bearing of zero five seven degrees from your present facing,' Van Der Decken's voice said. Ed checked the head up display inside the face mask. A stylised human figure floated in the centre of a compass rose.

'Got it.' He struck out in the indicated direction.

'Gotcha!' Beckett felt the last bolt give. It fell, suddenly, disappearing beneath the waist-high water, the faint splash inaudible over the torrent rushing in from the damaged pipe. He forged ahead, breasting the rising flood.

And the cuffs snagged again. The sudden jerk took him by surprise; the spanner fell from his hand, and vanished with a splash.

'Oh, you're joking . . .' He craned his neck to get a closer look. 'You've got to be.' The bracket had shifted, opening up some clearance between the pipe and the hull, but it still wasn't enough. The linking chain was firmly wedged.

He was running out of options fast. Maybe if he tried moving back the other way . . .

The lights went out. He wouldn't have believed darkness could be that intense. The rising water must have shorted out one of the main power conduits, he thought. Then the emergency lighting kicked in, shocking in its suddenness. The dim red light was like a foretaste of Hell, flickering like flames as it reflected from the rippling water around him.

This did not look good at all.

'I can see it!' Ed kicked out towards the dim shape, looming up out of this silt-clogged darkness. The mini-

234

ature sonar in his helmet guided him in, the blip clear in his head up display. Large. Metallic. 'I'm getting all the right readings.'

'Good. But be careful.' Van Der Decken's voice was loud in his ears. His breath hissed, bubbles rising with every exhalation, the demand valve clicking quietly every time he inhaled.

'I'm right above it now. I'm heading forward, where the escape hatch is. If I can't use that, I'll try getting in through the work hatch in the forward compartment.'

'Roger. We copy that,' Van Der Decken said.

His helmet beam picked out a discoloration on the metal, off to one side. He swam over to investigate it.

'There seems to be some kind of lettering here,' he said.

'We see it too,' Van Der Decken confirmed. She didn't sound at all happy. Ed swept the beam of the helmet light along it.

C.A.L. . . .

'Oh no.' Despair hit him, darker and more suffocating than the surrounding water. He stared at the treacherous letters, willing them to change. They didn't.

*Callisto.*

He'd dragged them on a wild goose chase after all. Wasted precious time.

Time Beckett didn't have.

'I'm coming up,' he said.

# « Twenty »

Ros hit the foyer of Jacobs Doyle at a run. There was no time for subtlety now. The more attention she attracted the better. The receptionist looked up as she approached the desk. The clatter of her feet against the marble floor echoed loudly in the open space. In her peripheral vision, Ros could see a couple of uniformed security guards closing in on her from opposite sides.

She reached the desk ahead of them.

'Get me Gilbey. Now!'

'Do you have an appointment?' The girl's voice quavered a little, plainly upset at such a breach of decorum. Or possibly the guns the security guards had produced. Ros didn't care much about either.

'No. But he'll see me. Unless he doesn't mind losing a quarter of a billion pounds worth of diamonds.'

'I most certainly do.' Gilbey materialised at her shoulder. How does he manage to move so quietly? she wondered. Recognition sparked in his eyes as he studied her face. 'You again.'

'I'm a security consultant.' Ros handed him her card. 'Working for Kamen and Ross. Graeme Hurry called you earlier this morning.'

'Yes, he did.' Gilbey made an almost imperceptible gesture with his hand. The uniformed guards reholstered their weapons. Ros suppressed a sigh of relief. At least he was listening.

'We have reason to believe there's a fraud in progress. Right now.' She pulled her palmtop computer out of her pocket. 'There's a woman here buying diamonds on a phoney credit transfer. From Fokker Dolenz in Frankfurt.'

'Frankfurt?' Gilbey looked troubled for a moment. 'What's that got to do with Kamen and Ross?'

'The transfer originated with them. It was intercepted *en route* to Fokker Dolenz, and the signal duplicated. Then the duplicate was bounced back to you, with the German Bank's authentication codes attached.'

'That's not technically possible,' Gilbey said. A note of doubt crept into his voice. 'Is it?'

'Why not ask her?' Ros called up a video still of Juliet Brody on the palmtop. The same image Graeme had shown her, Ed, and Beckett a few days before. 'She's here, now, isn't she?'

Gilbey came to a decision.

'Excuse me a moment,' he said. He picked up a phone on the desk, and dialled an internal number. 'Mr De Courcey? Gilbey. We may have a slight problem with the credit transfer after all. Could you ask the lady to wait a moment? Thank you.' There was a short pause. Then he dropped the handset, and sprinted across the foyer. After a moment's nonplussed confusion, the guards followed.

'What's happened?' Ros caught up with him easily. But then she had been a fifteen hundred metres champion a few years before. Gilbey's face was grim.

'Gunfire,' he said.

* * *

'No. Wait.' Van Der Decken's voice echoed tinnily inside Ed's helmet. 'Stay where you are for a moment. The submarine must be close by. Too close for our sonar to distinguish it from the wreck, maybe.'

'Maybe,' Ed agreed. It sounded plausible. 'But what good can I do down here?'

'Try swimming a search pattern. Spiral out from the wreck,' Van Der Decken said. 'It's possible the short-range system in your helmet can tell the echoes apart. You're much closer, after all.'

'Bit of a long shot, isn't it?' Ed asked. But he was already moving to comply. Long shot or not, it was the best chance they had.

Alarms were going off all over the building. Ros burst through a fire door and hesitated, looking for some clue as to where Gilbey and his guards had vanished to. She might have the edge in speed and fitness, she thought, but Gilbey and the others knew the layout. She'd fallen behind rapidly once they left the foyer for the maze of corridors and offices behind it. Keep going down, she told herself. The vaults must be below.

She paused, listening for footsteps, but the thick pile carpet muffled everything, and the alarms were drowning out whatever sounds were left. Carry on in the same direction, then; if only there was some obvious shortcut.

'Aha.' Her eye fell on an emergency exit sign. When in doubt, take the fire stairs, she told herself. They're always the quickest route to anywhere. She pulled the door open.

'You.' Juliet Brody had obviously had the same idea. She had a handbag slung over her shoulder, and a gun in her hand. She pointed the weapon at Ros. 'How do I get to the parking level?'

Ros breathed a sigh of relief. For a moment she

thought the woman had recognised her from their meeting on the quayside.

'I don't know,' she said. 'I don't work here. I'm just in for a meeting.'

'Oh, great.' Juliet's eyes flickered heavenward in a 'why me?' gesture. But her aim remained fixed firmly on Ros's torso. No chance of grabbing the gun, then. Not if she wanted to live, anyway. 'Well, we'll just have to improvise.' She seized Ros's elbow, and stepped in close, jamming the muzzle of the pistol up under her ear. Right on the nerve cluster. On purpose, too, the bitch. Ros flinched. 'Get moving.'

'Which way?'

'Any way. You think I care?' The woman was losing it, Ros thought. All the indications they had were that she wasn't too stable at the best of times. And she had a gun. She tugged on Ros's elbow, hustling her down the corridor.

An office door opened ahead of them, disgorging a secretary with an armful of papers. She caught sight of them and froze, her mouth dropping open. The papers fluttered to the floor.

'You. Where's the parking?' Juliet ground the barrel of the gun against Ros's jawbone. 'Tell me. Or I'll blow her head off. Then yours.'

'Down there.' The girl pointed, her voice a strangled squeak. Juliet hustled Ros in the indicated direction.

'You certainly have a way with people,' Ros said.

'You just have to know how to get down to their level,' Juliet said, without a trace of irony.

There was a lift at the end of the corridor. Juliet made for it like a homing pigeon, dragging Ros with her.

'Call it.' She watched carefully as Ros pressed the button. 'No tricks.'

No tricks? Was this woman paranoid or what? Ros waited for the doors to open. Where was Gilbey? He must know where they were, surely. These corridors must be riddled with surveillance devices.

The lift arrived with a muted chime. The door slid open. Hordes of heavily armed security goons failed to pour out of it. Juliet relaxed visibly as she saw it was empty, and bundled Ros inside.

'Press the button.' The pressure of the gun barrel against her ear grew a little more insistent. One of the levels was clearly labelled PARKING. Ros complied.

The door slid open to the unmistakable car park smell of old rain and exhaust. Juliet shoved Ros hard in the small of the back, forcing her through the gap. Ros looked around. Cars in neat rows, most of them expensive, sporty, or both. Concrete pillars supporting the roof. A couple of fire points, marked in yellow paint. No sign of anyone.

Correction. Bryan Brody was standing just outside the entrance. It was blocked by a metal security grille. Solid. Immovable. Beyond him was an expensive saloon car, its engine running.

'Bryan!' Juliet ran towards him, dragging Ros.

'Over here, Sweetheart.' He waved. 'Who's your friend?'

'Just some office drone. I needed a bit of insurance.' She stared at the metal barrier separating them. They weren't going to get through that without a cutting torch, Ros thought. 'What's this?' She kicked the grille in frustration. The gun moved slightly away from Ros's head.

I need a distraction, Ros thought. She glanced round, catching a flicker of movement behind one of the parked cars. The security guards were waiting until she was out of danger before making their move.

'It came down when the alarms went off,' Brody explained. He looked sheepish. 'There was nothing I could do about it.'

240

'Then think of something!' An edge of hysteria was entering Juliet's voice now. 'Get me out of here!'

'No problem.' Brody smiled confidently. 'I've got a plan. Have you got the rocks?'

'Yes. Right here.' Juliet slipped the handbag off her shoulder, and pushed it through the mesh. Brody took it. She looked at him expectantly. 'Now what?'

'Now he runs off and leaves you,' Ros said.

'Shut up!' Juliet turned, suddenly, and backhanded her across the mouth. She was surprisingly strong for her size. Ros staggered.

'Bryan?' Juliet's look of eager expectation was almost pathetic.

Brody started backing away. 'I'm sorry, Snookums. But you know you'd do the same if the situation was reversed. I'll be back, I promise.'

'*No!*' The word became an elongated howl of utter desolation. Like a child who's just discovered for the first time that life can be unfair. Ros felt her hackles rise; the woman barely sounded human. Brody took another step backwards.

'I haven't any choice. I'll get you the best lawyers money can buy. And if that doesn't work ....' he spread his hands. 'Look what we've achieved so far. A simple little jailbreak would be child's play.'

'He won't take the risk,' Ros said quietly.

'Bryan!' Another inhuman scream, shrill with the edge of hysteria. Brody smiled, placatingly.

'Trust me,' he said.

This time the scream was wordless. Juliet swung the gun away from Ros, and pulled the trigger. Brody fell backwards, an expression of absolute astonishment on his face. The handbag hit the ground, scattering what looked like chips of coloured glass. Juliet fired again, then a third time, in a paroxysm of fury. She must have reloaded since shooting her way out of the vault.

Ros leapt forward, grabbing the wrist of her gun hand, and twisted it. Juliet fell on her face, dropping the weapon, as Ros pivoted on her rear foot, swinging her hips into the throw. She dropped her weight, driving the breath from Juliet's body with her knees, and applied an armlock. The woman squirmed beneath her, spitting and screaming obscenities. Hysteria had doubled her strength, left her apparently immune to pain. Ros hung on for dear life.

Running footsteps echoed in the cavernous space. Gilbey and his security squad. A couple of them helped her restrain Juliet and cuff her wrists together.

'You'll probably need a muzzle too,' Ros said, rising to her feet.

'Well done,' Gilbey said. Someone had begun to raise the barrier. One of the uniformed guards ducked under it, and knelt by Brody, touching his carotid artery with a couple of fingertips. He looked up, and shook his head. A couple of his colleagues began to collect the fallen diamonds. 'Are you all right?'

'I will be.' Ros took a deep breath. It shuddered in her chest. Reaction, that's all, she thought. Nothing to worry about. She stepped forward, to where Juliet was being hauled to her feet. Stepped back out of the way as the woman tried to kick her.

'Juliet.' She spoke quietly. Soothing and authoritative. 'Where's the submarine?'

'Submarine?' Gilbey began. 'What are you –'

'Sh.' Ros cut him off with a gesture. Tried to establish eye contact. 'It's very important. Do you know where it is?'

'It's a secret,' Juliet said. She looked at Ros from under her disarrayed fringe. The sudden switch to calmness was almost more unnerving than the spasm of insensate violence had been. 'Bryan hid it. He's very clever.'

Wonderful, Ros thought. The light's on, but no one's at home. She just had to hope that Ed and Van Der Decken found it in time.

'Look at this stuff.' One of the guards had the boot of Brody's car open. 'What would he want with a diving suit?'

Hope flared, suddenly. She sprinted for the car. Brody would have had to find his way back to the British coast after abandoning the sub. Which probably meant . . .

'Yes!' She grabbed the GPS handset. Now all she had to do was find a way to patch these co-ordinates through to Ed.

'You're very faint,' Ed complained.

'Well, what do you expect.' Even through the static in his headphones Ros sounded a little tetchy. He wondered briefly what was eating her. 'I'm on a phone connection to the radio at Gizmos, which is bouncing a signal to the boat, which is being patched through to you by Van Der Decken. You're lucky you can hear me at all.'

'Point taken.' He swam on, through indistinct darkness. So far, nothing. 'What have you got for me?'

'Co-ordinates from Brody's GPS receiver. They're right on top of your current position.' So he had been right after all. They could still be in time. He grinned inside the mask. 'Van Der Decken says she can patch them through to your head up display.'

'Go ahead.' The figures appeared in the corner of the mask. 'Got 'em!'

They were only a couple of hundred metres away. He swam in the indicated direction as hard as he could.

Beckett bobbed to the surface and gulped air. The tiny pocket was all but depleted now. He couldn't hang on

243

for much longer. The handcuffs were immovable. The pipe wouldn't budge. He had barely another twenty minutes, he thought.

Less than that, probably. The air was becoming stale, unbreathable with his own exhaled carbon dioxide. Maybe he would suffocate before he drowned after all.

He refused to give up. If he could just work one wrist out of the cuffs he could still make it. Hold his breath long enough to locate one of the breathing sets in the next compartment. He took a deep breath, and dived again. Braced his feet against the bulkhead, and pulled. If he could just get the loop of metal over the root of his thumb he would be home free . . .

Pain shot up his arm. Ignore it, he told himself. Concentrate . . .

It still wouldn't give. He surfaced again, gasping at the foul air. It would last longer if he rested, he knew. But there was nothing to rest for. If he was going to die, he'd go down fighting.

Something brushed his leg. A fish, perhaps? There was certainly room for something to get in through the open floor hatch.

Water foamed next to his head. Something large broke the surface. Slick, shiny, dark in the dull red light. Were there sharks in the North Sea?

'Boo!' a familiar voice said, distorted slightly by the microphone in the mask. Ed. In a diving suit. 'Is my timing great, or what?'

'An hour ago would have been better.' Beckett sucked gratefully on the breather unit Ed held to his face. The sudden rush of fresh air was intoxicating. He'd never take being able to breathe for granted again. 'Or two.'

'Everyone's a critic,' Ed said. He slipped the retaining straps of the mask over Beckett's head. 'Now let's see.' He ducked below the surface, and examined the handcuffs. Selected a bolt-cutter from his toolbelt. 'Manicure?'

'Where did you spring from, anyway?' Beckett asked, through the communicator in his mask.

'It's a long story. But I got a lift from the Dutch Coastguard. They lent me the diving gear. Ah, that's got it.' The chain of the handcuffs parted.

'What about Brody?'

'Dead. His wife thought he was about to double-cross her, and shot him.'

'Charming.' Beckett followed him down, and out through the floor hatch. 'Whatever gave her that idea?'

'Something to do with him running off with the loot.' Ed struck out for the surface. Gradually the water began to lighten around them.

'And Juliet?'

'Sounds like a candidate for a rubber room, according to Ros.'

'No change there then.' His head broke the surface, and he squinted reflexively at the sudden burst of light. A sleek, grey naval vessel was rocking gently a few yards away. He struck out towards it. Welcoming hands reached down to help him aboard.

'This is getting to be a habit.' A young woman in uniform was waiting to greet him. 'I'm Captain Van Der Decken.'

'Ah. I take it you don't get ashore much.' Beckett pulled the mask off, and met her eye. He turned to Ed, who was smirking visibly. 'What? What did I say?'

'Nothing I haven't heard before,' she said, in a tone of long suffering. Oh. Well, it had been pretty obvious, he supposed.

'What about the crew?' he asked. 'There are still a dozen men down there.' Her expression softened.

'We've managed to get a line down to them. It's a bit awkward having to route everything through an interpreter ashore, but they seem to be all right. And we'll have a rescue submersible here by the evening.'

'Will they be able to get out?' Beckett asked. He inhaled deeply. He'd never known fresh air could taste so sweet. 'The escape hatch is flooded.'

'The rear hatch opens all right. It's only the pump that's broken. And they won't need that once the submersible's docked.'

'All the same.' Beckett shook his head. 'I wouldn't want to be in the captain's shoes.'

'Why's that?' Ed asked.

'Can you imagine how long it's going to take him to pay for losing a submarine?'

# « Epilogue »

The wind was cold again today, carrying a faint taste of the sea even this far inland, but Chief Petty Officer Stokes was in no mood to appreciate it. It cut keenly through his coat, stirring the branches of the trees in the churchyard. The rustling of the leaves sounded uncannily like waves on the seashore.

'A fine turnout,' he said. His midshipmen, impeccably attired in full dress uniform, formed up an honour guard around the gun carriage. Empty for the moment; Windette would be joining them shortly. 'Well done.'

There was a faint sussuration of gravel behind him. He turned in time to see a car pulling up next to the lych gate. Large, black, official-looking. A late arrival for the funeral service. Stokes fought down a pang of irritation at the breach of protocol.

A man climbed out of the back seat. Dressed in black, his overcoat flapping in the wind. The driver's window hummed down.

'Sorry we're so late, sir.'

'Don't worry. It wasn't your fault.' The man turned, and began to walk towards the church. He hesitated as the driver called after him.

'Mr Dent. Do you want me to wait?'

'No. Go on to the house. I'll travel back with the family.'

A close friend, then, thought Stokes, as the car pulled away. Dent hesitated as he passed the honour guard, and caught his eye.

'You're doing the boy proud, Mr Stokes.' His eyes scanned the group of midshipmen. 'They're all a credit to you.'

'Thank you, sir.' It took him a moment to realise he'd been addressed by name. 'Have we met?'

'I don't believe so. But I read your report.' The man's eyes moved to Stokes' face. They had a peculiarly colourless quality, Stokes thought. 'Admirably succinct.'

He was something official, then. Security, perhaps? He didn't look the type. But then Stokes wasn't exactly sure what the type was supposed to look like.

'I didn't think a routine accident report would be so widely circulated,' he said.

'Ordinarily, no. But there wasn't anything routine about this one, was there?' The man's voice was dry. 'And I took a personal interest in it. The Windettes are old and valued friends.'

A look of mutual understanding passed between the two men. He doesn't believe it was an accident any more than I do, Stokes thought.

'Would that be an active interest?' he asked.

'I'm a civil servant, Mr Stokes. A glorified filing clerk. I don't indulge in vendettas.'

So. Whoever killed Windette had got away with it. Something of his feelings must have shown on his face, because Dent's expression softened a little.

'There is, however, a young man who used to work for me. He has something of a quixotic streak, and some rather unorthodox friends.'

'I see.' Stokes nodded. 'And he likes you enough to

do you the odd favour. For old time's sake.'

'On the contrary. I believe he dislikes me intensely.' The flicker of a wintry smile. 'But a client of his had an interest in a related matter. It wasn't difficult to nudge him in the right direction.' The grey eyes turned momentarily hard. 'You may rest assured, Mr Stokes, that the people responsible have paid the price. In full.'

'Thank you.' Stokes paused fractionally. 'For telling me.'

'My pleasure. Now if you'll excuse me, I must be getting in. I'm quite unforgivably late as it is.' He disappeared inside the church.

Stokes felt his mood lift a little. He returned his attention to the honour guard. Leave them alone for five minutes, he thought, and they go completely to pieces.

'Groves. Your cap's crooked.'

'Sorry Chief Petty Officer. It's the wind.'

'Don't apologise, straighten it. That's better.' He gave her a quick nod of approval.

Windette was still dead, he thought. But not unavenged. The scales had been balanced. By a young man with a quixotic streak, and some unorthodox friends.

He'd never know who they were, but he wished them well.

'How's the invalid?' Ros asked.

'Oh. Bearing up.' Beckett stretched out on the sofa, a video game conveniently to hand. 'I should be back at work in a day or two.'

'Or three,' Ed said solicitously. 'You don't want to rush these things.'

'That's true,' Beckett agreed.

He's absolutely shameless, Ros thought. It's only a sprained wrist, for heaven's sake.

He looked up, doing puppy-dog wistful. 'I think I could manage another cup of tea.'

'Oh, right away,' Ros said. She didn't move.

'What's that?' Beckett sat up a little, supporting his weight on his elbows. Ed moved fully into his field of vision, carrying something concealed in a cloth from the kitchen.

'We thought you deserved a little present,' Ros said. 'For suffering so bravely.'

'So we got you this,' Ed said. He moved closer to the sofa. 'It's cold. It's wet. And it bubbles.'

'Champagne,' Beckett said. He grinned. 'You shouldn't have.'

'That's all right. We didn't.' Ed pulled the cloth away. Inches from his nose.

Beckett stared at the goldfish. The goldfish stared back. Then it blew a bubble at him.

'I suppose you think that's funny,' Beckett said, with all the wounded dignity he could muster.

Ros looked at Ed. Ed looked back at her.

'Yes,' they said in unison.

**BUGS – The TV Series**

This book is based on two episodes of the TV series BUGS: 'All Under Control' written by Duncan Gould from a story by Brian Clemens, and 'Down Among The Dead Men' written by Stephen Gallagher. These episodes were first broadcast on BBC1 on 15 April and 22 April 1995. They were directed by Brian Farnham and Andrew Grieve respectively.

Producer – Brian Eastman
Co-Producer – Stuart Doughty
Production Designers – Rob Harris and Mark Raggett
Script Consultant – Colin Brake
Executive Producer for the BBC – Caroline Oulton

BUGS is a Carnival Films production.

Read the full story in Virgin's non-stop action novels

Available from all good book shops!